Breakout
By
A P Bateman

Facebook: @authorapbateman

www.apbateman.com

Rockhopper Publishing Limited

2019

The Alex King Series
The Contract Man
Lies and Retribution
Shadows of Good Friday
The Five
Reaper
Stormbound

The Rob Stone Series
The Ares Virus
The Town
The Island

Standalone Novel
Hell's Mouth

For my wife, Clair

For her unwavering support and understanding.
Writing a novel is like balancing between sanity
and insanity. It's self-indulgent and time-
consuming, and while you are immersed in your
characters and plots, the real world sometimes
gets left behind. It isn't nine-to-five and when
the words are flowing, you're working. When
the flow dries up, you fear it will never return.
Like a spectre, a writer hovers between two
realms, thank you for snatching me back
occasionally into the real world. I know it isn't
easy.

Chapter One

Washington
Seventeen days ago

Four months had been building up to this point. Four long months of training – both in the field and the classroom – and in his mind. The mental strength, tacit stoicism needed for a task such as this was immeasurable. Certainly, his toughest assignment yet, and in a career spent plotting and fighting in the shadows, that meant a lot.

Alex King had paid for the room using a stolen credit card. The cardholder's body would be found, but only when the time was right. Only when all his ducks were in a row. The man had been a prolific terrorist. He would not be missed. Certainly not by the right people.

The rifle had been purchased at a gun show in Texas. A Barrett M82, 12.7x99mm NATO, or in these parts - .50 cal. It was stripped and folded, strapped in the carry box with the sights affixed to the sight-rail, pre-zeroed to two-thousand-six-hundred metres. King had put five-hundred rounds through the weapon and was confident that he could make the shot. Today's wind was light and drifting in from the Potomac in a steady South-westerly.

Congressman Willard Standing III was a fifty-nine-year-old veteran of Operation Desert Storm, where he ranked as Major and served with distinction. A lot of people had, America was long overdue a war and medals had been light on the ground since Vietnam. He terminated at Colonel with a few more decorations from Iraq and America's second attempt to bring peace to the region, and he entered politics two years after leaving the army and a short stint with a veteran's charity followed. He had accumulated a wealth of over two-hundred-million in the metallurgy industry, specialising in the smelting of gold. King wasn't sure how much the stolen Kuwaiti gold had helped him along, but he was willing to bet it had a more positive effect than negative on the company's earning potential. Standing Industries had been on a healthy climb since it was founded, first gaining the contract to buy weapons and military vehicles, both domestic and obsolete, and captured Iraqi stock, smelt them and return them to metal producers around

around the world as finished billets to create everything from cutlery to washing machines to premium vehicles. King realised that the man's contacts within the military had helped him get through the pentagon, but nobody had ever found anything untoward in the man's dealings. Still, if it walked and quacked like a duck...

Standing had been ahead of the game and cashed out of steel and into gold before India and China dominated the steel industry. At the right time. Conveniently so. Standing Industries was set to do nothing but climb, and the world-wide stock markets were indicating substantial stock growth over the next year. With wealth and influence came the need for more of both, and he had run through mayor and governor easily enough, faltered for a while because of an investigative journalist's questions about missing Kuwaiti gold his unit had liberated from the Iraqis, but was back on course for senator and congressman in a short seven years. The investigative journalist had been shot and killed in a Seven Eleven robbery gone wrong. Or right. It depended on your point of view. The perpetrator had never been found.

King checked his watch. It was a black digital and analogue affair, guaranteed to withstand shock and Gs. It wasn't his type of watch, but it had been worn by the cardholder

and that would provide a trail. Another breadcrumb. It was ten-twenty-seven AM. Eighteen minutes until Congressman Standing took to the podium.

King plugged in the hotplate and made himself another cup of tea as he waited for it to heat. He took the cup over to the table and looked down at the rifle. Taking a deep breath, he adjusted the latex gloves he was wearing and started to assemble the parts with well-practised precision.

Chapter Two

Thames House, London

"It's been over two bloody weeks!"

"I know."

"And not a word?"

"Nothing." Ramsay shrugged. "He checked in before Standing's speech. We know there were multiple shots fired and even saw Standing down on the stage. The whole world saw it. No arrests made, and no further word from King."

Amherst steepled his fingers under his chin. He was a young man to hold the position of Director, but the MI5 chief felt older today. Older these past two-weeks. He would swear that there had been more grey hair at his temples when he looked into the mirror at the ageing figure who stared tiredly back at him this morning. "Simon?"

Simon Mereweather shrugged. "There hasn't been any chatter. GCHQ has tasked Echelon with tapping the right channels. The CIA are denying an arrest was made. The FBI have been silenced through an order of National Security."

"And the Washington police?" Amherst asked, but to no one in particular.

Ramsay said, "But they won't know anything. Silenced."

"Can we at least make some intelligent guesses as to King's whereabouts?"

Simon Mereweather hesitated, then said, "It's a big country…"

"I know it's a big bloody country, Simon! But there are places where he could be. Some more obvious than others…"

Neil Ramsay was Mereweather's deputy. And even though Simon Mereweather was joint Deputy Director – the other being an administration only role – this in no way made him number three in the Security Service. Ramsay always joked that being the deputy's deputy merely made him overworked, underpaid and forever in the firing line. Even so, as a good batman, he took the pressure off his boss and said, "The Mid-West."

"Why so sure?" Amherst asked dubiously.

Ramsay had thrown a bone, now wished he hadn't. He hated backing up statements with nothing more than a hunch. But so far, his hunches had played out. "It's vast. And it suits their purposes. You can drive for days and avoid seeing a town."

"And that's it?"

Ramsay shrugged. "It's a calculated guess. But it makes sense."

"Oh, well that's okay then…"

Mereweather and Ramsay both knew sarcasm when they heard it, but neither man made the mistake of saying anything.

"So, we just have to wait?"

Mereweather nodded. "It will happen soon enough. We'll hear something about King, and we'll be ready to move."

"I hope you're right," Amherst said. "For all our sakes." He picked up a sheet of paper from his in tray and said nothing more.

Both men gave it around ten seconds, Mereweather making the first move and getting to his feet. Amherst seemed oblivious as both men headed for the door. Outside, there was an office with Amherst's PA typing quickly and expertly at a laptop. She smiled at them as she typed. She did not know Alex King. Nobody on this floor, or any floor within Thames House would recall the name or recognise a photograph. Mereweather held the door open for Ramsay and the overhead lighting illuminated the corridor. The building had been hit by anti-aircraft gun fire and incendiary ammunition in a terrorist attack and this level had been entirely rebuilt. It had lost what little character it had, and that wasn't saying much. Controlled by sensors, the lights ahead of them switched on and the lights behind them switched off as they walked. No matter the time of day, the experience was eerie.

"A hunch?" Mereweather asked. "Or an educated guess?"

"They're usually one and the same."

"But enough to go on?"

Ramsay shrugged. "I heard talk before, years ago. South Dakota, Wyoming – that sort of postcode."

Mereweather scoffed. "What's that? Three or four times the size of Britain?"

"A bit more."

"How much time will it save?"

Ramsay shrugged. He had a feeling too much was going to rest on his hunch. "A few days, at least."

"And if it turns out to be Florida?"

"Then I guess I get another job…"

"Or King dies…"

Ramsay nodded. "Sorry, yes." He felt a little foolish at his flippancy.

"Go with it," Mereweather said decisively. "Get back out there and see what you can find out. I won't tell the big cheese, not just yet. Get things in place for the Mid-West."

Ramsay nodded. He wasn't about to tell the Deputy Director that he had put both a plan and personnel in place a week before King had even deployed. It was a layered plan, borne of both hunch and intelligence gathering. A man's life was at stake. A friend's life. The plan the top floor had instigated had been difficult enough, but in Ramsay's mind it hadn't been sufficient. Too many variables. Ramsay's counterplan would give King some security and a buffer. But it would make terrorists and saboteurs out of them all. But King was a friend and he deserved a fighting chance. But not only that, what King had been working on held ramifications for the rest of mankind.

Chapter Three

Two months earlier

King watched her draw and fire the pistol. She wasn't altogether a natural – she did not get enough practise for that - but after a few rounds she found her groove and settled into the discipline. From his position above the firing line, he couldn't see where the bullets were grouping on the paper figure 11 target some thirty-metres further forward, but the strikes in the building sand of the back-stop behind the row of targets indicated that her shots were at least consistent. By the time she fed the third magazine into the Glock 19 pistol, her movements were both relaxed and fluid.

"I do find it a bit of a turn on," Rashid commented. "A hot chick with a gun. Kind of like when you see a fit bird driving an Aston Martin or a Ferrari on Oxford Street. A balding bloke in his forties or fifties just looks like a tosser, but a fit woman? There's a huge difference."

"I ought to punch you right now," King said flatly. "Anyway, Caroline drives a Mini."

"She's handling that weapon really well…"

"Could you get any more innuendo into that sentence?"

"There's no innuendo in that."

"Not what you say, just the way that you say it."

Rashid smirked. "You sound like my other half now."

"You have another half? Surely not…"

"Marnie," Rashid replied.

"The chubby bird in analytics?"

"You see, when I say something, it's funny. When you say it, it's downright nasty."

King smiled. "Ah, did I hurt your feelings?"

Rashid hauled the bag out of the rear of the Land Rover and bundled it at King. "Well, I won't tell Marnie you said that," he said and looked back at the firing line. "I might tell Caroline, though. She'll love that, what with all the women power and all that…"

"Now *that's* nasty. What did I ever do to you?"

"Plenty," Rashid paused. "Now, what range are we starting at?"

"Is it zeroed?"

"Not at all."

"Well, let's get a few on at a hundred and work backwards."

Rashid nodded and picked up the ammunition box. He hesitated and nodded to the firing line. "Look, Ramsay's up."

King watched as Caroline holstered her weapon and guided Ramsay around the Glock 17 in his hands. It was larger than the model 19 and would fit his hand better, recoil a little less. She started him off pointing at the target and getting used to the blade safety on the trigger. Ramsay then worked the action and she handed him a loaded magazine. She showed him how to drop the slide and make the weapon ready and aim at the target.

"I'm glad he's finally getting some training."

"I know," Rashid smiled. "But who'll carry my shit in a gunfight now?"

King laughed and headed towards the rifle range.

"This is from Hereford," Rashid said as King took the Barrett .50 out of the gun bag. He knew Rashid was an ex-SAS Captain, and the man still had his contacts. "So, don't break it."

"And this is definitely the weapon?"

Rashid nodded. "From the grooves and twists in the bullets recovered from the bodies – or at least near the bodies after over penetration - it was definitely a Barrett used in the assassinations."

King had used one before, and he set about assembling the barrel into the receiver. He could hear Ramsay on the 9mm. It sounded as if the desk-jockey was getting excited. The sharp reports were closer together and it sounded as if Caroline was encouraging him to double tap.

The range ahead of them spread out to almost three miles of uninterrupted Hampshire countryside. Rashid had earlier set out the figure 11 man-sized targets at various distances, although he had not told King what they were.

"First is at two-hundred," he said. "Forget zeroing on a hundred, the bullet is still rising at that range." He settled onto his stomach and raised the Zeiss field glasses. "I'll sight you onto the target."

King settled down beside him and put the ear protectors on. He hadn't loaded the magazine, simply placed a dozen of the bullets on the mat and dropped one into the breech. He closed the bolt and sighted on the centre of the paper target. The weapon was fitted with a two-stage trigger and King took up pressure until it gave, and he knew the tiniest contact would now make the weapon fire.

The gunshot was loud, even through the protection of the ear defenders and the recoil through his shoulder was like a hard punch.

"Off the paper," Rashid said looking at the plume of soil that had exploded into the air. "A foot right and I'd say a good foot high."

King fired again. He worked the bolt, dropped in another bullet and fired once he had settled his breathing. He wanted to establish a grouping before he adjusted the sights.

"Yeah, same place. You can plant some potatoes in those holes later if you like…"

King adjusted the top turret. The dial was ratcheted, and he spun it round half a dozen clicks. He did the same with the turret on the right side of the scope. He settled down, loaded the huge bullet into the breech and closed the bolt.

He fired again.

"On the paper, six inches high and ten right."

King could see for himself at this range, but he enjoyed the man's company. He also knew the man next to him was the finest sniper he'd ever encountered, and any pointers would always be appreciated, even after all his years in the field. He fired twice more.

"Tight grouping. That's nice."

King adjusted both turrets and fired another shot.

"Vee bull. High. Twenty-five points, buddy."

Another shot and the bullet clipped the last hole. King adjusted the top turret two clicks and the elevation three down. He loaded another bullet and closed the bolt. He fired again. His shoulder feeling the kick against the stock now.

"Bullseye! You win the cuddly toy…"

King put two more through the bull and there was nothing left to fire at. He changed his aim to the next target. He estimated four-hundred metres. He fired again.

"Bullseye!"

King fired three shots and tore the bull out of the target.

"Try one thousand," said Rashid.

The sight was fitted with an off-set to accommodate shots at various distances. King switched to the next aperture and took a steady aim. He fired.

"A little low," said Rashid. "You're more or less bang-on for point of aim."

Over the next ten-minutes, King brought the bullets into the bullseye. He re-set to the third aperture. He now had the rifle zeroed to four-hundred and one-thousand metres respectively. He could choose either setting to fire at six-hundred metres – simply aim a little high for the first aperture or a little low with the second.

"It's a shit plan," said Rashid.

"It's the only one we've got."

"Too many variables."

"You could say that."

"I just did," he paused. "How much does Caroline know?"

"The general premise."

"And that's enough?"

"Not nearly," said King. "But when it happens, you and Ramsay will be there for her."

"And that will be enough to get her through?"

"It'll have to be," King paused. "It will work. I'll make it work."

The two were silent for the next half-hour, save for Rashid guiding King into two-thousand and three-thousand metres. At three thousand, King was not concerned with the bullseye or the second ring in from the centre known as the V-bull. He settled for every shot making it into the black. This area was the size of a soccer ball. There were no impressive bullseyes past fifteen-hundred metres.

"Good shooting," Ramsay said from behind them.

King had no idea how long he'd been watching. He left the bolt all the way back and the breech open and got to his feet. The barrel was steaming. If he touched the metal it would singe his skin. He looked at both Ramsay and Caroline and smiled. "So, how did our man get on?" he asked.

"Excellent," Caroline said. "But he had a good teacher," she smiled.

"Bloody brilliant fun!" Ramsay beamed.

"Happier now?" Rashid asked.

"Much."

"But I've lost my bagman and sidekick…"

"Oh, fuck off," Ramsay chuckled. "I can't say I ever want to use one for real, but I feel happier than I did on the job in Finland..."

"Are you done?" Caroline asked.

King was about to answer when Rashid cut in. "He is for today, but he will be down here for the next two-weeks until he can close his grouping down by at least half."

"What he said," King shrugged.

They made their way back to Rashid's Audi RS4 where King stowed the rifle in a soft carrycase – this time keeping it assembled and the sight covered by dust-caps at either end.

"Don't lose it," Rashid said, handing it to him. "Lock it in the boot of your car." He looked at Ramsay and said, "Going to show me what you can do?"

"Oh, okay," Ramsay replied, a little too excitedly.

King smiled and rubbed his shoulder. He'd fired enough for one day, but he quite liked the idea of seeing how much Ramsay had picked up in his hour one-to-one with Caroline. As they approached the army range officer and his table of assorted small arms and ammunition, King couldn't help thinking what a fun break from the norm and monotony it had been. A drive into the country, the blue sky and warm sun of early summer. The promise of a decent pub lunch on the drive back to London. So reassuring amongst the anguish of formulating the plans for the impending operation, and the nagging doubt that he could even pull it off.

Chapter Four

Seventeen days ago

Congressman Standing had taken to the podium. King had studied the man intently for four-months. He had chosen him, not least because of the previous assassinations by an extremist group and that the man fitted their MO, but because of the question mark hanging over him. He had a secret. And while he was setting up his patsy, he couldn't help thinking that the question mark over him would soon be addressed. And the chance and unfortunate killing of an investigative journalist in an unsolved murder case, might well be taken more seriously.

The Secret Service cordon had kept the crowds back some fifty-metres. The veteran's band was playing to the man's right, and the press occupied the ground directly in front of him. The World's press was assembled, more so than they would have been on another occasion, but this memorial was tipped to be special. Not for the veterans or memory of the dead, but because Congressman Standing was expected to announce his run for President. He was starting his Presidential campaign today. What better way for a war veteran to throw his cap into the leadership ring, than to piggy-back a celebration of war heroes? It came as no surprise to King – politicians were the same the world over.

King had the rifle ready, steadied on the bipod and resting on the dresser. He had positioned the firing point six-feet back inside the room and worked out the distance first by using dead-reckoning and experience, then by measuring with the laser distance finder. He had two-thousand-six-hundred metres. He had previously zeroed the rifle to that exact distance at a rifle range in Ohio. He had taken bets from other shooters whether he could hit the target at that range. The bets got bigger as the targets got smaller and King had made a good deal of money and enemies in a single afternoon. They certainly wouldn't forget him in a hurry. Which had been part of his plan.

Standing was well into his speech, the cameras flashing and the film rolling. Flags were waving and sentiment flowing. King opened the window, eased the curtains back and returned to the dresser. He leaned over, shouldered the weapon and flicked off the safety. Unlike the British army version that Rashid had acquired for him, this US civilian version was semi-automatic. King had loaded it with just five rounds of .50 calibre Hornady A-Max, 750 grain match-grade ammunition at ten-dollars a bang. He settled in behind the stock, rested his chin on the adjustable cheek-piece and centred the crosshairs of the scope on the centre of Standing's head.

He breathed in, exhaled steadily and held for a second. There was a critical point where the lungs were not starved of oxygen and the pause in breathing created a moment of stillness needed to take a shot like this. King didn't quite have it. His heart was hammering against his chest. He took a deep breath, willed himself to calm. He focused on the centre of Standing's forehead, imagined the bullet finding its mark. He took another breath, felt calmer now, and as he reached the point that his lungs did not crave the air, but every part of him was still, he slowly, steadily, squeezed the trigger.

At this range, King had time to resettle the rifle and watch the bullet strike the plexiglass ten-feet in front of Standing's face. He squeezed off the second shot before Standing even flinched. He thought back to one of the many briefings, the report from the French manufacturer of the ballistic glass. King fired twice more, his finger hovering on the trigger as he watched Standing fall backwards from the podium and the Secret Service bullet-catchers burst onto the stage as if they were going to pick up a ball and go for a touchdown.

King had fired four rounds, his finger still hovering over the trigger. The target was down.

He was done.

Chapter Five

King unloaded the weapon and slipped it into the carry bag. He breathed deeply as he poured water into a glass. He took a sip, topped up the glass and readied himself. There was no going back now, and he stepped up to the dresser, slipped off the latex gloves and pressed all the digits of his left hand onto the hotplate. He flinched away but steadied his hand with his right and pressed down harder. He screamed, but used the energy to roar, as his skin smoked, and his nostrils were filled with the acrid aroma like that of burnt hair. He plunged his hand into the glass of water, then pressed the fingers and thumb of his right hand onto the hotplate, avoiding the five smouldering patches of skin. He did not scream this time but panted through the pain. He had known what to expect, and as he had been briefed, the burn was so deep that the nerve endings were destroyed. He dipped his fingers into the water, grit his teeth and wiped the tears in his eyes with the sleeve of his left arm. He had never felt an initial pain like it, but he knew there would be more to come. He had tossed the snowball down the hill. There was no stopping the momentum now.

He shouldered the rifle case and tucked the latex gloves into his pocket. The door handle was difficult to grasp, his fingers sore and throbbing. They felt hot. If he'd done it at home on the stove, then he would have held them in iced water for half an hour. But he did not have that luxury.

Outside his room, the corridor was empty, but he could hear screams and noises downstairs. The Secret Service had reacted quickly. Either that, or the Washington DC police department were on the scene. He doubted that, but there were no hard and fast rules, no clue just how this would play out. The rifle would have woken the dead from where he had fired, and he was in no doubt that somebody would have phoned it in before he had put the rifle away. Events were set now, but King needed to do two things before it was too late. The first was ditch the gloves, which he did in a housekeeper's trolley bin on the next floor down. His finger prints would be on the inside of the latex. His DNA also. The second thing was to avoid getting shot. King figured the lift would be his best bet and he rested the rifle against the control panel as he selected the lobby. He watched the floors count down from eight to G. The doors parted, and King could already see his opportunity. A uniformed female police officer was checking with the desk. There were Secret Service agents gathering in the entrance, and police officers were heading for the stairwell. King made eye contact with her as she looked towards the lift. The other officers and agents were looking now, but King did not look at them as he raised his hands and slowly eased himself down onto his knees. He focused on the female officer, her weapon now drawn and aiming at him.

"I am unarmed!" he shouted. He eased himself onto his stomach, his hands stretched out in front of him. "Unarmed!"

The doors of the lift closed behind him, although he could not hear them above the screams, shouts and roars of the other officers and agents, each scrabbling to draw their weapons and aim, some taking cover, some forgetting their training altogether. He kept eye contact with the woman, not daring to look at any other law enforcement officer. He could not give them an excuse to open fire, and he knew the woman would be more level headed than the testosterone-fuelled men looking to get their guns off at some domestic terrorist.

King braced himself and felt the metal of multiple pistol barrels dig into him, handcuffs grip his wrists – unimaginably tight – and his limbs wrenched backwards. He felt his shoulder pop and grimaced as he realised it had been dislocated. He howled in pain, over emphasising it, but not by much. It was an agonising ache that made him feel nauseous and close to vomiting.

His face was pushed hard into the marble floor and he could no longer see the female police officer. Someone had the lift doors open, had announced they had the weapon. A police officer started to Mirandize him and read him his rights, but the officer faltered and trailed off. What looked to be a senior Secret Service agent was shouting for people to leave the area and sited jurisdiction and Pentagon powers of secrecy.

So, this was it, King thought. There were two ways this was going to play out. He would be uncuffed, pulled to his feet and shot 'while trying to escape'. Or he would feel a hood over his head and the game would begin.

The lobby was becoming more and more quiet. King was aware of footsteps and hushed tones. He could hear his own breathing, but at least the pain of his dislocated shoulder had taken his mind off his burned fingertips.

Silence.

An uncomfortable silence interrupted only by the thudding of his own heartbeat.

Two men, tentative. Hushed tones. A muffled phone call.

King felt someone at the handcuffs. His heart sank, but he always told himself there was a chance. His shoulder was out of action, but if they got the cuffs off him, he would be ready. He wouldn't die like a dog. He thought of Caroline, their last moments together, he couldn't leave her like this…

He felt himself pulled harshly to his knees, his shoulder exploding in pain. He caught sight of a man in a dark suit. Seasoned, professional and tough. Receded hair, close cropped. Dark sunglasses. And then darkness, as the hood was put over him, and he knew, that here at least, he would remain alive for a little while longer.

Chapter Six

King did not know how many hours had passed. He guessed at eight but knew from experience – both on his escape and evasion courses with the SAS, or for real in some of the world's less likely tourist destinations – that time was immeasurable. After three hours, it all merged into one long period of hell.

They had worked him well. A few punches and kicks, but he could cope with that. He had once made his living as a boxer and prize fighter and he hadn't fought in the best venues with the kindest opponents. In many of his fights there hadn't even been a doctor on call. But what these people lacked in harshness and viciousness, they made up with technical skill. The hood had remained, and he had been put into various stress positions. He was fit and supple and could cope with most, but he was tiring now, and his burned fingertips were causing him huge discomfort. But it had worked. They had not been able to take a set of fingerprints from him, and that kept them out of the international databases the CIA had unlimited access to. It had bought him precious time.

"Your name…"

She was back in the room. King hadn't spoken yet, but he knew for survival he would have to change that soon. He was weakening, needed the pause that information would give him. Time to rest while they went and checked.

"What is your name?" she repeated.

"Get somebody to pop my shoulder back in and I'll tell you…"

Naturally, he did not see the blow coming from behind, and it was a shock to his system, but he told himself he had taken worse. He had sprawled to the ground. Hard concrete, unfinished, cold. A warehouse perhaps? Certainly not a federal or law enforcement building. There was concrete dust as well, indicating it wasn't a room that had ever received more than a perfunctory sweep after construction. It was prevalent enough to smell through the hood.

"Mike," he said. "My name is Mike!" He eased himself up and settled onto his backside. "We'll get along a whole lot better if I don't have to think about my shoulder." He braced himself for another punch, but it didn't come.

Conference. Hushed tones. The door opened and closed. A moment later, maybe a minute, perhaps ten, and he was lifted by two pairs of rough hands. His right cuff was released and almost instantly locked onto something firm and metallic. Fingers pressed into his shoulder while another pair of rough hands pulled one way, then pushed another. It took a great deal of force, but the relief when it found its place back in the socket was euphoric. Agony to ecstasy, then comfort. King knew it would be greatly weakened, could even find a way of popping back out until the ligaments contracted back, but for now, he felt back to normal.

The cuffs went back on, but the hood came off and he blinked at the light. The room was much as he'd expected. No windows, plain block walls and a steel door. A single low wattage light bulb hung from the ceiling, but it was high enough to be out of reach even standing on a chair. Of which, there were three. Two for his hosts and one for the guest. But this place wasn't getting a great score on *TripAdvisor*.

"So, Mike," she paused. "Mike what?" The woman was thirty, dark-skinned. Perhaps part Hispanic. She wore her hair in a thick ponytail. She was attractive, and that was probably her strength for interrogation.

"Hunt."

"Michael?"

"Just Mike."

"Mike Hunt."

King smiled. Behind him, one of the pairs of rough hands sniggered. She looked at him, and the glare said it all. She turned her stare back at King. "Cute."

"I'm sure it is…"

"Hit him," she said.

King ducked his head and the punch skimmed his scalp. The second punch didn't miss, and nor did the third. The man had hurt his own knuckles. She nodded for him to continue, but the next punch was far softer than what had gone before it. King was making more of it than he needed to. It had hurt, but he'd had worse over the years. He'd have a thick ear, but the thing about those was you never really felt the next blow. Otherwise boxers would never get into the ring.

"So, it's not Mike?" she looked at him coldly.

"Philip," King said.

"Philip what?"

"McCavity…"

"Philip McCavity?"

"Sure, why not. Doesn't look like I'm going anywhere…" King grinned, but he knew he'd overdone it. The punches rained down on him, and the other pair of hands joined in.

The woman watched him throughout. Impassive. King lost interest in her, tried his best to take the blows. They were tough men, or at least vicious. King suspected if he were not shackled then he could show them what tough really was. But for now, he took the beating. He had decided he wouldn't talk after this. He'd close his eyes and play unconscious. He just needed a sufficient enough blow to take him to the cusp, then he'd allow his body and mind to do the rest.

The blow never came. The door opened and the man in the dark suit with the receded hairline and the tough face came in. He'd ditched the sunglasses.

"What the fuck is this? Amateur hour?" he dropped a file and photos on the table. The woman glowered but checked herself. The man was clearly senior to her.

"Casey M. Grant," he said. "We've got your credit card records, CCTV footage of you using that same rifle on a range in Ohio. Not so smart, are you? Bought your ammunition there using the same credit card. But you left a trail, dumbass. That's how I know your fucking name…"

King stared at him but said nothing. His heart was beating. Pounding against his chest. He could feel his blood pressure rising.

Make or break.

"We've now linked that card to the locations of the assassinations of three Congressmen, and the attempted hit on Congressman Standing. Gas stations, motels, In and Out Burger, Denny's, Seven Eleven, Dunkin' Donuts," he paused. "And the shining star? A Cabela's. A God-damned firearms and outdoor sportsman's store. You even bought your ammunition with that same damned card! Right there in Louisiana and again in New Jersey. The day before a congressman was killed in both those states using a point-fifty. And now, we have a fifth link. Only you're not as good as you think you are…" The man pulled out the spare chair and sat down heavily. "Congressman Standing was unharmed. You fired four shots at him through that plexiglass and it almost gave way. Another bullet and it would have shattered the glass and the death toll would have been five congressmen. You had that bullet, could've used it if you were more professional. So, you failed. And now your ass belongs to me..."

Chapter Seven

Four months earlier

"I don't see how the death of a US congressman is anything to do with MI5," said Ramsay. "Not when the assassination occurred on US soil."

"The FBI and the Secret Service are working hard to find the gunman. Three victims so far. They are seizing CCTV footage at gun ranges and the NRA are filing for civil liberty violations. The CCTV is there for the operator's safety, not to keep tabs on gun owners. It's all in the second-amendment."

"They had CCTV when the founding fathers wrote the constitution?" Ramsay smiled.

"Neil…"

"Sorry. Well, the yanks are a bit touchy on that subject."

Simon Mereweather picked up the sheaf of papers and handed them across the desk. "We suspect we know the identity of this vigilante. A team working on links to Islamic terrorism on US soil…"

"What?" Ramsay interrupted.

Mereweather held up a hand. "Please permit me to finish, Neil," he paused. "I know we shouldn't be there but matters escalated. And dealing with the Americans has become tiresome lately. They are fast becoming a shuttered nation…"

"But are our friends and allies, nonetheless…"

"There are no friends or allies in intelligence, Neil. Merely countries or organisations with common interests. And at present, some of our views are not shared by the Americans. They have distanced themselves under this current administration. Presidents come and go; we'll all be on each other's Christmas lists again soon."

"So, we're operating out there without sanction?"

"Yes."

"And how has this link with the gunman been established?"

"The Islamic terrorists have been subtly recruiting a sniper."

"They can't train their own?"

"Not to the extent they wanted," he paused. "They wanted to score a moral victory as well. They wanted to recruit a disaffected US serviceman. Better PR, so to speak. It was an odd approach but makes perfect sense when one thinks about it."

"And the target?"

"The US President, amongst others. Start low, build momentum and publicity, then take out POTUS."

Ramsay shrugged. "So, we could just sit back and watch the show then."

"Neil…"

"Sorry." He glanced at the top copy of paper, more out of discomfort. He had surprised himself. He wasn't normally obtuse. Not up the ladder, at least.

"A domestic investigation led a team to the states. Islamic terrorists were trying for a three-pronged attack using British, American and French ex-soldiers to assassinate key politicians who supported the war on terrorism in the Middle-East. A crowning victory for their PR machine. Soldiers so disaffected that they pick up arms against the very people who sent them off to war," he paused. "We thought our sniper was heading out there to get some range practise and procure a weapon and ammunition. It's quite possible for someone to buy what they need, and all you'd have to do is find a way to get it back into the country. Anything bought on the black market here is either old Soviet stock or stolen and well-used rubbish. The ammunition in most cases is home-loaded. In the US, match-grade equipment can be easily obtained and with some ingenuity, smuggled back here. We had identified our sniper and it was merely a case of poor operational security that led us to the American sniper. The terrorists did not operate a tight enough cell system."

"What happened to the British sniper?"

"We kept him in play," Mereweather paused. "He's back here and he's under constant surveillance."

"And his weapon?"

"We let it through."

"So, he's active?" Ramsay asked incredulously.

"Until we choose otherwise," Mereweather said. "SCO19 are on standby; four teams of watchers are in place and Special Branch are onside. We have the SAS on speed-dial, so to speak. The guy won't get close enough to his target."

"And the French?"

"We've handed them what data and intelligence we've found," Mereweather sighed. "They'd lost him, the last I heard. They think he has used the open border policy of the Schengen Agreement to slip into Belgium and hide among the huge Islamic community there."

"And the yanks?"

"Haven't told them, old boy."

"But…"

"But, that is where you come in. You and your team. Our first team of watchers have him under surveillance and he doesn't look in a rush to do anything just yet."

"But four congressmen have been killed!"

"That predates our involvement."

"But they will want to know what we know, arrest him, charge him and throw away the key…"

Simon Mereweather steepled his fingers, his elbows firmly on the desk. He smiled and said, "Precisely. And that's what we're counting on."

Chapter Eight

He had been moved three times. Each time, he got the impression that it would be temporary. He had gotten over the fear of being executed. He couldn't change that, and the longer he remained in captivity and the longer he divulged his cover story – one layer at a time – the more chance he had of remaining a viable commodity.

He had been hooded for much of the time and whenever it had been removed, he had been kept in the light and left alone with white noise. He had been subjected to all three but couldn't pick his favourite. Hooded would be close, but that usually accompanied interrogation and beatings. It was more difficult to take a beating when you never knew what was coming and could not brace yourself for the blow. The first strike always landed with enough shock to threaten his heart with stopping. If only they knew. Because the second and third strikes always seemed to revive him. The white noise stopped him from sleeping, and that was the worst torture of all. True sleep deprivation drove loving parents to do unspeakable things in the heat of the moment, so as a form of coercion, it ranked right up there with ripping out fingernails.

It was the waterboarding that drove him to talk, though. The feeling of water seeping into his airway, the sensation of drowning was enough to get anybody spilling the information they held. Or at least, that is what his interrogators thought. King had received training, had the method shown to him, performed on him. He had even used it once on a Russian terrorist. He knew how to resist, how to act and when to divulge. His cover story was multi-layered. And he knew when to bring it in, how much to peel away and when to beg for his life. All the while, remaining calm and fighting the illusion of drowning with what he knew it to be. The sensation built upon fear of the unknown and one's own fragile expectation of mortality.

They had what they wanted, but they would be back. And now, as he ate a burger and fries from the tray and sipped on a paper cup of cola, he had been rewarded with some carrot. Having only eaten microwave sachets of rice or day-old bread rolls for an insurmountable period of time - that he guessed at with the amount of rudimentary meals he had received - as ten days, the burger and fries was going down extremely well.

Now no longer shackled or hooded, he was incarcerated in a cell no larger than eight by eight with a mattress on the floor and a bucket to defecate in, but it provided him with an element of freedom, nonetheless. He had managed to keep check on time, as one of his interrogators and one of the guards had left their watches on. Both were set on the same time, and he had worked out from the pattern of the meals, that it would now be the afternoon. He was aware that he had probably lost track of entire days, but as he sat on his bare mattress and ate the meal, aching and tired, left near exhausted after the last bout of waterboarding, he knew it was approaching evening and he had a good chance of maintaining his equilibrium a little more now that he could distinguish between night and day, and build back in the rest he needed.

He had lost weight, but he had been carrying a little more than normal. Normally somewhere between thirteen and fourteen stone, depending on exercise regime or the mission, he had purposely topped half a stone over, now suspecting he was somewhere between his middle weight. It had been enough to give him the energy he needed, the resolve to get through what was hopefully behind him for a while. He could lose another stone without losing muscle tone, and he would now start tensing his muscles in a pattern to retain strength. A workout without equipment, but he was aware he would be under surveillance and he would refrain from squats, sit-ups and press-ups. It would work in his favour to appear broken and beaten.

Chapter Nine

Boston

It was a black bag operation. Just like he'd seen in the movies and on his favourite TV shows, but this was real and there was a very real chance he could be caught or killed. He never really thought such things existed. Not in today's age. But the world was a complex place, and his position in it was towards the bottom of the pile.

He had served in the marines and the Navy SEALS and had taken a well-paid post at Paradigm - a highly secretive civilian security contracting firm - after his third tour in Afghanistan. He had no idea what the name stood for in terms of its being, and nor did his colleagues, but the pay was good, the leave was regular, and the equipment and resources had been second to none. In fact, it seemed better organised and funded than his SEAL team. Not altogether surprising, given its benefactor, but the CIA had virtually unlimited funds available to pump into outlets such as this. The new way to fight terrorism was through subcontracting deniability and mortgaging morality.

He had killed countless times. But that had been for God, corps and country. Now that it was for money, it didn't feel so good. A numbness to the senses, a detachment that he hadn't felt in the heat of battle, or in the adrenalin build and release of special operations. Tainted. But he would get over it. The fifty-thousand bonus wired to his off-shore account would help with that.

The woman lay on the floor where she had fallen and hugged her dying husband. She had screamed at him, and as he shot her, he had known they were neither words of forgiveness or begs for mercy. Her eyes had said it all. As he walked near to inspect the other body in the kitchen of the open-planned apartment, her left leg shot out. Nerves possibly, but he made sure by planting another .22 bullet in her skull. He wouldn't have normally chosen such a small pistol, but it hadn't been his choice and it worked well with the suppressor – almost silent. The other man – the third in the terrorist cell – had fallen over the sink. Cole couldn't see the man's hands, so he put a bullet into his back, left of the spine and just below the shoulder blade. The body didn't move. He reached out with a gloved hand, pulled the cadaver away from the sink and allowed it to fall heavily to the floor. Satisfied that they were all dead, he slipped the pistol under his jacket and into the shoulder holster, before taking out his phone and taking a picture of each of the corpses. He focused on their faces and then moved the bodies so that he could photograph the wounds. Next, he took out a small set of garden shears, or secateurs and three clear plastic evidence bags. He removed the right index finger of all three corpses and labelled each bag with the code name he had been given for all three targets. He placed the bloodied secateurs and the empty bullet cases in a fourth bag and checked the apartment over for any traces he may have left. As he did so, he caught sight of himself in the mirror. To his surprise, he seemed different somehow. Not so much aged, as weary. He was short and stocky, around five-seven and twelve stone, but well-muscled. His black skin was as dark as imaginable, which emphasised the whites of his eyes, and his large, straight teeth. His close-cropped hair showed no grey, so why did he feel the reflection looked different? It couldn't have merely been the act of what he'd just done, could it? It hadn't so much been murder, as an execution. Maybe that was the difference. He couldn't be sure, but as he tucked the grisly contents inside the bags into his jacket pocket, and picked up his phone, the final glance at the bodies filled him with no further emotion. They had been terrorists. Plain and simple. He did not know of their crimes, couldn't care any less. They had been in the chain, and now they were not.

Cole opened the door and closed it carefully behind him. There was no movement in the corridor, nothing to indicate his actions had disturbed the other residents. He would remove his gloves once he was back on the street. His visit had taken just eleven minutes and America was now a safer place because of it.

Chapter Ten

Cornwall, England
Five weeks earlier

The beach was deserted, and the sea glistened in the rising sun, a rare millpond day on the North coast of the Southwestern-most county.

King enjoyed May, not only his birthday month, but it signalled the start of summer. He had been granted a week's leave of absence to recover from minor surgery, and he was determined to enjoy it. He had left Caroline sleeping at the rental cottage and taken the opportunity to walk the cliffs in the dawn light and make his way down to the beach. The tide was dropping and only his footprints marked the sand behind him. Ahead of him – a blank sand canvas, cool under his bare feet. He dropped his shoes he'd been carrying and stripped down to his boxer shorts. An impromptu dip beckoned him, and what better way to feel alive than to feel cold water on his skin? He jogged the short distance and did not hesitate as he reached the water, and ran up to his knees, hurdled as best he could as the water deepened and cut his losses with a shallow dive into the crystal-clear water. The sea was freezing, his heart pounding and his breath shortening as he started to crawl out into the depths. After fifty-metres, he took a breath, dived down the eight-feet or so to the sand and flipped onto his back. The water was crystal-clear, the sky blue above. He blew out a bubble ring, watched it rise and grow to the surface where it dispersed in a scattering of tiny bubbles. He had perfected the art, though in much warmer water than this. He pushed off the sand and as he broke the surface, he turned to watch the shore. The cliffs rose dramatically out of the sea on both sides of the tiny bay and the beach gave way to dunes and the small hamlet beyond. King could happily move here. Or at least buy his and Caroline's ideal holiday home. A crash-pad for R&R between assignments, with a view to take early retirement to in the not too distant future. He smiled to himself, knowing pipe dreams seldom panned out. But he had seen a cottage for sale further up the valley which had looked ideal. He shook the thought from his mind, took a breath and started to crawl down the bay until he'd swam around a quarter of a mile. He looked up at the cliff towering above him, then started for the shore. The sun was edging above the land to the East, and as it broke over the horizon, it flooded the bay with bright yellow light, and he welcomed its warmth as he walked back to his clothes. He ditched the boxers and pulled on his jeans, covering his brief nakedness, then wrung the boxers out and pocketed them before picking up his shoes. He fingered the healing scar on his abdomen, just below his left ribcage. Keyhole surgery, a miracle of modern science. Shrapnel from a wound on his previous assignment had been detected and removed. He looked down at his right side, where the picture told a different story. A bullet had taken part of his rib, caused massive internal bleeding and the surgery needed to remove the shattered bone and damaged bullet had left him looking as if a shark had taken an exploratory bite and discounted him in the same mouthful. Over two-hundred stitches to his back and abdomen. He slipped his shirt over him. He didn't really mind the scars. They meant he had lived to tell the tale.

He jogged his way up the beach and stopped before the sandy car park. Rashid was perched on the bonnet of his Audi, a coffee in his hand. Another cup sat beside him, along with a paper bag.

"Nice day for a swim," Rashid paused. "Somewhere in the world, but not here. Must have been bloody freezing."

"It gets the blood flowing and the heart pumping" King said and picked up the cup. "Tea?"

"White and one."

"What's in the bag?"

"Sausage rolls and some croissants."

"You really are a crap Muslim," he said and sipped some of the tea through the gap in the lid.

Rashid shrugged and took out a sausage roll. "I got these from a bakery and deli in Padstow," he said. "Weird place. The harbour's full of water and the tide is nearly out."

"They have a loch."

"Oh." He took a bite of the sausage roll and spoke with his mouthful, "That's a bugger if you miss the tide," he said.

"Why are you here?" King rummaged through the bag and retrieved a sausage roll. "Besides breakfast, that is?"

"Director Amherst wants me to assess your shooting."

"Piss off!"

"I know," Rashid laughed. "But he's worried about the shot. He wants three in the bull, no misses or he's changing his mind about the entire operation."

"Idiot."

"I've got the rifle in the boot."

"You're really going to test me?"

Rashid was grinning. "There's a military range on Bodmin Moor at Milpool, but it's only rated to six-hundred metres."

"Wasted trip, then."

"There's another club on Bodmin Moor, but it's civilian and rated to twelve-hundred metres."

"Like I said…"

"I've set something up," Rashid interrupted.

"I'm sure."

"A couple of thousand metres, at least. I used Google Earth and found a disused airfield. It's at a place called Davidstow. Not all that far from here, near Camelford. It's all ready, just need to drive around a bit and make sure there's no random dog walkers, or doggers, or whatever the hell they do down here for kicks."

"Caroline will be expecting me," King said tersely.

"Don't worry, I've cleared it with the boss. I got her a cappuccino and a nice sticky Danish with a cherry on top, she's good to go for a couple of hours," he smiled. "Besides, we don't want you in your comfort zone, or anything like that."

King sipped some more tea and picked up a sausage roll. "Come on, then," he said. "The sooner we do this, the sooner you can piss-off back up the line and let me get on with my sick leave."

Chapter Eleven

There were several points of access to the area surrounding the airfield. A forest was gated off against vehicles but allowed enough room for access to walkers and horse riders. The airfield itself had been abandoned since the end of the second world war and the runways were largely potholed and overgrown. A fence restricted access, but somebody had cut through the chain link. King could guess who.

"I've measured out the distance," Rashid said.

"Which is?"

"Your problem."

"Thanks," said King. "And what's the target?"

"You'll see."

"You're not being helpful."

"Well, maybe I'd like to see you fail."

"What, so you get my job? It's not all that."

Rashid dropped down from the branch of a large pine. He handed King the binoculars. "It looks clear," he said. "Do you want to take a look?"

"No."

"And I don't want your job," Rashid said sullenly. "I don't particularly want you to have this one, that's all."

King shrugged. "It's a sound plan."

"It's suicide."

"Come on," King replied. "I've got good back-up."

"Well, I hope so."

"Well, make it so. Just be where you've got to be and stick to the timings."

"Easier said than done."

King turned and led the way back to Rashid's car. Rashid popped the boot and King took out the fully assembled rifle, housed in a soft rifle slip.

"I have faith in you, the rest of the team," King said. "Have some faith in me."

"Oh, I've got that," Rashid shook his head. "But I wouldn't trade places with you for anything."

"Thanks."

"Go find the target," Rashid said. "I'll time from your first shot. Three bulls. And I'll give you ten seconds seeing how this model is bolt-action and the one you'll be using is semi-auto. But I've changed the parameters. The target area is smaller than you'll be used to. No big black bullseye this time."

"Setting me up to fail?"

"Hopefully."

King took the rifle out of the slip and checked the magazine. He could see from the inspection holes that it held three rounds. He eased the bolt, saw the chamber was empty. He kept it that way and headed out to where Rashid had indicated he should take up position.

The ground was heathland, made up predominantly from heather, gorse and bracken. King watched his step, a nice time of year for waking adders full of venom and protective of their territory. Certainly not lethal to a healthy adult, but one of the moodiest and fastest-striking snakes on the planet. As well as having an incredibly painful bite. It was an old Cornish saying when someone was in a particularly bad mood that they were 'teasy as an adder'.

King found a decent laying-up spot and got down into a prone firing position with the rifle. He pulled down the spring-loaded bipod and studied the ground ahead of him. He used the scope to scan the hedgerow some two-thousand metres distant. It was only now, as he searched for the target, that he considered what a ridiculous distance this was to make a shot. But then he was reminded of the ballistic capabilities of the .50 calibre round.

King had been over the area twice, but as he slowed his scan, took in the hedgerow metre by metre, the target eased into view. He adjusted the sight aperture and smiled. A full head and shoulders photograph of Congressman Standing that had been blown up as a life-sized poster. A grey suit, crisp white shirt and even whiter teeth. His sandy blond hair sat atop his head like a bad wig and his face had an unusual orange tint to it, the product of a tanning salon and some poor advice.

King could already ascertain that it was a life-sized impression. The foliage and exposed pieces of shaped and cut hedging stone in part of the hedge lent some scale and perspective to the picture. He sighted the rifle, eased the bolt back, then pushed firmly forwards to chamber the big round. He watched the bracken and the movement of the gorse on top of the hedge. The wind was consistent with how it felt against his cheek. South-westerly, no more than five-miles-per-hour but enough for the bullet to travel two inches to the right over two kilometres. To compensate the wind, he adjusted the top turret two clicks. The turret on the righthand side was dialled back four clicks for the distance. He re-sighted and took a deep breath, gently squeezed the trigger pre-set. On the exhalation, he waited until two-thirds of the air was steadily exhaled and slowly finished the trigger squeeze. The mighty rifle boomed and kicked back, its recoil like a decent punch to his shoulder. He knew Rashid would be timing him and he worked the bolt and ejected the massive brass shell. He drove the bolt back home, closing the breech and taking up the pre-set on the trigger. Again, he breathed steadily out and fired at the point just before he had no air left. He re-sighted, could see the grouping through the powerful scope. He went through the motions again, fired the third bullet before Rashid had counted to eight.

King picked up the rifle and the spent brass cases and made his way back across the heath to the gap in the fence. Rashid had the binoculars and looked pleased with himself.

"Not like you to miss." He smiled. "Finally seeing sense?"

"Bollocks," King retorted.

"Close, but no cigar," Rashid grinned. "I'm taking my findings to Mereweather and

Amherst. Both you and Caroline can thank me. You'll live to fight another day. Now, go and get some leave, the two of you."

"Check the target," said King.

"I'll get it when we drive around the airfield. But I saw through the binos. You missed. Good grouping though."

"About two inches to the right?"

"Yep."

"And an inch high?"

"Yes," Rashid frowned at him.

"Well tell Mereweather and Amherst I wasn't briefed to take Congressman Standing's life. I was briefed to miss, but make it look convincing. A near miss is more difficult to achieve than a direct hit. So, that's what I can do. But I imagine the plexiglass will do the rest on the day."

Chapter Twelve

The guards were rough, but then guards usually were. They relished the power. They were usually strong men who lacked toughness or resilience. King always found them to go down easily enough in a fight and stay there.

He was shackled with his hands behind his back. Each time he was taken to the interrogation room they would unlock one side of his handcuffs, push him down into a hard-backed chair, and put the shackles through a metal loop bolted to the desk. King had no doubt he could choose that moment to overpower the two guards, but there was no point. He needed to know more about his surroundings first.

Both guards left the room and the door closed behind them with an ominous clunk. Metal on metal. Once that door closed, there was no breaking it down. King relaxed his breathing. It was the unknown that was entirely out of his control yet looming dominantly over him. He hadn't seen a mirror, but doubted he looked pretty. Over the course of time he had been incarcerated he had both eyes bruised and swollen shut, his nose broken, and his teeth loosened. His ribs had been cracked and his shins beaten with pieces of wood. He now had lumps on his shins like splints on a rescue horse. However, since he had spilled his cover story under waterboarding, he had been left alone. King knew he had convinced them, and that people were checking out his story. With any luck a terrorist cell operating in Boston and on MI5's radar had been shut down. Three dead terrorists and no minutes of sleep conceded. This had bought him time and provided him with credibility to his story. He had straightened his own nose using the edge of the doorframe in his cell, and his teeth had firmed up. It hadn't been like he'd had much food to chew. His ribs would be ok, he had broken them before and knew how long they would hurt for and how they would limit his abilities. He had resigned himself to a month of pain with those, and along with his shoulder and the threat of the joint slipping, he knew he could be in better shape.

Hunger was key, though. The food had become irregular, but King knew that it was to mess with his head and make him lose track of time. One of the guards still wore a wristwatch and he started to wonder if it had been a ploy all along to get into his head. His mentor Peter

Stewart had always said that he should listen to his subconscious voice, the voice of reason. The fact that he knew the tricks of the trade could only help him. He would eat again soon, and he would rise above their tricks and foibles, because he still had more to give them and this time, it would be his chance to send a signal.

The door opened, and King looked around to see who had entered.

"Eyes front, shithead!"

King did so slowly. He called this one Tommy Lee. Because he looked like Tommy Lee Jones' character from the film Men in Black. He was the man from the lobby of the hotel and King suspected he was something more wide-ranging than Secret Service.

"Good information," he said finally, after sitting down and sipping coffee from a paper cup. "We've closed the loop. You shitheads want to kill our politicians, you get what's coming to you."

"Nice and clean?"

"Who gives a rat's ass?"

"I won't get paid."

The man studied King for a moment. "You're not a believer?"

"Only when I saw her face," King paused. "Not a doubt in my mind…"

"Smartass, eh?"

King shrugged. "Come on, I gave them up to you. You've got to give me something back."

"I haven't got to give you shit."

"I have plenty more information where that came from," King said.

"Really?"

"Yeah, really."

"So, for the record, you're not a disenfranchised ex-soldier?"

King smiled. He bore a slight resemblance to Casey M. Grant, at least from the man's file photo with a military buzz-cut and ten years of youth expunged from him. It had been close enough, but he was surprised it had stuck. The ruined fingerprints had seen to that. They were sore still, and rough. Like he'd gotten superglue all over them. But they would serve another purpose. He needed to drop Grant from the cover story. He was going to drop the American accent now. He just hoped he could after two arduous weeks. "No. I'm a gun for hire," he said, his accent neutral British with a slight hint of South London that he had watered down over the years. "I was with the Secret Intelligence Service for around fifteen years." He was surprised at his voice, like a stranger's. He wasn't even sure it was natural. He guessed he'd slip into that as he went on.

The man smiled. "Well, that will be easy to check, buddy. Are you sure you don't want to change your story? Again, that is."

"You may not find the department I used to work for on any database."

"We've got people all over MI6," the man sipped his coffee and smiled. "If you worked for SIS, I'll know within the hour."

"Good. Go and check. And bring me back another cheeseburger meal, will you? I'm not responding to your line of questioning anymore. Anymore rough stuff and my lips will be tighter than a clam's arsehole, got it?"

"Tough guy, eh?"

"No, just options. I don't seem to have many sitting here. But I will if you move me somewhere a little more… permanent. I'll barter information for my freedom. A long game, I imagine, but a workable arrangement. Or I'll die here. That's the game, the flip of a coin. I'm ready and okay with that. So, do your waterboarding and beat me, and you'll end up with fuck-all. Feed me, treat me with a little respect and I'll mortgage you some information."

The man looked at King, but had trouble holding his stare. He took out a pen and a piece of paper. "Okay, then. Name?"

"Mark Thomas Jeffries, but my alias is Alex King," he paused. "You'll have to dig deep. See if those CIA moles are worth what you're paying them." King watched the man's expression. He didn't respond, not even a flicker. "Or is it NSA?"

The man smirked, but he wasn't admitting to anything. He didn't need to, King knew right off the bat. "Alright, Mister King. I'll get onto it."

"And a shake," King said. "To go with the meal…"

Chapter Thirteen

Hereford, England
Four weeks ago

It was a quiet and unassuming cul-de-sac. Freshly mown lawns, decent family vehicles. SUVs, people carriers and hatchbacks. Mainly new, but there were a few two or three-year-old German marques there, too. These were nine to fivers. Home owners. Workers with mortgages and aspirations. The backbone of Britain. They paid their taxes, spent their money and didn't claim benefits.

Rashid smiled to himself as he parked his car three doors down from the house he wanted. He had driven past, performed a U-turn and was now parked up what he called nosey-out. Able to get out of trouble quickly. He wondered what the neighbours would make of the person he'd come to visit. But then, he knew what secrets suburbia held. A place where most people did not really know their neighbours. Where pop-up brothels operated without detection, where drugs could be grown and harvested without suspicion. Because these very same people who worked and held onto their aspirations seldom knew the world around them. They drifted in and out, spent more time at desks than in their gardens. Which was why the person Rashid had come to see had operated without suspicion for so long.

Rashid got out and crossed the road. He always parked on the opposite side to provide him with a better view. Not only could he keep an eye on his car, but he could see fifty-metres in both directions from the house.

The garden was untidy, but the grass had been cut. He doubted the occupier had performed such a task. Perhaps a kind spirited neighbour had intervened. Most likely looking to keep the value of their own property buoyant. Rashid noticed the ramp, but took the steps, nonetheless. He rang the bell, stepped back a pace and waited.

There was movement behind the door. Rashid couldn't see anything through the frosted decorative glass in the top quarter of the door, but he suspected he was being watched somehow.

"Fuck off, Paki..."

Rashid smiled. "I thought you'd settle in Wales," he replied. "Someplace with a lot of frightened sheep."

"I go on day trips…" The door unlocked, but it took a while for it to open. "That way I don't wear them out…"

"Not with that little thing of yours you won't," Rashid fired back. He looked down at the former SAS Sergeant. "Good for the special forces chat up line, though."

The man looked up from his wheelchair and grinned, "I got my wife with that one. Or ex-wife, the fucking bitch…" He shrugged. "Fancy a shag, love? Don't worry if you're not in the mood… I'm special forces, I'll be in and out before you know anything about it!"

"Good to see you, Taff." He ignored the man's missing limbs and stepped in past him. He had known it had been bad but had not expected anything like this.

"I've not seen you, since…"

Rashid shrugged. "Been busy, you know how it is…"

"No bother," the man replied and pushed the door closed with his one remaining arm. "Well, you're here now." He turned the electric wheelchair around and scuffed some paint off the wall. From a metre downwards there was barely a flake of paint left.

Rashid walked through to the lounge. The house was an open-plan bungalow that the former Welsh Guardsman and SAS soldier had bought after his life-changing injuries in Afghanistan. "Liz not here, then? You said; ex-wife…"

The Welshman laughed. "Nah, fucked off with someone else soon afterwards. I can't blame her, really." He raised the stump that had once been his left arm. "Who the fuck wants to be stuck with this?"

"Well, not even those sheep now, I guess," Rashid said, looking at the wheelchair. "It's not like you could catch them in that thing."

"Still a twat, then?" He shook his head. "I'll never know how you made Captain," he said. "Oh, wait… the twat thing, that's how."

Rashid grinned. "I'll get a brew on."

"Help yourself."

Rashid walked into the kitchen and looked in one of the top cupboards, but it was empty.

"Bloody Ruperts," Taff said, shaking his head. "How the fuck am I going to reach up there?" Rashid got the message, looked in the lower cabinets. He found tea bags and sugar, a couple of mugs. "Can you believe Liz moved all the things into the top cupboards just to piss me off? Or that she'd purposely move the toilet roll and make herself scarce when I needed a dump? She didn't have the guts to tell me she was shagging another bloke, thought she'd just make my life hell and force me to push her away."

"Best rid, then." Rashid put the kettle on to boil and took out some milk from an under-unit fridge.

"I still can't believe it…"

"What? The fact you stepped on an IED, the fact she cheated on you and left you," he paused. "Or that you're going to save a hell of a lot on socks, shoes and gloves? Get on with it, man. Shit happens."

Taff looked at him for a moment. Rashid wasn't sure if the man was going to cry, but he started to chuckle and before long the pair were laughing loudly, with Taff wiping tears from his eyes.

"You're a git," Taff said. "But to be honest, I've missed the banter. Everyone is so on edge around me, never know what to say."

"I'm sorry I didn't visit sooner," said Rashid. He'd never actually left the regiment, just found himself seconded and sequestered and signed up to MI5 because of his association with King, who had needed his help at a time he found himself on the outside of the usual channels. Rashid had never done the rounds, visited friends and comrades before leaving for a new career. His life in Hereford had simply slipped by unnoticed.

"Guys like me are an inconvenient reminder. We're what guys like you could have been if your luck had run out, too." Taff shrugged. "What difference did it all make?"

"None."

"Then why?"

"Ours is not to reason why, ours is but to do and die..."

"Kipling was a twat."

"I'm sure he was, but it was Tennyson."

Taff shrugged. "Whatever. He was a twat, too. Now, are you going to tell me why you're here? Apart from giving me a motivational kick up the arse?"

Rashid finished making the tea and handed him the mug. He took a sip of his own, placed it down next to him on the counter. He noticed the dishes in the sink, the dirt on the countertop. He wondered whether Liz had ever felt guilty at cheating on him, or if she ever would. Rashid had never liked the woman and had once called her in to his office along with a Corporal she had been sleeping with. Taff had never known, but Rashid had poured iced water on the affair. He'd had the corporal posted far and wide. He guessed she was just the type of woman who would always be sleeping with someone else.

"I need six men," Rashid said. "It's black-bag stuff. You have my word there will be no double-cross, no expendable shit. They do the job, get out and get paid. I just need six top-notch operators who will take the risk."

"How risky?"

"It's not quite suicide…"

Taff laughed. "You're not selling this well."

"I'm being up front."

"Specialisms?"

"I want men from the regiment. It won't be good enough to have well-meaning gung-ho ex-Royal Marines or Paras. They must have hostage rescue experience. Not just trained but to have served a tour in CRW. And to have worked undercover is crucial."

Taff raised an eyebrow. The Counter Revolutionary Warfare group was a specialist posting. Everybody going through SAS training would do their drills in the killing house, learn what needed to be done, but specialising in it was a different matter. With all the deployment in the Middle-East over the years, the hostage rescue element was depleting. The role of the SAS trooper had reverted to its essence, its formation as a hit and run unit in a desert theatre of war. Captain David Stirling had formed the unit in the Second World War from rag-tag, gung-ho soldiers in North Africa who were up for near-impossible missions and would go the extra mile to see some action. The regiment seemed to have gone full circle.

"In fact," Rashid added. "In light of the terrain and scenarios, men who have put their time in all troops would be favourable."

"Really?"

"It's undercover and the opposition will be US ex-special forces. But the terrain could well be mountains, urban or even need aerial insertion."

"So, they'll be up against SEALs?"

"I imagine SEALs *and* Delta."

"Jesus… What the hell are you doing?"

"You know better than to ask that."

"Fair point," Taff sipped some tea, then said, "I'll need the timeframe, bounty and comebacks."

"It will be in a fortnight's time. There will be a two-week refresher and training programme, then the job should be done within a week. Say, four weeks in all to be safe. Travel expenses and accommodation will be taken care of. The bounty is fifty-grand. Ten-thousand on sign-up, forty-thousand upon completion. Next of kin to receive the full bounty if it all goes tits-up."

"Holy shit! That's some money for a month's work."

"You get me the best, fulfil this deal on time and without a leak, and it's one-hundred thousand for your fee."

"You're fucking kidding, right?"

"No," said Rashid. "But here's the thing. The opposition will be Americans. Ex-soldiers, at that. We've served with these guys, got muddy and bloody with them. This may be a problem for some. Not only are we cut from the same cloth, they will be as well trained as we are. These aren't shit-kickers or goat-fuckers with thirty-year-old AK47s, no formal training and fighting in their dressing gowns. These are as good as it gets. And the other matter is deniability. There are no comebacks. I won't tell you who this is for, and nor will I tell the guys you put in place. If they get caught, mess things up, get injured – there's nobody to run and cry to. They will have to accept their fate."

The Welshman nodded. "I'll get the file," he said. "The trouble is, anyone suiting that criteria are going to be as mad as you are," he smiled. "Either that, or a bloody psychopath that you wouldn't want to fight alongside…"

Rashid watched the man power the wheelchair out through the scuffed doorway, then turned and ran a sink of hot water. He squirted in some washing-up liquid, then started on the dishes and wiping the surfaces where his old Sergeant could no longer reach.

Chapter Fourteen

Appalachian Mountains, Virginia
Two weeks later

The camp was like many throughout the mountain range. Although while other campsites catered for obese teenagers or yoga retreats, or team-building executives, this one was used by a private security company to train close protection personnel. Fifty-acres of privately-owned woodland, a three-acre lake and a series of log cabins that were divided into the main house, accommodation blocks for up to ten people and a recreation room come restaurant. A concrete and metal-lined building built into a hollow made a first-class killing house and pistol range. A series of small-arms ranges had been constructed throughout the woods, making use of natural depressions and sandbags and scrap vehicles positioned to shoot from, or sometimes at, as well as a five-hundred-metre rifle range cut through the woods with targets set every one-hundred-metres.

Throughout the woods a series of obstacles made for a hellish assault course that the fittest of individuals would take twenty-minutes to complete.

Rashid had been here for three days. He had set up targets, designed a training and evaluation programme and prepared the classrooms. He was aware of the enormity of the operation, realising just how last minute it would be. Objective clear, target unknown. He watched the first vehicle pull into the gravelled clearing. Neil Ramsay at the wheel, Marnie in the passenger seat. He could see two men in the back seat, didn't know who they were yet. The second car, an identical GMC Yukon followed closely, driven by Caroline Darby. He had his reservations about her being involved, and had voiced them to Ramsay, who had shouted him down quickly. He couldn't do anything more. He had tried to put King off the mission, and felt that Caroline was far too emotionally involved, given her and King's relationship. He wouldn't go there again, simply had to get on with it. A man was seated next to her with another in the rear. The third Yukon brought up the rear of the convoy, two men in the front. They parked in a line and everybody got out. They stretched and swayed, loosening up from the drive. Rashid walked down the wooden steps.

"Guys, welcome," he said. "The sleeping quarters are over there…" He pointed to the row of cabins. "The rec-room is just down there, help yourself to snacks and drinks. Unpack and unwind. We'll reconvene in an hour." He looked at Ramsay, Caroline and Marnie, who had migrated toward each other. "Come up to the main house."

"Nice place you've got here," said Marnie. She tossed Rashid her bag and he caught it and smiled. "You said you'd take me away to the countryside one day…"

Rashid waved a hand towards the forest and said, "We can have a walk later, I'll show you the sights."

Ramsay pushed past and said, "Briefing, now. Get the kettle on."

Caroline walked up behind him and pulled a face, "The poor love doesn't travel well," she said. "He needs a shower and a coffee." She turned and watched the six men make their way to the recreation room. "An interesting bunch," she commented.

"Handpicked," said Rashid.

"By whom?"

"An intermediary. Why?"

She shrugged. "Maybe it's nothing... Let's get that kettle on." She looked up at the sound of an approaching engine. A motorcycle. High-revving and loud. It appeared over some rough ground adjacent to the road. She recognised the build of the rider, even if she couldn't see his face through the helmet. "Alex..."

King turned a circle and brought the powerful trail bike to a halt facing back out. He kicked down the stand and got off, carrying only a small rucksack. He removed the helmet and hung it from the handlebar by the chinstrap.

"Thought I should meet the team," he said. He hugged Caroline, where she met him at the bottom of the steps. They kissed but were professional enough not to linger. "Missed me?"

"Not much," she chided. "I wasn't expecting to see you."

"A surprise."

She shrugged, punched his arm as they climbed the steps. "I almost wish you hadn't come. I have to say goodbye again; not sure I can handle it. It was bad enough back in England."

"It won't be for long," he said and smiled at Marnie as they reached the top. "Hi," he said.

He looked at Ramsay and nodded. "I wanted to put my face in, thought it might be wise."

Ramsay nodded. "We're having refreshments, and a briefing. The hired help are on an hour's downtime."

"Neil's not a fan," Caroline said. "There's a few that seem okay, but…"

King nodded. It was a special assignment and would undoubtedly appeal to only a few. The private security industry was a mixed bag. He turned to Rashid, who was helping Marnie get the coffee and tea on the go. "Have you vetted them?"

He shook his head. "No time," he said, a little defensively. "But I trust the intermediary. He saved my life once."

"That doesn't mean much," King said. "You saved mine once, too. And look at you…"

"Once?" Rashid frowned. "Oh, how quickly you forget."

"Once, twice, whatever," King smiled. He looked at Caroline and asked, "What are your misgivings?"

"A couple are really up for it," she said.

"Psyching themselves up? A bit of excess bravado?"

"Perhaps," she said, taking the cup of coffee from Marnie. She sipped and shrugged.

"Are they troopers, NCOs, what?" King asked.

"All of the above," Rashid said. "Without being funny, officers seldom sign up for mercenary stuff."

"But they're all experienced in multiple theatres of operation?" King asked, taking his cup of tea from Rashid.

"Absolutely. They all completed selection, served for at least four years, some of them closer to twelve years. They all came up from the Paras or infantry units as well. All have done tours of Afghanistan. And as I stipulated, they've all done a tour in counter revolutionary warfare."

"What's that element?" Ramsay asked.

"Hostage rescue and urban assaults," Rashid replied.

"It's the Afghan thing, isn't it?" Caroline said. "I think a few of our soldiers got a taste for killing."

"No doubt," Rashid said, a little tersely. "But these guys have been around the block. And I wasn't tasked with hiring child minders. To fit the parameters of the assignment, you got killers. Plain and simple."

"Fair enough," Caroline said quietly. She turned to King, "Can we talk outside?"

"Sure." King put down his coffee and led the way out through the Western-style saloon doors. The building had been built to effect, but also had sliding double-glazed doors that had been pulled back. King dropped down the steps, waited for Caroline then walked towards a wood-bark pathway. "What's up?"

Caroline caught hold of his hand and squeezed. "Don't do this..."

King went to pull his hand away but relented. He squeezed back, annoyed it had gotten this far, but feeling for her all the same. "It's too far down the road."

"It doesn't have to be. We can leave, right now."

"And drop out of MI5?"

"If we have to."

"We can't," he said. "And besides, this is too important. What we are going after here is the link that could save us all."

"Is it?" she said sharply. "Or is it just another tiny battle that will soon be forgotten, and soon realised to make no difference? Like almost everything else."

"This matters," said King.

"You're so sure?"

"I'm positive."

"Or is it merely unresolved business?"

"It was resolved," King said. "And now things have taken a different course. This is important."

"Enough to risk your life?"

King shrugged. "It's what we do."

"Then, maybe we shouldn't do it anymore," Caroline commented flatly. They had walked through the trees, the path making for smooth, clean progress through the forest. To her left, a man-sized target was shrouded two-thirds by sandbags. The target and sandbags had been peppered with bullet holes and the paper sheet of the wooden cut-out had been newly pasted on. She waved a hand at the target. "But it's not only targets, is it? We're on the other end of the gunfire as well."

"Like I said, it's what we do…"

Caroline stopped walking and hugged him, leaning her cheek into his firm chest. "Bullets are one thing," she said. "Fighting an enemy is altogether different to what you're going to do. This is like rolling a snowball downhill and hoping it doesn't gather more snow. It's unavoidable. Inevitable."

"We have intelligence," said King. "Good intelligence. We have a sound plan. I'm not denying we need some luck…"

"Luck?" she interrupted. "Don't sell this to me on luck!"

"Luck is half of everything we do."

"And what's the other half?"

King did not answer. He had been close to saying fate, but he realised it was no time to be flippant. He hugged her close and said, "It will be okay."

"Promise me?" She looked up at him, her eyes glossy and her entire demeanour one of child-like vulnerability. He couldn't remember seeing her even close to this.

"I promise," King said somewhat emptily. He had started to doubt himself now, but too much was resting on this to back out now. "We'll be fine. *I'll* be fine. And we'll get the job done." He looked down at her, saw the frightened girl within the smart and confident women he loved. He loved her but had the terrible feeling he may never see her again.

Chapter Fifteen

"This is the Bora Arms BR99 tactical shotgun," Rashid announced. "A Turkish-made weapon based on the M16 or M4 rifle, but a little more substantial in terms of weight and size."

Seven identical weapons rested on the table in front of him. All black and lethal-looking. The weapons were new and fresh out of the box. Rashid had removed the foresights and tactical carry handles, which housed the open sight arrangement and had replaced them with 4x40 tactical optics with illuminated reticle display and a luminous open sight system on top.

"The sights have an open channel with luminous markings that I would recommend for under twenty-five metres, the scope will be good for one-hundred and fifty."

"Fuck those, where are the *real* M4s?" a brash Scotsman named Macintosh asked.

"Wait until I've finished," Rashid said curtly.

"Aye, okay," Macintosh said, visibly taken aback. "Don't get your knickers in a twist, pal."

"If you want your fifty-grand, you'll shut up and listen, *pal*," Rashid retorted. "Anybody else want to fuck off now?"

A collective round of grunts, and Macintosh scowled. Ramsay glanced at Caroline, but she had remained impassive.

"The BR99 is semi-automatic but will fire as quick as you can squeeze the trigger, or as fast as your shoulder will allow for the considerable recoil. In short, it kicks like a mule and ejects the shells about thirty-feet. So, don't be too close to the man firing next to you. It's loud as well. Obscenely so. But I have chosen the weapon for a number of reasons. Firstly; confines. It will knock a rhino on its arse, but because of its low velocity it won't over penetrate walls or ricochet off into next week. Secondly; ammunition combination. Now here's the deal – we're up against American special forces. At the moment, the yanks have something we want, and we can't seem to agree on who should have it. But we will next month, or next year. We've all served with them, too. We don't want to kill these guys, but we have a job to do, nonetheless. I have configured two types of ammunition consisting of rock sea salt and a semi-hardened ballistic gel. Now, don't get me wrong, the harmless rock salt fallacy of a farmer shooting someone in the arse in *Carry On Camping* isn't strictly true. It will blow a person wide-open at close range. But after twenty-metres or so, it will knock them on their arse, and the salt will dissolve leaving no fragment, shot or shrapnel. Yes, it will break the skin, but the person *should* be okay…"

"I don't want a plane ride home with no wonga, but I ain't about to go up against Navy SEALs or Delta with a shotgun full of salt. If I want salt, I'll put it on me fucking chips! And this ballistic gel bullet sounds like a bloody Nerf gun!"

Rashid knew the man as Yates, and he was a cockney through and through. The type who thinks *EastEnders* is a documentary on the middle-classes.

"Let the guy finish," said a man at the back. He had a quiet demeanour and was clean-cut. He looked more like a car salesman than a former SAS soldier. Rashid remembered him from his time in the SAS and knew him as Adams. He was a good operator and a bit of a player with the women. As an officer, Rashid had not socialised with him, but he had seen him around and not heard anything negative.

"What the fuck is it to you?" Yates retorted.

"You're wasting time," replied Adams. "And I want to get busy on the range with my new toy."

Yates scowled, but the calmness of the younger man seemed to unnerve him somewhat. He leaned back in his chair, drumming his fingers on the desk.

"As I was saying; I have also loaded shells with a semi-hardened ballistic gel," Rashid continued. "Now, hit someone in the heart or head at under twenty-five metres and they're not getting up again. But place your shots, and you'll knock them down at up to one-hundred metres." Rashid held up a substantial magazine. Twice as thick as the standard AR magazine on which it was based. "It's simple. These are ten-round magazines. Blue cartridges are salt, and the red cartridges are gel. Now, here's where it's up to you – I have clear cartridges and black cartridges. The clear ones are double-oh-buck. Now, that's nine balls of shot around eight-millimetre in diameter, so think of it in layman's terms as something close to nine Walther PPK bullets hitting the target every time you squeeze the trigger. Now, that's firepower. And they're good in this weapon's three-inch magnum guise for sixty-metres, with a fair amount of spread. The black cartridges are .700 calibre slugs. They are one-ounce of hardened lead and zinc, externally rifled to spin in the smooth bore of the shotgun. They'll take down an elephant. And they're bullseye accurate to one-hundred and fifty metres. I have given you a moral choice. You can take down the opposition with non-lethal force, or you can go another way. If we get into trouble, then we may all feel the switch to lethal rounds is a viable option."

"What about sidearms?" a Northerner asked. Rashid knew him to be a Geordie called Powell. He was knocking on the door of fifty, but that only made him the most experienced soldier in the room. He was as fit as most twenty-five-year-olds in the regiment and carried barely a trace of fat under his weathered mahogany skin.

"Beretta 92fs nine-millimetre pistols," Rashid said. "Again, I will give you one magazine of rubber sub-sonic bullets and the rest will be live-ammo."

"No choice, really," said Yates quietly. He looked at the rest of the men. "Come on lads, do you really want to go up against Delta Force with rubber bullets? It's bogus…"

"Let's get out there on the range," Rashid interrupted, ignoring Yates before the man could turn people's persuasions. He thought back to Taff in his partially modified bungalow and wondered if he'd made a mistake in trusting his old Sergeant's judgement.

Chapter Sixteen

Westfield, New Jersey
Two weeks later

"The timings are bang on," Rashid said as he climbed into the passenger seat of the Yukon. He handed Ramsay the sandwich wrapped in paper. "It's to the day, but there's no telling how long King held out. Whether torture has broken him down, or whether he managed to keep a clear head."

Ramsay looked at the sandwich. "What have I got?"

"Fried breaded chicken with balsamic vinegar glaze."

"What, they didn't have cheese and onion?"

"This is the United States," Rashid replied. "They don't do basic sandwiches over here. Besides, the place is called *Feast Catering*. They're hardly going to do a floppy service station sarnie on thin white bread, are they?"

"I suppose not. What have you got?"

"The same as you, but with brie."

"So, they *did* have cheese."

"It's brie. It's not a safe guess. How was I meant to know you'd like brie? Half the time it tastes like ass."

"I don't even want to hear how you know that."

"Or like ass smells," Rashid clarified.

"You need a doctor if your backside smells like brie."

"I mean, like roast lamb smells like farmyards."

"It does?"

"Oh, forget it."

"Do you want to swap?"

"If I wanted to swap, I would have got what you've got."

"But I would have got your order," Ramsay shook his head. "Look, I'm in charge, swap sandwiches with me."

"You're in charge of lunch, now?" Rashid smirked. "Like a lunch monitor, or something?" Rashid took a bite of his sandwich, looked at Ramsay as he licked around the open edge. "Whoops, too late."

"Git."

"There's a car," Rashid said, putting the sandwich down on the centre console. "Black

Ford, basic trim with an aerial on the rear quarter. Definitely feds."

"Are you sure?"

"Going by the movies, yeah. I haven't been to the states before, much less worked here."

Ramsay nodded as he scribbled in a notebook in his lap. "Looks viable, though."

They watched the man get out. He was stocky yet moved freely. He looked like he did weights. He got out of the car and checked his jacket.

"Armed," Rashid said.

"Everyone is out here."

"Fair point." Rashid glanced down at Ramsay's notes. "What's that?"

"My notepad."

"I know that, but why have you written Afro-Caribbean?"

Ramsay looked up and watched the man walk between the two buildings which led to a courtyard, beyond which two buildings of apartments stood out of view. "But why not just write *black*?"

"It's a bloody minefield," Ramsay said. "Whatever you say ends up upsetting someone. You can't say coloured…"

"What's wrong with you? Of course, you can't say *coloured!*"

"What difference does it make?"

"Loads."

"So, what are you?"

"Human."

"You know what I mean."

"Oh, right," Rashid said. "British."

"But you're coloured…"

"What? For fuck's sake, Neil. Why don't you just stick with IC-four. The Guy over the road is IC-three and you're, I don't know, a neo-Nazi…"

"Hey!"

Rashid watched a woman walk past the black Ford and drop her purse. She started to pick up spilled items and another woman bent down to help her. He looked back at Ramsay and asked, "Well, how many ethnic friends have you got?"

Ramsay took the monitor out of the footwell. He switched it on and frowned as the screen flickered. "Alright," he said. "None."

"Oh, thanks!"

"You know what I mean."

Rashid tried not to smile. He enjoyed

winding Ramsay up. "So, we're just colleagues now, nothing more?"

"I didn't mean that. We just live in a…"

"Decent area?" Rashid shrugged. "Well, I was going to invite you over for dinner when we've got some downtime. I'm not sure I'll bother now. You and the rest of the team. Just for a curry and some ethnic dishes, like. You know, in my flat above my uncle's corner shop…"

"Bloody hell, Rashid!"

"Don't worry about it," Rashid said. "I won't tell anyone."

"You're winding me up, aren't you?"

Rashid nodded and smiled. "It's my new hobby."

"You really can be an idiot sometimes," Ramsay steadied the monitor. "He's going in, look…"

Rashid watched as the man hesitated by the door, the thumb-tack camera he had installed a week before catching him clearly in the fish-eye lens above him. The man knocked, waited then knocked again. He glanced around him, then took out a leather pouch and removed a set of lock-picks. He worked quickly, unlocking the door in just a couple of minutes.

The man put the lock-picks back in his pocket and drew a tiny automatic pistol with a large, bulbous suppressor.

Rashid looked up at Ramsay and said, "This guy's a pro."

Ramsay switched the monitor onto multi-screen. The man worked his way from room to room. They only had four cameras installed, so he disappeared a few times, then came back into view.

"King's in deep," said Ramsay. "This guy would have killed anyone in there."

"But King is *alive*. And his timing is still good. He's only a day off. I was worried when nobody showed yesterday."

"Me too."

"Do we follow this guy?"

Ramsay watched the man's car across the street. Caroline was getting back up from pretending to search for her credit card. Marnie appeared to hand her something and they parted, Caroline thanking her. They had the tracker in position, held firmly in place by a magnetic pad. They walked past the sandwich, salad and soup bar where Rashid had bought the sandwiches, Marnie stopped inside for something while Caroline headed back to the

Yukon further up the street. By the time the man had got back on the street, Adams had pulled up outside the restaurant and picked up Marnie, while Caroline drove past in the third Yukon ready to take the lead. It looked clean, but Ramsay reflected that the area had been a bit Yukon heavy. Perhaps different vehicles would have been more desirable, but the other two cars had gone now, and only the one Rashid and Ramsay were in remained.

The man got in his car and drove away, unaware he was being followed by three vehicles at a safe distance, each following the tracker on an identical monitor.

Rashid drove, eating his sandwich and glancing at the red dot on the screen of the monitor, which had now been synced with the transponder that was receiving a pulse signal from the tracker, or transponder underneath the target vehicle's wheel arch. Ramsay sipped from a Big-Gulp of Mountain Dew that he'd gotten a taste for.

"You really like that shit?"

"Wouldn't drink it if I didn't like it."

Rashid pulled in behind a truck and waited at the lights. The red dot of the tracking device was making its way down the 28 towards Roselle. They caught every light on red and the distance increased. The dot took the 613 Garden State Parkway and the speed increased. Rashid took the on ramp and accelerated. He looked across at Ramsay as his mobile phone rang.

"Hello?" Ramsay said. The international numbers replaced the names in his address book. It was annoying not knowing who was calling.

"Neil, Caroline. Are we happy to follow the tracker, or do you want a visual?"

"I guess it wouldn't hurt."

"I'll slide in behind you, while you take a look see."

Ramsay said, "Okay," and put the phone back in his pocket. He looked at Rashid and said, "Get out in front and I'll check as we pass him. Caroline is taking our place."

Rashid nodded, quietly pleased to do something more pro-active. He stepped down on the accelerator and the massive truck lurched forward, its big V8 engine bellowing as they gained speed rapidly. He frowned as he watched the monitor and looked up as he closed in on an old Ford Bronco pickup truck. "Where's the bloody car?" He pulled in behind the truck, glancing back to the monitor. "Oh, shit…"

"He's played us," Ramsay said. "He's planted the tracker on that old banger!"

Rashid nodded. "And that means we've got some serious competition."

Chapter Seventeen

King couldn't decide whether it had gone to plan or not. Tommy-Lee came back in and studied a file for a while without talking. The cheeseburger and shake never materialised, but he hadn't been beaten. Not in the interrogation room or his cell, at least.

Tommy-Lee had eventually closed the file and looked at King. "Your second tip-off was bogus. Our operative discovered he was under surveillance."

"Another law enforcement agency," King offered.

"Perhaps, perhaps not," Tommy-Lee replied, studying the file. "But no sign of a terrorist cell."

"They must have bugged out."

"Or were never there."

"Whatever." King shrugged. "My last tip-off panned-out. I can't promise anything as a certainty locked up in here."

"What are you up to?"

"I told you," King said. "I was hired to take a shot."

"We heard back from MI6," he said. "Not a lot of detail, but what we got told a story."

"I like a good story."

"No doubt. But we are interested in what you know."

"About what?"

Tommy-Lee shrugged. "Everything. But not now," he said. "With someone like you, we could have it on tap."

"Someone like me?"

"Yeah. Someone on the wrong side of the law. Someone that MI6 doesn't care for, nor apparently want back," he paused. "I suspect when they realise what we have, they may pay handsomely for your silence. Not numerically, of course. More quid-pro-quo."

King shrugged. "Am I not getting my burger, then?"

Tommy-Lee smiled. "There's a great deal you will not be getting anymore, Mister King, but a burger and a shake is the least of your concerns."

When he had finally succumbed to sleep after being returned to his cell, he had been rudely interrupted, shackled and hooded. He had been unceremoniously dragged down echoing corridors and bundled down hard concrete steps. Two vehicle rides followed. The first had felt like a utility van. Echoing, metallic.

The ride had taken over an hour. There had been two guards. One had decided it would be fun to take out his gun and press it into the back of King's head. He had heard the click of the hammer striking the empty chamber, but he hadn't flinched. He had pointed out that only a moron would shoot someone in the back of a van. That DNA, fibres and general transference of particles would make the killer easily detectable. That cleaning out a van full of blood and brain splatter was almost impossible. He had received a beating for his troubles, but as he suspected, there had been no further gun-play.

The next mode of transport was the rear seat of a quiet and powerful car. What the Americans would call a sedan. He could feel that the seats were made from soft leather. King suspected it had been a domestic brand, with a luxury package and a powerful engine. The gear changes were clearly automatic, but not as refined or with as many ratios as a German marque, and the size of the interior was substantial. King had been seated between two new guards, and he wasn't rubbing up against either of them.

Time had become immeasurable. The men inside the car did not speak. King could tell there was a passenger up front, a brief mumbled conversation regarding the route, but nothing more. The car had eventually swung into what King suspected to be a multi-storey or underground car park. The wheels squealed at the low-speed turn, highlighting the probability of the car being a domestic make. Americans had power and luxury down, price and value as well, but not handling. Not in their sedans, at least. The turn built up enough inertia for King to lean into the man on his right, and a quick jab of the man's elbow pushed King back upright. He had started to feel motion sickness, the hood delaying his senses and making him reactionary to the vehicle's manoeuvres.

The car drew to a halt and before the engine switched off King could tell they were at an airport. A jet, its engines straining on take-off, roared somewhere in the distance and a light aircraft with propellers taxied past what King now suspected to be a hangar keeping them from view.

King was pulled out of the car and dragged across the hangar, where he was guided onto the first step. He was pushed forwards, but without knowing how many steps there were, he sprawled at the top and fell into the aircraft. Somebody laughed as he struggled to get up with his hands shackled behind his back. Nobody helped, and he got back to his feet, his ribs aching and making him wince, his expression thankfully hidden from his captives.

He was pulled backwards and dropped into a seat. He could already tell it was soft, sumptuous leather. Like nothing he had previously experienced on any aircraft. His hands stopped him from sitting properly in the seat, and as if to accommodate this, he was pushed forwards and two pairs of heavy hands unlocked his cuffs and reattached them around his front, but he felt them threaded through a loop in his seatbelt. His hood was removed, and he blinked in the light of the aircraft. He exaggerated his discomfort for long enough to take in his surroundings. The window shutters were down. They knew how to play the game. A bottle of water was thrust in front of him and he had just enough slack in his wrists to take the bottle and drain it in one go. He asked for another and to his surprise a young man in a dark grey suit uncapped another bottle and he drank that one down, too.

King looked at the two men sitting down ahead of him, across the aisle. They looked tough and quiet, ex-military would be his guess. They would be the muscle. The younger guy would be the junior agent. Further up the aisle Tommy-Lee Jones looked through what appeared to be a log-book and conferred with the pilot. He never once looked at King. The agent went through the notes, nodded at something the pilot said. King knew that in the world of deception and secrets, this could be a ruse. They could simply take off, fly some circuits or a generous loop and land back at the airport. Deception complete. But King hoped – would go so far as to pray – that they took off and flew due West for four hours. That would be his favourite scenario. He figured they were in a private jet, most likely a Learjet registered to a company that was a front for the NSA. He knew the CIA operated a private fleet, so there was no reason why the more secretive and often more powerful intelligence service should have their own, too. And he guessed that the aircraft would cruise at somewhere around four-hundred and fifty miles per hour. So now it was time to pray. King had never been religious, but he was willing to hedge his bets. Because if he was somewhere around Washington DC then a four-hour flight due West would land him at Rapid City, South Dakota. And if the intelligence MI5 were working from was correct, the plan was working. If they landed elsewhere, then he would have to resign himself to fate. And if that was the case, then he was as good as dead.

Chapter Eighteen

"I don't know how he suspected," said Caroline. "We were subtle, weren't we?"

"We *were*, weren't we?" Marnie asked, looking at Rashid. She wasn't a field agent, and this had knocked her confidence in her abilities. Her work in the field to date had been reactionary. Borne from necessity and the situation of their assignments escalating.

"Silky smooth, babe," Rashid reassured her.

"Well, he cottoned on," Ramsay said. "And he found the transmitter, got it off and planted it on another car while we waited at the first set of lights. The guy was fast."

"Unless…" Rashid sat back in his chair and smiled knowingly. "He was being watched By a third party that was aligned with our target. Somebody out there had his back. And we were so focused on him, that we didn't notice anybody else watching him."

"And in turn, watching us," said Caroline. "Jesus; we could have been hit. We were so wrapped up in him, his being there confirming Alex was alive and well…" she paused, wiped a tear from her eye, hoping nobody had noticed. "That we missed his team." She shuddered, the thought of being watched and vulnerable making her feel uneasy.

Rashid nodded. "From now on, I'll get two of the SAS guys shadowing us, watching our backs. It was stupid, really. We're operating on foreign soil. We're on the back foot. It was sloppy and we're lucky to be alive. We could certainly be under surveillance now, so we need to put in counter measures."

"What's worse," said Caroline. "Is that whole set-up was all so we knew that Alex was sending a message. The fact that someone showed up meant that they were listening to what Alex had to say. It was telling us he was still alive…" she trailed off, wiped her eye with the end of her sleeve again. Marnie offered her a clean handkerchief and she smiled at her in appreciation. She had flushed red, embarrassed she hadn't been able to hold it together. There had been a question mark hanging over whether she could do this, and now she was proving them right. Ramsay had pushed for her to be on the team, and she wouldn't let him down now. "Now we've lost the guy."

Ramsay shook his head. "Let's not get bogged down reading too much into this. That guy was a bonus, but he wasn't necessarily an asset to us. We know the intel on this, the premise of the operation. We're here in New Jersey, King was arrested, or detained, in Washington DC. We suspect where they'll take him, ball-park, at least. Forget this guy. It's up to King to send the next message."

"That's what I'm afraid of the most," said Caroline.

Nobody said anything. They all had their reservations, it was all down to King, and not one of them would have even considered taking the risk he was about to take.

Chapter Nineteen

King had been expecting an airport, but the runway they landed on was short and the pilot used a tremendous amount of reverse thrust and brakes to bring the aircraft back to a manageable speed. It was taxiing less than thirty seconds after it had thumped down hard on the tarmac.

The flight was in the ballpark of four hours. He had not been hooded until they started the descent, and by then he had taken in enough through the windows to see that he was in a place of expansive grasslands with rising rocky and wooded mountains. The intel was spot on. He was in the Great Plains, almost certainly somewhere around South Dakota and Wyoming.

He had been allowed a toilet break and given a sandwich and more water. There had been no questioning, but King knew there would be more to come. He tried to use the time to rest, but sleep eluded him. Knowing it could, and probably would be shattered, left him in a state of semi-alertness. Instead, he tried to pick up snippets of information. The two men up front, the muscle, were called Carl and Tony, although he had not been able to ascertain who was who.

They were Redskins fans and had their own ideas on a player's worth and how aligned advertising was with the league. One of them did three tours of Afghanistan. No mean feat, considering a US serviceman's tour was around a year to fifteen months, depending on the branch of service, compared to the UK's six to eight months. The other man didn't mention service, but King could tell he knew his way around the block. The younger man spent his time alone, working through a file and occasionally jotting down notes. He had mentioned to one of the men that he was flying straight back to Washington DC. Tommy-Lee had kept himself to himself. He had eaten a sandwich and slept for most of the journey. This told King he was ex-military with a good deal of time behind him in his current job. The type of man who knows that there was work to be done and he had better be well-rested and well-fed when it starts.

King could see a Blackhawk helicopter taxiing, its rotors turning. There were no markings, so he assumed it was a military aircraft. It looked like it was heading in rather than getting into position for take-off. The hood went back on and finally King knew which man Carl was. A quietly spoken instruction. Which by default told him which man Tony was. It was a simple task as he pulled King forwards and they firmly applied the cuffs behind his back and slipped the hood over him. King had snuck a look at Carl's watch. A decent Tag with the date at the three o'clock position. He'd lost a day, but he now knew the time and the date and could recalibrate his senses. And he could confirm the time of day with the light sneaking in through the gap of one of the window shutters. The knowledge lifted him. Because they had not broken him, not managed to wreak havoc with his senses.

The aircraft stopped, and the engines shut down. There was a whirling of electrical noises and movement from around the cabin. Hand-luggage carry-ons pulled out of stowage and belts being tightened. Knee joints clicking, muscles stretching. King was gripped firmly under both arms and pulled out of his seat. The door clunked open and the steps were unfolded electronically. King was greeted with a cool, dry air, the cleanest he'd ever breathed. It was like nectar in his lungs. As he was led down the steps, he could feel the warmth of the sun on his back. He imagined a big, blue, cloudless sky. He did not have to walk far and was bundled into an open-topped vehicle that was low on comfort and refinement. As it started up and sped across the tarmac, he could tell it was a military vehicle. He had no seatbelt and felt as if he was about to fall out of the open side at every turn.

The vehicle drove for several minutes, then King was aware of shadow through the hood, of a chill and echo as they entered a hangar or building of some description. The vehicle pulled up to a sudden halt, sending King into the dashboard. He recovered, but several pairs of hands pulled him clear of the vehicle and he was bundled onto the ground. He was aware of scissors cutting into his clothes and he was pulled and pushed about until every piece of fabric was ripped from him. He was searched quickly and expertly, felt the rubber gloves and the hands of a seasoned medical practitioner. He barely had time to take in what was happening as the hood was torn off, making him choke as it tugged against his windpipe. He looked up at the men. A slightly built man with dark features and wearing a white medical coat was snapping his leather case shut. He walked away towards a partition wall where medical equipment was stacked on shelving. King ignored him, looked around at the other men. Carl and Tony were there front and centre, but so were two more and they were built like the NFL poster boys. The backrow ones. Six-foot-five and eighteen-stone-plus. They wore combats, but no insignia of rank or unit. They looked at each other and smiled. King knew what was coming before they did it, and as they launched upon him with kicks and blows, he kicked one of the bigger men in the balls with a solid strike that was more reflex than anything else. He followed up with another kick to Carl's kneecap. Not through reflex, but because he was going to get beaten anyway and he was damned if he was going to lay down and take it. Both men went down, and as the other two looked on for a moment out of sheer surprise, King dropped his heel down with all the force he could muster into the side of Carl's temple. He felt something give under his foot and Carl went still.

He looked up defiantly at the other two and scowled. "Come on then, you pair of fucking pussies, let's see what you've got!" It was done now, so he would go out fighting.

Both men hesitated. The big man in the battle fatigues was getting unsteadily to his knees. Carl was going nowhere. They all checked each other, eyeballing that they were all in agreement, then paced around King until they had him inside their triangle. Satisfied the shackled, naked man on the ground was covered, they cautiously closed the gap.

"Stop this shit at once!" a voice hollered. It was a seasoned voice accustomed to giving orders. The men hesitated just long enough to make their impending attack a disregard for the order. Maybe so they could save face. King didn't care. He strained his neck to see Tommy-Lee striding across the hangar floor. Beside him a black, compact man carrying a kit-bag looked on with amusement. When they stopped walking, the black man was smiling, or at least trying to suppress a smile.

"He put Carl down, Sir," Tony said rather feebly, as if he could suddenly hear his own words and how absurd they sounded given King's position.

"Has he been searched?"

"Yes, Sir."

"Well, get him cleaned up and into the chamber," Tommy-Lee snapped. He looked down at King and said, "Pull that shit again and it's a nine-millimetre bullet in the back of your skull and an unmarked grave." He glanced at the man beside him and said, "My man here will not lose a minute's sleep over it."

Chapter Twenty

Appalachian Mountains, Virginia

They worked as a team. Fluid and in conjunction with one another's actions and reactions. If one of them moved too far to the left, the man behind would close the gap. They breached the door, moved inside fanning out left and right, the last man walking in backwards to keep the arcs of fire to three-hundred and sixty-degrees. They were both an intimidating and undeniably aggressive unit. With their Kevlar body armour and steel trauma plates, Kevlar helmets and knee and elbow pads, they made for an impressive show of force. The BR99 shotguns did the rest.

Maligned at first, the soldiers had grown to appreciate them. Not only could they breach door locks or hinges with just one shot of double-oh-buck, but the men had consistently scored bullseyes at one-hundred metres with the solid rifled-slugs. They used the quarter choke – a screw-in adjustment at the end of the barrel which set the shot pattern - to get the best results for spread patterns and slug usage, and to attain the best accuracy from the ballistic gel, or what had been adopted as the 'Nerf' rounds. Yates had remained vocal in advocating live or lethal ammunition, but he had still declined to stand on the fifty-metre line and take a shot to the torso with one of the non-lethal rounds when Rashid had suggested he either put up or shut up.

Rashid had assessed the men and noted their strengths and weaknesses. He couldn't say he liked them all, but they weren't here to make friends. Yates and Macintosh had become inseparable. But they had failed to gel with the rest of the group. The other four men were decent blokes and he had started to ask more of them as a result.

After an arduous training session, the men sat down, leaning against the wooden ranch fencing that separated the parking area from the woods. They were steaming from the gaps in their loosened clothing, their BR99 shotguns resting across their legs. The morning had been filled with multiple assaults on the killing house and target clusters in the woods. Their shoulders were sore from the savage recoil, and the barrels of the shotguns were too hot to touch. But the actions and magazine springs had loosened up and were feeding the heavy .12-gauge cartridges without incident. Each man was equipped with foam earplugs fastened with fine paracord and were hanging loose from their necks. They sipped water from their personal bottles and wiped perspiration from their brows.

"So, what's the job?" Macintosh asked.

"Need to know," Rashid replied, then drained the rest of his water.

"Yeah," said the biggest man among them. "And you don't need to know. What's with all the questions, anyway? It's always been the same; the less you know, the better." The Scotsman shrugged but didn't argue. The other man was known as 'Big Dave' and rightly so. He stood six-foot-four and weighed somewhere between seventeen and eighteen-stone. He was black and spoke with an accent and nobody ever dared to ask where he was from, but Rashid knew him to be Fijian. He had operated with him years ago and he had been part of a British Army recruitment drive around the Pacific British Commonwealth. He liked the big man but would confess at not truly knowing him. Only that he had been tried and tested in battle and not left wanting. "It's hostage rescue, innit?" he said and drained the rest of his bottle.

"It's a heist," said Yates, looking at Macintosh as he smiled. "Obvious, really. Non-lethal ammunition, and such a good paycheque for a month's work…"

"I'm all for a good heist," Macintosh agreed. "But I want a fair crack at the loot. Bollocks to fifty-grand if there's a shed-load more up for grabs."

"Too right," agreed Yates. "What is it, a gold mine? That would make sense. Little security, remote location. That's why that bloke was here putting his face about, him with the wolf eyes. So's we know who he is and don't go blowing him to kingdom come. He's working on the inside."

"It's hostage rescue, you bozzos," said Mick. He was small and sinewy, covered with tattoos and had a freshly shaved crew-cut. He was mild mannered and well-spoken, blowing his appearance all to hell. Rashid didn't know him, but he liked what he saw. The man wasn't afraid to throw himself on point or cover the rear. Nobody liked to cover the rear. "And that bloke is going to be a deep cover asset. The inside man. Right, Rashid?"

Rashid said nothing. They would know soon enough. He looked up at Caroline and

Marnie, who came out of the cabin and leaned against the rails. They both nursed cups of coffee, Marnie working near-constantly on her smartphone.

"Oi, tits!" Yates shouted. "How about getting a brew on?"

Caroline didn't hide her anger or distaste for the man. She turned her attention back to Marnie, who looked equally taken aback.

"You heard me, tits!" Yates laughed and grinned at Macintosh. "White and two sugars, luv!"

Caroline strode down the steps and walked over. Marnie looked unsure, stayed where she was on the porch deck. Caroline walked up to Yates, who was still grinning lecherously.

"Wrong pair of tits," he said as she reached the group and stood directly in front of him. "I was talking about your mate. Her with the curves and about ten pounds more in her bra…"

"Aye, on each side!" Macintosh exclaimed wolfishly.

Rashid stood up and looked down at him. "I can think of fifty-thousand reasons why you should apologise," he said. "But I'll give you just one. She's with me, so take it back."

"Whoa! Take it easy, mate," Yates grinned. "I'll take it back. Blondie can run and fetch me a coffee instead."

Caroline smiled and said, "Milk and two sugars?"

"Yeah."

She tipped her coffee in his crotch and he jumped up to his feet, patting himself down in a panic. "Have mine," she said. "Want me to fetch you some sugar?"

Rashid smiled at Caroline. "He doesn't know how you serve sugar…"

"I bet."

"Fucking bitch!" Yates snapped and took a step forwards, his fists clenched. Caroline didn't move, but she'd dropped lower into a fighting stance. She wasn't going anywhere. He stared at her, expecting her to have flinched away, not stand for a fight. He hesitated, then decided he had better soothe his balls and took out his water bottle and doused himself. He glared at her as he did so. "Just a bit of bantz, luv!" He snapped. "Just some banter you fucking psycho bitch! What are you? Pre-menstrual or what?"

Big Dave stood up, towering over everybody. He gave Yates a gentle shove and the man took off and stumbled ten-feet into the fence. "Shut up, you twat!" He stepped over Macintosh and caught hold of Yates by his shoulder. It appeared friendly, but Yates was going nowhere except for where Big Dave was taking him. "Come on guys," he said. "Let's call time for thirty minutes and get some scran."

The rest of the men seemed to think it a good idea and got up. Big Dave's and Yates' weapons were picked up and the group took off towards the cabins. Macintosh didn't look Rashid or Caroline in the eyes as he walked past them.

"What the hell?" Marnie said as she walked up to them.

Rashid shook his head. "There's always one," he said.

"Or two," Caroline added. "That guy Macintosh is one and the same. They've bonded as a partnership. It might affect the rest of the team."

"I thought your old SAS chum hand-picked these men?" Marnie said. "You trusted his judgement."

"That's the thing," Rashid replied. "I would have trusted his judgement with my life. But I'm not so sure, now."

"Well, it's too late to change things," Marnie said. "But I'm not happy with that guy, Yates. And the Scottish guy is just as bad."

"And there's me thinking the SAS were a cut above the average soldier," Caroline commented. "Peter was an SAS Captain..." she said distantly, trailing off, her eyes glossy. Her fiancé had been an MI5 officer and ex-SAS. He had been killed shielding her and others from a suicide bomber. She looked at Rashid, her eyes glistening in the light. Rashid didn't say anything, hadn't seen her like that before.

Marnie rubbed her shoulder. "I don't think any of those blokes are former Captains," she said.

"Well, they're just long-time Tommies," Rashid said. "They have served for years without promotion, not above Sergeant, at least. Always getting into scrapes, but under the parentage of the British Army. They made the SAS because they were tough and sharp. I guess they enjoy the situations that go with the regiment. More chance of action. I suppose a few of the wrong characters get through. More so considering we've been at war, in one theatre or another, since the nine-eleven attacks. The SAS has never turned over so many soldiers."

"But I'm surprised your contact didn't know quite what these two were like," Caroline mused.

"I think they'll do the job required of them," Rashid said, a little defensively. The men knew their way around hostage rescue and were supreme marksmen. He didn't want to over-think it so near to the objective. So, he wasn't fond of Yates or Macintosh, but they were still good at their job. He wasn't happy about his old Sergeant's decision, though.

"We don't want a bloodbath, Rashid," said Caroline. "Those two aren't on board with the non-lethal loads."

"I've given everybody the choice," he replied. "Personally, I'd feel happier with an assault rifle, too. But whatever our conflicts of interest now, the yanks are our friends and we can't just go in there and mow them down. But by the same token, the security in this facility is rumoured to be made up from ex-special forces. If the tide turns during the assault, then we need to be able to change the odds in our favour."

"I'm with you," Marnie agreed. "But it's also unclear whether serving soldiers are there as well on a clandestine attachment. This could end up getting extremely messy diplomatically."

Rashid raised his hands in despair. "What the hell am I meant to do? King's in play now! We *have* to stick to the plan!"

"I'm all too aware of that!" Caroline snapped. "But Marnie's right and those two men are simply too unpredictable to put Alex's life, and the operation at risk."

"So, what do you suggest?" he asked, still perplexed. "Go to the CIA and say, 'we had an idea, but it's not worked out and please can we have our agent back?'"

"Of course not!"

"Then what?"

"Cut them loose," she said.

"Just like that?"

"It might not be such a bad idea," said Marnie. "Ramsay and I could take a role on the fringe, perhaps observation and communications, and Caroline can get up to speed with one of those bloody great cannons."

Caroline nodded. "The other men seem decent. I can do it," she said. "Ditch the possibility of the lethal loads being too readily used, drive those two idiots to the airport. Pay them off. Give them their fifty-grand and tell them no hard feelings."

"I'm with Caroline," said Marnie. "Two rotten apples can ruin the entire barrel."

"Okay," Rashid relented. It was one of those moments where a great weight was lifted at the merest hint of a solution. He could hone Caroline's skills in the few remaining days. Her training in Army Intelligence had taken her through six-weeks of basic infantry training, and she had also done the small-arms course that had been put together by SAS instructors for MI5 officers working on attachments abroad. She had also proven herself in the field. "I'll do it now," he said.

"I'll go to town and get the funds wired," Marnie said. "I can draw them within the hour. The sight of cold, hard cash will make your job easier." She tipped her cold coffee onto the ground as she walked back to the cabin.

Caroline exhaled deeply. "God, I don't know how Alex got himself into this."

"I know," Rashid agreed. "I tried to talk him out of it. I even made it difficult for him when I came down to Cornwall and put him through that marksman test."

"He just can't resist a challenge," she said quietly.

Rashid shook his head. "Is it that, or is it just a case of unfinished business?"

Chapter Twenty-One

Rashid watched the big man eat. In a country renowned for its food and the size of its citizen's expanding waistlines, Big Dave really could take them to school. Rashid had chosen fried chicken and salad. He was washing it down with Coke, his concession being that he had been burning calories with all the training. The man-mountain had two plates in front of him. One full of breaded fried shrimp and fries. What he would have called scampi in a pub back home. The second plate was loaded with three hotdogs. A New Yorker with mustard and ketchup, a weird white coloured hotdog Rashid had never seen before, topped with burned onions, and a Chicago – a beast of a thing topped with onions, pickles, celery salt, peppers and mustard, and all wrapped up in a poppyseed bun. Next to his plates was a full condiment rack that had been all but emptied across the trencherman's buffet in front of him. Dave had also worked his way through three refills of various sodas. Rashid smiled, estimating the man at seventeen or eighteen stone and six-four. He doubted his muscle-clad frame contained a shred of fat.

"I appreciate you coming."

"No bother," said Big Dave. "Glad to see them gone, to be honest. Two divisive.
Good to get off the reservation and have some decent scran for a change."

Rashid watched the man digging into the loaded hotdog. "Yeah, I can see that you've been missing out."

Dave shrugged. "Never know when the meal you're eating will be your last."

Rashid said nothing. He knew there was plenty of truth in that statement. He ate some chicken, drank some cola. He was glad he had got rid of Yates and Macintosh. Marnie had collected the wired money and Rashid had given the two men the news they were surplus to requirements. He hadn't dressed it up, simply ordered them to leave their weapons and equipment, take only what they had brought with them, and had Big Dave act as driver. Both men seemed embarrassed rather than angry, and Rashid had made it clear from the start that they would have their bounty in cash at the airport with no hard feelings, but it was about gelling as a team, and they simply didn't. The drive had taken a little over an hour to the airport and the two former SAS soldiers had simply skulked off into the crowd. Dave had said he was hungry, and Rashid felt a huge relief that it had gone well and could go a lunch that didn't include tinned meat, cheese in a can and long-life sliced white bread.

"I think we will work better without them."

Big Dave shrugged. "Those women from box didn't like them much."

Rashid nodded. He hadn't mentioned that it was an MI5 operation to the men, but they had all been around the block enough to know. Rashid had also referred to MI5 as box before he had joined, too. Going back to the Security Service's wartime address of PO Box 500. If it had stuck after seventy-odd years, it always would. "Those women, as you say, are critical to the mission. Marnie…"

"Who you're shagging…" Big Dave interrupted.

"That's an aside."

Dave shrugged. "And that King bloke is with the blonde."

"They're engaged."

The man-mountain shrugged and swallowed a mouthful of who knew what.

All Rashid knew was it was either deep fried or meat-based. "Cosy."

"It works."

Dave didn't appear to care less. "What are their roles?"

"Marnie is tech. She knows just about everything there is to know about computers and networks and bypassing technical security." He did not elaborate further, but Marnie had been a first-class technician at GCHQ and was poached by MI5 when she worked with them on a task. She jumped at the chance and preferred to be in London than semi-rural Cheltenham.

"And the blonde?"

"She's a field agent," replied Rashid. "She's pretty handy in all scenarios."

Big Dave nodded and finished his mouthful. There appeared to be no slowing down his appetite. "So, she'll be stepping up now the chuckle brothers have shipped out?"

"That's the plan." Rashid had finished his chicken and couldn't be bothered with the rest of the salad. He washed it down with the cola and surveyed Big Dave's empty plates. He took out his wallet and thumbed out forty-dollars. Big Dave looked at him, his stare boring into him. Rashid felt uncomfortable, cocked his head and frowned. "What's wrong?"

"What about pudding?"

"Seriously?"

"Always."

"Well, they call it dessert. Pudding is custard out here. Or chocolate mousse, I think."

"You're shitting me?"

"Nope. But, really? After two meals?"

"I've had one meal, but they just don't have big enough plates."

"Even in America three hotdogs doesn't constitute as a side dish."

"Well, Taff said you were picking up expenses on top," he said. "So, I guess you can take it up with him if you're going to get all cheap on me."

Rashid smiled. "So, do you know Taff well?"

"I knew him in the regiment, never served with him, but he seemed okay. Shame about what happened up in Tora Bora."

Rashid had been there. Fighting in caves and leaving the Taliban with no opportunity of escape. It was a joint operation with US Navy SEALs, Delta Force and the British SAS, and it had been bloody and brutal, fought with knives and bayonets and determination. Taff had stepped on an IED in the mouth of a cave and tunnel complex. Time had stood still for Rashid and the men who had gathered around the twisted and broken body of their Sergeant. The men had rallied round and thrown everything at treating the casualty, to the annoyance of their American counterparts who were leaving their injured and pushing forward with the objective. Rashid reasoned that there was no escape for the Taliban, that they were cornered and as a joint operation they had the advantage and could afford to regroup and take the caves later. He managed to get Taff evacuated on a helicopter before returning to the fight, where multiple American casualties were stacking up. Rashid's troop turned to medics and saved more than twenty US soldiers that day. When SEAL and Delta forces were depleted and ineffective, the SAS continued to fight on alone for five more days, joined for the last three days by members of the British SBS – the Royal Navy's special forces counterparts. Rashid earned the DSO, or distinguished service order, Britain's second highest medal for valour. He had tossed the medal in a drawer and not looked at it since. The price of pride too heavy for him to bear.

"It was a lottery out there," said Rashid.

"Worse towards the end. There were IEDs everywhere."

Big Dave nodded. "I was being taxied by the Royal Anglians when someone stopped up ahead because they thought a kid had been involved in a hit and run. Turned out insurgents had killed the kid, scooped out his insides and packed him with two T55 tank shells and buried the command wire." He looked up as the waitress approached and said, "Hi, love, two of the battered and deep-fried cheesecakes, please." He looked back at Rashid and shrugged. "Never gonna beat fuckers like that. Not truly. They'll always be there, and we won't beat them by chucking a billion bullets on them or raining missiles from the sky. They're welcome to it out there. Bloody shithole."

"What happened to the Royal Anglians?" Rashid asked, still thinking about the Tora Bora and a boy's body on the side of an anonymous dusty road.

"Three dead, another three with a few fewer limbs, two more broken up and too many to count who got damaged inside."

Rashid nodded, knowing that many casualties of war had injuries you couldn't see. PTSD and mental health were every bit as debilitating as loss of limbs. He'd once talked to King about PTSD and depression and King had told him not to be so bloody self-indulgent. Have a beer and get on with it. But King was a relic, and Rashid supposed King dealt with it by shoving it all aside. He assumed one day it would overload and had told King so, but King responded that he probably wouldn't live long enough to reach that day. Maybe not even to the objective of this operation. The thought made him uneasy and he thumbed out another twenty to include a tip and stood up. "I need some air," he said. "Don't take too long over your cakes."

Chapter Twenty-Two

The guards had beaten him, and they had humiliated him. They had forced him at gunpoint to empty his toilet bucket with his hands, then lick the shit off his fingers. They had defecated on his food and they had urinated on him as he had finally succumbed to sleep. The beatings carried on for two weeks, and when he had not weakened to their interrogations, the fake executions and the starvation, they had cut him slowly with dirty knives and still he had not talked. Only when they had covered him in petrol and paraded a gas lighter had he given in and told them what they wanted to know. Peter Stewart had told him how long he should hold out for, and if he did as the tough Scotsman said – played it to the letter – then they would believe everything he said. They would not question his story, and that was what they were counting on.

King had taken everything they had thrown at him. The fuel and the flame were to be his limit, and only because he had held off for so long, would they truly have known they had broken him. But they had broken nothing. They
had played into his hands and when Stewart and the Israeli commandos had stormed the camp

and rescued King, he had shot his kneeling captors through their heads without a second thought. The operation had retrieved a stolen Soviet stock weapons grade uranium from Hezbollah and his duress under torture had given the Israeli commandos time to find him, and time to organise an assault. It had needed a volunteer, a special kind of person to take the abuse and hold out. And here he was again...

King swung his legs off the solid concrete bunk and sat up, staring at the walls. He had been through hell once before. And now he was back for more. But he had learned something at the hands of his Arab torturers. He had learned how much pain and mental abuse he could take. And after a while, he even liked it. The test of it. The competition. Who would break first? Who would have the guile to ramp it up another level? King had given the Americans some information but had shut down quickly at torture. These were not the ragtag terrorists he faced ten years ago. These were people from a civilised world, and although ruthless and driven, they had different morals and sensibilities. Not that he would ever underestimate them, but he had been in the intelligence game long enough, worked with enough allies to know that the West were different to the East. He had allowed enough for the similarities between them, common interests and values. He spoke of names they knew, operations the United States had been involved with. And then, when the water boarding started, he shut down completely. Only when they had fed and watered him, given him some rest, had he gone ahead with his cover story, and finally with his trump card. That he could prove he had not been involved in the previous shootings, and that he had taken the shots at the plexiglass, stopping before it shattered in order to miss the Congressman and retain his MI6 deep cover working to infiltrate an Islamic extremist terrorist cell. Now they had to check through proper and open channels. Now they had a new line of investigation. Now they had the chance of an agent from a friendly nation being in their custody and the potential for a political and diplomatic backlash. But they would also meet closed doors, dead ends. King knew enough about MI6 to back-up his story, but MI6 would never officially sanction such an act. He could hide behind the legend of being a black-ops agent, working for a department that did not officially exist. And the agency behind this unofficial prison, this secret gulag would understand that. MI6 could deny Alex King and this operation as much as they liked, but they simply wouldn't be believed.

The flap in the cell door opened and a guard ordered him to back up to the door. King complied, and the guard asked for him to bunch his fists and put his arms behind his back. He felt the cold steel of the cuffs and the flap closed and the steel door opened.

"You are prisoner three-eight-one-four-B. It says so on the front and back of your jumpsuit," the man paused as he pulled King around and walked him through the doorway and down a long, narrow corridor of concrete and natural stone. The corridor was hewed from rock, which to King looked like granite. There was a steep gradient and they were heading downhill. King got the impression they were deep underground. The rock was semi-smooth, with drill holes all over where dynamite had broken out the larger pieces at some time. Maybe in the goldrush. "You will not look directly into a guard's eyes. You will not address any guard as anything but Sir, understand?"

King nodded and said, "Sir." He humoured him, but he felt he was making progress here and wanted to see what was at the end of the tunnel.

"You will be allowed in general population for two hours a day. You will take your two hots and a slop in general population for a duration of no longer than thirty-minutes. Do you understand?"

"Yes."

King felt a dig in his spine. The guard used the end of a baton. King stumbled, turned out of reflex. Two more guards flanked the monotone guard. King hadn't been aware of their presence before now. He lowered his eyes from the guard's and said, "Sir."

The guards were dressed in military fatigues with a desert camouflage pattern. There were no names or insignia anywhere to denote rank, unit or an individual's identity. They all looked the same with buzz cuts and tattoos. King could see from their faces that the men were battle hardened. They would have done tours of the sandbox for sure. He turned back the way they had been walking. The guard shoved him forwards and they continued down the corridor.

"You will notice two yellow lines on the floor. You treat it like an American road. You will walk on the line closest to the wall at all times. We are heading downhill; the wall is on your right." The guard was monotone, as if he were reading from a sheet and had read it too many times before. "When you return, it will be uphill, with the wall on your right. Do you understand?"

"Sir."

"You will be assigned a cell. You will be responsible for that cell. You will keep that cell clean and respectable. You will share with one other inmate. Do you understand?"

"Sir."

"Any questions?"

"When can I make a phone call and see my lawyer?"

The guard brought his baton down on King's shoulder and he crashed down onto the hard floor, his face contorted as he writhed in pain. "Oh, you're in for a fun time in here..." The guard looked down at him and the two escorts grinned. "Your life is over. You don't get a call and you don't get legal representation. You belong to the US of A now!"

One of the other guards grinned and added, "You want to off a politician then go back home, there are more than a few of yours that need culling."

King forgot the pain, concentrated on his reaction. This was school playground stuff. Silly taunts and bully boy antics. It didn't bother him, not after what he had been through back in Washington, and a decade ago in Palestine. He could take their jabs and punches and kicks. He could take their lack of intelligence and integrity. He needed to get out of confinement and get into general population and what he did now would decide the course he was to take.

"Yes, Sir," he said without eye contact. He got back to his feet and turned his back on them. He waited. Either it would be a shove, or the men would have their blood up and want a bit of violent interlude. They seemed low-ranking, so hopefully they wouldn't go too far. He felt the push and remained silent as they walked the fifty-metres or so to the steel door at the end of the corridor. King could already hear the hum of voices, of shouts and of clatter. He braved himself. He had been in prison a long time ago.

Another lifetime. And as he breathed deeply to steady himself, he wondered why in God's name he had taken such a risk to be here.

Chapter Twenty-Three

They had chosen a mid-sized SUV from the Hertz desk at the airport and driven South. Stopping at a mall they had bought boots, camouflaged hunting clothes, Bowie knives, water canteens and light backpacks. They even found camo-cream for their faces. Virginia state law ruled that without proof of residence, they could not purchase firearms, but they could buy ammunition. And then it hit them that a shotgun was not under the same firearms infringements. So, they stocked up on .12-gauge slugs and buckshot and legally purchased two Remington pump-action shotguns with no ID.

God bless America…

Their next stop was at an electrical outlet that had a good selection of electronic surveillance equipment. Most of the standard goods were sufficient for the task at hand, but with Yates' specialist experience he was able to cobble together something more satisfactory to their requirements. With some powerful magnets, Tupperware, glue and a soldering iron, he made short work of creating the items he needed using the 12v auxiliary power outlet and the boot of the vehicle as a workspace.

The terrain was too undulated and the cover too thick for field glasses to be effective. Instead, Yates and Macintosh had parked the SUV a little over a mile away from the campsite and came in on a wide arc to the rear of the camp. They had then pincered the property and waited in their individual positions around a hundred metres from the buildings. Not chancing the sporadic cellphone reception, they had bought a set of outdoorsman walkie-talkies, leaving them switched on at low volume and communicating through a code they were used to with the SAS, using the contact switch. This would allow a coded reply before they spoke, negating the chance of giving themselves away if someone was nearby.

A double click and Yates picked up his handset. He clicked once in reply to indicate it was clear.

"I'll go for the first hut, check there are no sudden surprises," said Macintosh. "You take the vehicles."

"Roger that, out." Yates slowly drew himself to his feet, his eyes on the huts and the main house. There were no lights on within any of the buildings. He carefully stepped through the undergrowth, mindful of dried branches and twigs that could give away his position, but also aware that rattlesnakes could be nestled up against the larger fallen branches. In the poor light of a half moon, he took it slowly and steadily.

Each device was linked to a separate receiver by its own frequency, and as Yates planted the first, he made a mental note of the pairing. The large SUVs were the same make and colour, so he memorised the last three letters and digits of each license plate. He already knew which vehicle Ramsay had designated to the MI5 team, and he couldn't care less about the other ex-SAS men. There was no brotherhood now that he had worked for ten-years in the realms of mercenary. He cared only for money and convenient alliances. Satisfied he knew which device was assigned to each vehicle, he set about sliding under the first and securing it in place. He found a sweet spot beside the exhaust silencer, routed in the middle of the vehicle. The device locked tightly in place, and as he tested it with a wiggle, he was immediately satisfied it would remain in place. Unless the vehicle bounced and grounded on a rutted track or exceeded a hundred-mile-per-hour on the freeway, he was sure it would remain in place indefinitely. He wriggled free, checked the direction of the huts and crawled across the gravel to the next vehicle.

Macintosh had drawn his twelve-inched blade Bowie knife and held it firmly in his right hand. In his left he held a tactical torch capable of a strobe setting, which would temporarily blind any would-be attacker long enough to sheath his blade in them. With the giant, razor edged blade, one thrust was all he would need. But he was never one to stop short of a twist and slash when he took a blade to someone.

Despite the men inside being trained in one of the world's leading special forces units - some would argue the best - he could hear the men sleeping fitfully inside. They were only men, after all. Big Dave in particular had been an excessive snorer, only he was simply too big for the other men to complain too seriously to. He shared the hut with Tattooed Mick. Another snorer. Macintosh eased the door open, and as he suspected, Powell and Adams had shipped out to the other hut after both he and Yates had been cut loose. Maybe they would get some sleep now.

Macintosh looked at the forms of the two

sleeping men in their bunks. Mick was half the size of Big Dave, whose feet stuck out a good ten inches from the foot of the bed. The perverse side of him thought of slitting their throats, but he needed them for now. Perhaps later. He had done it before to men as they had slept. A job in Rwanda had seen him do worse to the women. But he took what he was paid and never questioned anything. The British government had invested hundreds of thousands of pounds into his training, and then discarded him in a round of budget cuts that had seen the SAS slashed by over one-hundred personnel, only to reinvest in numbers with the next Prime Minister. It had been too late for him then, and the British Army always liked to fill the SAS with twenty-something Corporals and save on the salaries of men in their late thirties with several ranks under their belts. They always sighted fitness but in reality, it was just a way of controlling the purse strings. The thought made him angry. He had given his entire adult life over to serving his country, and now for the past ten years he had had to rely on handouts. An overzealous mission had seen him excluded from the international bodyguard circuit – you were only ever as good as your last job in that game - and now he took the jobs nobody else wanted. Handouts from that Welsh cripple who lost three limbs and his dick in an IED he should have been able to avoid. Well, he had forced his way into this job, and even though Taff insisted it wasn't a heist, he knew better. And that "mouthy-Southey" Yates knew it too. They would turn this around in their favour and they would get what they deserved. Or what *he* deserved, because the cockney chatterbox would get what was coming to him as well. He needed a partner in this thing, and Yates had gone too far insulting the women. The other Hereford guys would take the money and do the job as if the government were still calling the shots, and not some rogue unit out for their own gains. He had fallen in with Yates because he needed him, and now they were on the outside. But not for long.

Macintosh could see the tactical shotguns stacked against the wall. Two tactical vests hung on a peg, both with Beretta pistols in the integral holsters. It was tempting to help himself to two of the vests, but it would only let them know they had been here. And there were ways to get revenge on somebody, and ways to make people pay. Big Dave turned over in bed and the

Scotsman saw the whites of the man's eyes, highlighted by his own black face. He took a step forwards, the knife ready, but Dave was still asleep, his eyes closing again as he let out a monumental roar that melted away in a nasal whine. Macintosh stopped in his tracks, because even though Dave was out for the count, his massive snore had woken Tattooed Mick, who was sitting up and scratching his stubbly head. Macintosh froze, the heavy Remington shotgun under his arm, the giant knife raised in his right hand. But Mick was too far away. If he saw Macintosh, then he would have a chance because he would have Big Dave's bed in the way as a barrier. By the time Macintosh cleared Big Dave, then he will have lost his advantage. And Macintosh had sparred with Mick during training, he was a handy boxer and wrestler. Well-spoken, looked like a thug and fought like a tiger that had been backed into a corner. Macintosh had heard that the man had a PHD. Another anomaly within the special forces. If he had stayed away from the tattoos, grown and combed his hair, then he may well have been a Colonel by now.

Macintosh relaxed as Mick flopped back

down and rolled onto his side. He backed away and damn-near stepped into Yates, who was standing to the side of the door with his knife drawn.

"Shit!" Macintosh whispered as he stepped off the wooden porch. "Are you done?"

Yates nodded. "All set." He edged away, then scurried over to one of the SUVs and ducked down. Macintosh followed the man's stare and saw a figure on the porch deck of the main cabin. He eased back into the shadows, choosing not to make any sudden movements that the person may well detect in the stillness of the night. He sheathed the knife and eased the Remington shotgun out from under his arm. He kept the tactical torch in his left hand, the strobe setting just a flick away. He had taped up the strap swivels on the sling of the shotgun, making it silent to move. He could see the figure stretching on the deck, one of the men, most likely Rashid as the desk man from MI5 seemed to do nothing more physical than drink coffee. Macintosh did not make the weapon ready. The Remington was a rugged and rustic weapon, and any working parks were metallic and clunky. Whether he worked the action of the weapon would depend on if he had to use it, and once he did, he would go into the huts and cut down the other men amid the chaos. He simply couldn't afford to be outnumbered in this company. And, whether he used it or not, depended on what the figure did next.

Rashid checked his watch. He had an uneasy feeling that he had not seen the last of the two men. An uneasiness he had learned to trust in the past. Dawn was an hour away. He stretched sideways, easing his tired and tight muscles. The training had been difficult, strenuous. Each man had been designated physical instructor on a rotation. You could never push yourself like someone else could. It was like training with weights at home or working with a personal instructor. Homes all over the world had clothes hanging from exercise equipment long-since pushed into the corner of the room. Powell had taken this afternoon's session after the firing disciplines, and the tough little Geordie enjoyed upper-body blasts. Rashid's abs and shoulders were on fire, and he stretched them off before taking a run through the myriad of pathways through the woods that would bring him back by sunrise. He looked to his left, sure he had caught sight of a movement. He stared for a while, then looked back to his right. He was in the Appalachian Mountains and there were deer, coyotes and foxes all over. They had seen an array of roadkill on the drive up. He checked to his left again, saw a light come on in one of the cabins and shrugged. Someone was on a pee-pee sleepwalk, and the light ruined his night vision enough for him to decide to head away from the buildings and jog down the steps and head off to his right.

Macintosh walked casually across the gravel and wood bark parking area and tapped Yates on the shoulder. "Let's get the fuck out of here while that Paki works up a sweat."

Yates shrugged. He wasn't overly-racist, just a casual bigot. He'd grown up on the East End streets of London, and as multi-cultural as it was, he'd mainly mixed with his own kind. The Paki slur wasn't something he'd usually be a part of, but he was easily led, and Macintosh was his partner now. He wasn't about to object.

They made their way back the way they'd came, a mile or so back down the hill to the logging road where they had parked the hired SUV. They had successfully infiltrated the enemy's camp and compromised the vehicles, and now the first part of their plan was complete.

Chapter Twenty-Four

King hadn't known where the man he was to share his cell with had gone. It was unlikely he would have been off on his own time, which meant one of two things. Taking the fact that he was being interrogated himself, or visiting the infirmary out of the equation, the man would be in front of the guards with one of two briefs – to befriend King and glean information or to give King a tough time. King knew how it worked, especially when imprisoned on enemy territory. He was out of the system. No charges had been brought against him, and he doubted they ever would. This was his future unless he could achieve his objective and turn his situation around.

He had eaten a meal of pork and beans and bread. As with prisons the world over, he queued for his food and was the attention of a hundred pairs of eyes. He chose the end of a bench nearest the wall, so he could put his back near it and face the room. He did not make eye contact with anyone, but he scanned the faces, worked out the exits and guard placements, looked for any hierarchy. There would be, of course, whether the guards wanted it or not.

Wherever prisoners mixed, a hierarchy would be in place. The law of the jungle. Usually the largest, but occasionally it worked differently. But ruthlessness was always the key. Whoever had the most followers, and whoever had the least to lose would usually dominate. He could have killed for a cup of tea, but there was only water on offer to drink, and he had drunk more than he needed to rehydrate himself. His injured muscles needed to heal, and dehydration would hamper that. There was no dessert, but given the brief of this place, the prisoners it contained and the secrecy of its existence, King was both pleased and surprised the meal had been more than just plain boiled rice. It wasn't like the prisoners could complain. King wondered what the terminal plan was to keep political prisoners after they had outlived their usefulness. The stark, cold reality hit him. The Great Plains was a vast place, where secrets could easily be buried.

The cell door clattered, and a large Asian man was pushed inside. He was well muscled, and the orange jumpsuit strained around his chest and biceps. He regarded King with distain and waited for the two guards to unshackle him. Once they had, the door closed, and the man sneered at King. "Pretty boy…"

"You need your eyes tested, mate," King replied, gently rubbing the side of his bruised and battered face.

"They work fine," the man said. "What's your story?" He couldn't place the accent, but it was Persian, or at least in the same postcode, but with a smattering of American. King perched down on the nearest bed. A solid concrete slab protruding from the wall, three-feet off the ground. A thin mattress, no more than a roll of sponge in a waterproof plastic cover, and a thick blanket. Nothing else. "That's my bed…" King shrugged as he stood back up and walked across to the other bed. The room was no more than eight by eight. "So is that one," he said. "You'll take the floor until I say so."

King smiled, sat down and said, "I know how this works."

"You do?"

"More or less," he answered. "But it won't work out like the guards said it would. I figured they'd get you to befriend me or give me a hard time. And that's fine. This is a prison, and everybody has a scam, a way of surviving. I don't know what they promised you, but I hope it's worth it."

"Smart ass."

"Smarter than you. So, I guess that makes you the dumb ass?"

The man lunged forwards, fists clenched and letting out a full battle-cry. King pushed himself off the bed, dodged left and low and tucked a solid round-house punch into the man's groin. The man released all his breath at once, but King wasn't finished and grabbed a handful, dropped to his knees and struck his own forearm with his left hand as he pulled down, doubling the force as he wrenched. Something detached inside the man's sack and he simply couldn't get the scream out, panting and dropping to his knees, all hope of continuing his attack gone. King let go and stood up and the man sprawled onto his back, clutching his groin and howling.

"Bastard..." the man eventually panted. He writhed and bucked on the floor, the pain so intense that King was surprised he'd even remained conscious.

"I am," King replied truthfully. "I bet that really hurts, doesn't it?" The man didn't reply. He was rolling from side to side, holding his testicles like they would roll down his trouser leg and across the floor if he let go. "Tell you what, how about some prison anaesthetic?"

King raised his foot and didn't give the man time to object as he stamped down into his face culminating in a sickening crunch. The man's hands flopped to his sides and his head rocked back onto the floor. King put his foot underneath the man's back, levered him over onto his side. No sense in letting him suffocate on blood or his own tongue. He stepped over the man's bulk and took the original bed. Laying on his back, his hands casually behind his head, he stared up at the ceiling and waited to have an answer confirmed as he started to plan his next move.

It took ten minutes for the guards to arrive and open the cell door. And that told King that the cell was under CCTV surveillance. The only place it could be was in the ceiling rose of the single light that had been trunked in to the middle of the roughly hewn rock, twenty-feet above his head.

"Prisoner three-eight-one-four-B! You will stand, turn around and place your hands behind your back!" the guard shouted. King noted it was the same guard as before, so he was ready for a beating, but it never came. The cuffs were placed on and reamed tightly, and he was pulled and pushed out of the door. He could see the same medic who had searched him when he had arrived working on the man on the floor, but not very convincingly. He knew the guy would come around eventually, but he would be in the infirmary for a while, and if he ever got out of here, then he wouldn't be fathering any children in a hurry.

The guard walked him up the corridor, flanked by two more guards brandishing batons. They passed doors, but most seemed suited for other uses, and not the purpose-built cell types King was being held in. After two-hundred metres King was yanked backwards and bundled through a plain door. Tommy-Lee sat behind a stainless-steel desk. King was pushed down opposite him in the empty steel and plastic chair. He could feel his cuffs locked onto the back of the chair. It felt and sounded like a loop and padlock. The guards left, and the steel door closed loudly in the confines of the ten by ten room.

"Settling in?"

"Don't hold your breath for the *TripAdvisor* review…"

Tommy-Lee smiled mirthlessly. "You're not fazed by this?"

King shrugged. "No, I wouldn't say that. I just appear unflappably calm and sarcastic when I'm scared."

Tommy-Lee shook his head. "I'm Johnson."

"Special Agent Johnson, of the Johnsons of Quantico?"

"No relation."

"So, your name's not really Lynch?"

"Wrong department. You know Mister Lynch?"

"I've met many men called Lynch. None of them who they said they were," said King. "So, you're not a Johnson from the FBI or a Lynch from the CIA," he mused. "Do you guys use your real names in the NSA, you're really called Johnson?"

"You seem to have forgotten how this works," said Johnson.

King shook his head. "Look, you're on two stars at best. The pork and beans weren't half bad. Get rid of the cuffs, get me a pillow to fluff and you're back in with a shout."

"I could have you shot," said Johnson. "There's enough hill-billies working here who would jump at the chance to put a bullet in the head of a man who has committed terror offences on US soil."

"I thought you had a special man for that?" King grinned. "The Navy SEAL."

"You know he was a SEAL, how?" Johnson asked incredulously.

"The tattoo on his left forearm."

"You were being beaten up at the time, I'm surprised you noticed."

"I notice things," said King. "And I don't think they were beating me up. But if two of your guys can be taken down by a man with his hands behind his back, well maybe your operation isn't all that."

"Maybe Cole should have a try?" Johnson smirked. "I don't think he'd have any problems killing you if I told him to."

"That's the thing, isn't it? The country you've become. Zero tolerance to matters you don't fully understand. A tough, some would say heartless stand on immigration, yet you are a country of immigrants…"

"We kicked *your* asses out of here two-hundred and fifty-years ago!"

"Did you?" King asked. "Or were political and trade factors enough for Britain to throw in their hand. Who else would they have traded with? Common language, new and untapped resources, and a country that needed stable treaties. Why bite the hand that feeds?"

"You seriously think that?" Johnson scoffed, visibly irked.

"Name a single battle you won after Yorktown and between the four years when Cornwallis surrendered."

"What?" Johnson asked incredulously. "You're kidding, right?"

"Was it a tactical failure not to foresee French ships cutting off and counter-attacking the British, or was Cornwallis merely following orders? This was America's deciding battle and it took less than ninety British. Bit strange, that. Given that the British had been outnumbered by three to one for the entire war and often drove the Colonialists to retreating because of the British soldiers' ability to keep marching towards what appeared to be certain death."

"So, you're saying you threw the war?"

King smiled. "I doubt it. But it's not a stretch to think that Cornwallis was following an agenda. Orders, so to speak."

"Thanks for the history lesson," Johnson said offhandedly. "Allow me to give *you* one. World War Two."

"Undoubtedly," said King.

"So, was your spiel about Cornwallis a euphemism?"

"In what way?"

"That things are not always as they seem," said Johnson.

"Where am I?"

"No comment."

"I'm figuring South Dakota. Or Wyoming. Somewhere in the mid-West."

"No comment."

"Not a high-security prison, although I'm sure this installation is escape-proof, but more like a secret prison. Somewhere that doesn't exist. Not on any map, at least."

"No comment."

"So, the National Security Agency runs this place? The Secret Service backed off back in Washington, so you have a higher clearance, which is difficult to imagine, given the Secret Service's remit."

"No comment," Johnson smiled wryly.

"I suppose that was a private jet I flew here in? Registered to a company off shore, funded entirely by dirty money?"

"You seem remarkably well informed," Johnson said. "Or think you are."

King shrugged. "I doubt this is NSA either. My bet is that this is a recent venture, funded by an amalgamation of US intelligence and law enforcement agencies, overseen by a newly conceived agency pulling money, resources and personnel from the darker corners of other agencies. Where the CIA, the FBI, the Secret Service and the NSA, hell, all the wings of the military, do their dirty work. And with a direct line to a controversial President who has little regard for immigration or human rights."

"You don't have anything like that in Britain?"

King noted that Johnson hadn't used the *no comment* line. Progress. "No, we generally go by the book."

"From the mouth of an assassin?"

"It's a thick and complex book," said King. "And we don't let many people read it."

"We dug about," Johnson said. "There were a few things our inside friends at MI6 found out about you."

"I'm sure," said King. "Good to know the old service is as watertight as ever."

"You didn't so much leave under a cloud, you simply disappeared. At a time when the entire service was restructured. A series of accidents claimed the top three people in SIS. Strange that you should disappear around the same time, don't you think?"

"Well, in my line of work, there was very little job security."

"There was more," Johnson said. "It was claimed you worked in Northern Iraq, Syria and Afghanistan."

"All the holiday hotspots. Check out my TripAdvisor account. Still, better than this dump, though."

"You killed high-value ISIS and Al Qaeda targets at long range with a rifle."

"No comment," King smirked. He'd killed more than this man would ever know, and certainly closer than with a rifle. He could hear his target's breath at times, feel the life leave their bodies as he twisted his blade.

"So how come you missed the Congressman?"

"I underestimated the shield," King said matter-of-factly. "I thought the first two rounds would break it. And then he was moving, and Secret Service agents were on him. At that distance, well, it isn't like knocking down ducks at a shooting gallery."

"I don't think you simply underestimated that shield."

"No?"

"No, I don't."

King shrugged. "So, why would I take the shot?"

Johnson stared at him coldly, the thinnest smile on his dry lips. "Why indeed?"

Chapter Twenty-Five

The man did not return to the cell. His blanket was gone, as was the thin excuse for a mattress. King knew he had called them, he simply had to wait to see what approach they would try next.

Using the single toilet had taken on a whole new meaning of low, now that King knew there was a camera above him somewhere recording his every move. As degradation went, it was bad enough not to have paper to use or a sink to wash in, now he felt the subject of voyeurism. He had to remind himself of his training and what his sensibilities meant in the grand scheme of things. What mattered, and what didn't. He remembered how women from MI5 acted as interrogators on his escape and evasion exercises with the SAS. How they sniggered at the size of his shrunken penis as he shivered naked in front of them - frozen, hungry, exhausted and disorientated. It meant nothing. He'd ended up marrying one of them, so she couldn't have been put off by what she had seen. It had been nothing more than power-play and designed to weaken his resolve. What did he care now if some guy watched him squat on a toilet? Everybody did it every day. His sensibilities meant nothing, and he ignored it now altogether.

Breakfast had been a sort of porridge made with water. He had eaten it without hesitation, knowing he needed to maintain his strength and weight. As he had chewed on the bland, rubbery substance, he had heard talk of showers today. He looked forward to that, but he'd been in prison before and knew that the first time in the showers was the last chance to prove himself. He would do what he had to do.

With the camera above him, King did not want to show whoever was watching him that he was keeping fit. Instead, he used a complex muscle separating system, tensing individual muscles and releasing in time with his breathing. He worked on sets and reps, alternating each side. He counted, estimating that he had worked his muscles for an hour. He aimed to do these three times a day. He stretched, making it more of a show of boredom. The process did nothing for cardiovascular exercise, but his muscles were still toned and firm after so long in confined spaces with no exercise.

An alarm sounded just once, and King

swung his legs over the bed and onto the floor. He told himself he would not become submissive or institutionalised but he simply needed to leave his cell and get on with why he was here. If indeed, *here* was the place.

The door opened mechanically, and King could hear a series of metallic clunks down the corridor. He walked to the door and looked both ways. Other prisoners had done the same. The alarm sounded a second time and each man left their cell. King turned right and walked along the yellow line. Men on the other side of the corridor crossed over and joined the orderly queue. By the time King had made his way down to the end of the corridor there was little more than a metre between each man. The door opened, and the men fanned out into an open chasm that had been carved out of the rock. Arc lights had been fixed into the ceiling fifty-feet above his head and an open viewing window had been made, with enough room for two guards to cover the room with a shotgun and an M4 carbine. The cave was two-hundred feet or so across. The guards could make mincemeat of them, especially when both doors closed, which they did right now.

King estimated three-hundred men. Did that tie in with his designated number? Probably, given that some would die under interrogation, others may have entered the penal system, but he doubted that, and others no doubt found a nine-millimetre bullet and a shallow grave somewhere in the Great Plains, as Johnson had outlined as something he could look forward to if he failed to cooperate. Maybe this was Cole's sole purpose, but he doubted that. The man would be Johnson's go-to guy. Either way, his own prison number meant a lot of men had passed through here, and he doubted they were anything other than fertiliser out on the Great Plains.

King walked slowly around the cave. He watched for groups, the hierarchy. Many of the men were bearded and had peeled off into clusters to pray. Muslim men, ISIS fighters or domestic terrorists. King didn't care what group they were, they were all as bad as each other. Deciding between Al Qaeda, ISIS and Boko Haram was like trying to decide which venereal disease was preferable. He could see the killers amongst the men, and he could see those who had been caught up and swept along for the ride. Cannon fodder for the ISIS commanders, largely disaffected youths sent to carry out the threats of the men preaching behind the firing lines.

As he walked, it was evident that all eyes were on him and he knew it would only be a matter of time before someone tested the water. In an attempt to blend in, he sought out other white males, but soon realised this was America's dumping bin for Islamic terrorists. A few heavily muscled and tattooed white men with large beards had congregated near the door on the other side of the cave. They looked like white supremacists or motorcycle gangs, and King wondered if they were militia who had declared independent status in the mountains of Wyoming or Montana. Such acts were to declare war on Washington and groups had been dealt with harshly in the past and many attempts to serve warrants had resulted in tragic standoffs and sieges that had ended in slaughter. Many women and children had died in those sieges and only went to increase the hate. It mirrored Middle-East problems, but in the American heartland. He sized the men up, deciding there was no preferable option in this room. He was in a class of one.

"Oh, what a quandary you are in?" King turned around and looked at the man standing before him. "You have no friends, no allies in here. You see the Arabs and the Asians, and the Persians and you know you will find no friends there. Not when they find out who you are and what you have done to their brothers. You see the Nazi scum bikers and know you will fool nobody. They will not accept you, and together they will kill you. Or rape you. Perhaps both? You are a tough and resourceful man, but numbers are numbers and when a man goes down to a large group, the training and the strength and the resourcefulness pales into insignificance. Numbers are everything. Like an army of ants that can overwhelm and devour the largest of snakes. The venom and the speed and the agility of the snake means nothing to a million ants. And so it is, in this room."

King could see the man had lost weight and looked like he had aged a decade since he had seen him last, less than two years ago on the same day he had proposed to Caroline on a Majorcan beach. The man was a former Russian Spetsnaz General, a retired KGB officer who served with the FSB. An old-school warrior who served under the banner of the USSR, and later with Russia as a federation.

"I'd like to say you look well, Zukovsky," King paused. "But you look like shit."

"I look better than my son, you bastard!"

"He was trying to kill me. Shit happens."

"But not, I fear, does a coincidence of this magnitude."

King started to walk. He glanced up at the window, saw that the two guards were chatting, weapons relaxed. "I see you fell foul of the CIA."

Zukovsky dry spat and said, "Your department was bad enough!"

"But this is a whole new ball game."

Zukovsky stopped walking and shook his head. "They dehumanise you here," he said quietly. "And they have executed prisoners. Many prisoners…"

"Coming from a former KGB officer, you don't mean to say the Americans are really the bad guys, do you?" he grinned.

"Everyone is bad," the Russian said sardonically. "There are no good guys left."

"Coming from the man who attempted to annihilate millions of people with a nuclear device, I think you had better dump the world-weary attitude and think about karma. Maybe what goes around, comes around and it all caught up with you. And in time, too."

"How's that blonde?" he asked, as he started walking again, this time towards the group of white supremacists.

"Well."

"She killed my lover."

"You had a bad taste in lovers," King said quietly.

"But a horrible way to go, would you not agree?"

King thought of the woman, gasping for breath as the skin burned off her face, the heat closing her throat and suffocating her slowly. "I couldn't give a shit," he said.

Zukovsky stared at him, his cheeks hollowed out and the life in his eyes offering no intensity, merely perpetual sadness. "I will not give you what you want. Whatever you are here for, under whatever premise, I will die here rather than help you. I will gladly die today, I would be happy going to my death safe in the comforting knowledge that you would be stuck here forever."

"And they say time heals," King chided. "I'll tell Caroline not to expect a Christmas card."

"You are a comedian, no?"

King shrugged. "A little humour tends to get me through."

"I will give you nothing," Zukovsky said adamantly.

"What makes you think I want you to give me something?"

Zukovsky regarded him curiously, his lips breaking into the semblance of a smile. "I tried to destroy your pathetic little country once before..."

"You failed. I was there."

"So, I told MI5 and MI6 everything about the weapon, my contacts, the extremists." Zukovsky stepped out of the way of a group of young, feral-looking men with menacing eyes and stubborn, jutting jaws. King thought they looked Pakistani. He thought briefly of Rashid, hoped he and the rest of the team were on track.

King shrugged. "And you told the CIA when we handed you over to them. And I bet you've told whoever runs this place all about it, too." King was aware how the Americans had screwed over the British government. MI5 had handed Zukovsky over to the CIA for questioning. Concerned that his attempted attack on UK soil could be, or was planned to be repeated in the USA, they wanted Zukovsky to fill in the blanks. They had merely kept him and denied any knowledge of the clandestine handover. He was in their system, under the radar and intelligence pointed to the Americans operating a secret prison. In the shadowy world of intelligence, the suspicion was common knowledge. Using hearsay and analytical data, combined with solid intelligence gathering, and MI5 had confirmed the ball park area. The rest was now up to King. He was going to get their asset back.

The Russian's smile emboldened. "So, in that case, you are here about something else."

King smiled, was about to say something, but Zukovsky shoved him into the group of white supremacists and darted away. King sprawled into the biggest of them and all hell broke loose. King rolled away, got to his feet as the man-mountain came at him like a three-hundred-pound gorilla. Except that he was closer to three-fifty and at least six-five. King was sure that if the man wanted to, he could kill a gorilla for breakfast. The man swung hard but missed. King backed away, saw that three more of the group had broken ranks and were flanking him.

"I'm sorry," King said. "I was pushed." He looked around for Zukovsky, but the Russian had fled and mingled into the crowd, which was now gathering around them. Nothing happened here, so everybody enjoyed a good fight.

"No," the gorilla said. "*Now*, you're going to be pushed."

He lunged forwards and King darted to his left. The man swung a backfist and King ducked as it sailed over his head. He stepped inside the man's guard and jabbed his index finger into the man's eye. He stopped short of a proper job and didn't hook or sweep behind the eyeball, simply wetted his finger up to the knuckle and gave the man something to think about.

Three-hundred and fifty pounds reeled backwards, howling and holding both palms to his eye. The other men looked on, some losing the stomach for a fight, but there was always one. And he came in swinging. King kicked him in the groin and smashed the palm of his hand upwards into the man's nose. He seldom punched – knuckles were easily broken, and some of these men looked like they'd been punched plenty of times before and were still here to tell the tale. The man stumbled, but in the close proximity of the crowd, he fell into onlookers and didn't go down. King kicked downwards onto the man's left kneecap and he folded in two, crashing down onto the ground as one of the guards fired two warning shots. It should have been the shotgun, but it wasn't. The 5.56mm high-velocity bullets ricocheted off the cave walls and only stopped when the twisted and flattened rounds found two unsuspecting prisoners. Both men fell, screaming. One held his bleeding arm, the other looked like he wouldn't be making it out of the cave for his shower. He started to fit, and his face became ashen. Most of the men in the cave had seen the scene before. Hardened ISIS fighters who had killed their enemy and lost their friends. Or done a hell of a lot worse to their prisoners. The men dispersed as well as they could inside the cave, and nobody tended to either wounded prisoner.

An alarm sounded, a long buzz like a claxon, and each man got onto his knees. King hadn't been briefed on this, but he was a quick learner and knew it could only be a bad thing to remain standing. The gorilla was whimpering, still holding his eye, but he managed to kneel and duck his head. His companion was resting on his side.

"Prisoners on their knees!" the warning came and the man with the broken kneecap tried to move. *"Prisoners on their knees!"* Again, the man struggled but failed to get his leg anywhere near where it needed to be. King watched, saw the man's face tear apart and heard the gunshot ring out. Two more gunshots rang out and the other two wounded men rested still. The alarm continued to sound and one of the doors opened. King risked a glance to the open window and saw Johnson looking directly back at him. The man seemed amused. He held his stare for a moment, then looked back at the three

bodies on the floor. Headshots. No mercy given. King closed his eyes and thought about Caroline. He hoped he would see her again, but a nagging sensation in his gut told him he was in trouble. Rashid had done everything he could to persuade King not to accept the mission, and for the first time since the initial briefing, he wished he'd passed it by.

Chapter Twenty-Six

After the alarm had ended, they were ordered back to their cells. The men did not move, and King who had started to stand had paused and hovered on his haunches, his eyes on the other men, until they were ordered from the kneeling position to their feet. The men seemed to know the score, like some macabre game of *Simon says*. King would have thought the prisoners would have been shaken by the killings, but their expressions were neutral, their emotions in check. Despite what King had done in his life, and what he had seen, he was aware that he was probably the only person to be shaken at the swiftness in which the wounded men had been dispatched. The man he had disabled by breaking his knee had been shot dead. He wouldn't have been able to kneel no matter how hard he tried. That was on King. But the two innocent bystanders caught up in events, injured by the guard's warning shots, had been shot regardless. And the agent named Johnson had calmly watched events transpire. His threats of shooting King and sending him to a shallow grave seemed more than plausible now that King had seen what could happen here. King had even wondered whether it had been turned into an exhibition for him. In fact, he was certain of it. A stark warning if ever it were needed.

King had passed the time on his bed, thinking about Vladimir Zukovsky. A man with whom he had history and had never expected to see again. Until the head of MI5, Director Amherst, had discovered Zukovsky's involvement in a Russian project, started under the ruling of the USSR, he had not thought about the man who had so very nearly crippled his country. Having discovered the project on a recent mission to Finland, close to the Russian border where he was to retrieve a defector and investigate an MI6 officer's murder, King now knew that to put the threat of a genetic-disrupting biological weapon to bed, he needed to find and interrogate the person involved with its conception. The British SAS had already infiltrated the facility and used explosives to make it look like geothermal and hydroelectric technology had failed due to flooding in the spring thaw and torn the power station apart – a cover for the secret laboratory operating underneath - but Zukovsky was mentioned in transcripts taken by the defector and he was the only link to a hideous and deadly virus designed to incapacitate entire nations.

He did not know how many hours had passed, but as the alarm sounded once, King knew what it meant. He slid off the bed and stood by the door as it opened. It sounded again, and he glanced outside. He couldn't see any other heads, but the message said loudly, *"Those who have been chosen, head to the showers."*

King didn't know which way to walk, but by the process of elimination, he guessed it was to his right, as he had entered the prison from his left, and that was also the direction of Johnson's office. At the end of the corridor downhill the door to the cavern opened and King hesitated, not yet seeing anybody else. He had a feeling that the guards in the open window may well be testing their aim again soon. Was that it? Like Jews marched to the showers in the Holocaust, would he simply meet his end there? He couldn't see what else he could do. He had no weapon, no way of escaping. He could stay in the corridor, but not indefinitely. He was under CCTV surveillance and the guards were armed and had proven they had no qualms about killing prisoners. He felt trepidation as he cautiously entered, his legs leaden and his heart pounding. He looked up at the opening, but the single guard appeared uninterested, his pump-action shotgun held loosely over his forearm. King walked down the steps and headed for the furthest door. It was the only one open, and he had missed it on his earlier visit. So many people, and so much happening. The first door was a double sliding steel affair, more suited to an aircraft hangar. It led to the mess hall, and from there only to the kitchens and service area beyond. It had been open both times he had been down here. The open doorway ahead of him led to a short walk through a narrow, roughly hewn passageway and another rocky cavern opened-up but this time far smaller than the general population cave. He wondered how long it had taken to construct, whether it had been done clandestinely as the airstrip had been constructed, or whether it was left over from a gold mining project that had been bored out underground. He knew that the Black Hills was the birthplace of the American goldrush and because of the ego of General Custer who was told by President Ulysses S. Grant to keep news of the discovery of gold quiet – America being both in recession and under contract of agreement with Sitting Bull and the Sioux nation to stay out of the newly formed Black Hills Indian reservations – it had spelt the beginning of the end for the Native American Indian's freedom. King had focused his research on the area and had learned a great deal. He had memorised topographic and geographical features, a potted history and reckoned he would know his way out of the vast area without a map. He just hoped he was in the right place to begin with.

A bank of showers ran along one wall, partially sectioned off by hardboard panel screens. There were stalls of warped plywood and dishes piled high with used soap bars. The floor was grated, and the place smelled of damp and urine and faeces. King guessed that many of the men would make use of the shower as they took the chance to defecate away from the cameras in their cells. With no paper in the cells, squatting and washing in the shower afterwards would have felt a luxury. Indeed, he imagined the many Muslim men preferring it to the Western toilet in their cell. King had found that once away from the larger hotels in the Middle-East simple squat toilets were the norm throughout most of the countries he had visited out there. But as he entered the shower area, it was clear from the smell that it hadn't been intended nor equipped for that purpose. A putrid, fetid obtrusion to his senses. It was enough to make him want to gag. He breathed through his mouth to nullify the smell.

"Prisoner three-two-eight, you will strip and shower…" The speaker system crackled above his head.

King was guarded. He knew that there were enough men here in need of a shower but couldn't work out why he was alone. He kicked off the cheap plimsoles, stripped out of the orange jumpsuit and took off his boxers. He switched the shower head on and picked up some soap. He washed the boxers out with the soap, rinsed them thoroughly and wrung them as dry as he could and flung them onto a hook. The hook was loose in its plywood setting and tipped slightly as it took the weight. He looked at the fixings, wandered if it could work in his favour. He then scrubbed and soaped himself all over, washing twice and allowing the tepid water to run over his aching neck and shoulders.

"Hey, look! Some fresh meat!"

King looked up to see the gorilla sporting an eye patch. He was flanked by two more men, who were similar in looks to him, though a little smaller. But still over six-foot and twice an average man's weight. To their credit, their size looked to be hewn from cheeseburgers and dumb-bells. Equal parts muscle and fat, but certainly strong and not underestimated.

"I want to thank you for the cheap shot in my eye," the gorilla said. "The doc says I'll be lucky to get my sight back, so thanks a lot, buddy."

"You're welcome."

The man's jaw dropped, but he recovered quickly enough. He snarled, "Oh, you're gonna be sorry! But first, my bros here want to get acquainted…"

"Prison gay?" King asked. "Or just gay?"

"Does it make any difference?" one of the men asked incredulously.

King smiled, started to soap his hands. Lots of lather going on as he looked at the three men. "Well, one type brings flowers, I suppose."

"It'll still go in the same way. Spit and determination," the man said coldly from behind a sadistic smile.

"You seen Deliverance?" the gorilla asked, smiling. He took a step towards King. The two men followed suit.

King nodded and smiled. "Yeah."

"Well?"

King shrugged. "A couple of hill-billies rape a man, get killed for their trouble. Should serve as a lesson to you."

The gorilla shook his head. "I meant the squealing like a pig part."

King smiled. "Well, I guess we know who's who."

"Meaning?" the gorilla asked. He was staring at King's scars, a network of lines across his chest and torso.

"Fuck me, you're not that stupid, are you?" King kept lathering the soap in his hands, the water still running down his back. "You think you've got one thing planned, but it's not going to pan out like that. Now, fuck off back to your cells, before it all goes wrong for you. Again."

One of the men shrugged. "No. You see, being here serves two purposes. We get a thrill, Chuck gets some payback for his eye and we get a serious amount of credit with the guards."

"That's three dumb-ass," said King.

The two men glanced at each other and pumped themselves a little. Their stances widened, like cowboys with a brace of six-guns on their hips, only it was a combination of fat and muscle that kept their arms out from their sides. They didn't quite manage it in unison, but they lunged forwards into the wet room, just as King threw the handful of the soap lather in front of them. Both men lost their footing, but one went down hard and the other slipped and slid and tried to regain his balance. King's hands were still lathered, and he slapped the man in the face with an open palm, the soap plastering his eyes. He started to howl and dig at his eyes with his fingers and didn't see King's knee coming towards his groin. He felt it though and went down, his partner taking the brunt of his weight as he fell on top of him. King dropped to his knees, caught hold of the man's ears and dragged his head over so that it lined up with his partner's face. He lifted and smashed three times, until both men lay still. He gave it one more for luck, then let go and stood up. Still naked, unashamed and ready to take on the gorilla.

The gorilla stood up straight and flexed.

King wasn't a small man at a shade under six-foot and although he had lost weight since his incarceration, he was still a well-muscled thirteen and a half stone or so. All useful and no excess fat that wasn't. But the man in front of him was a mountain. King had taken him on once, but as he sized him up a second time, the gorilla allowed a section of pipe to slide out of his sleeve. He gripped it firmly, the other end glinting in the light where it had been flattened and scraped into a makeshift chisel edge.

"Walk away," King said.

"Not until I've cut off your dick," he replied, eyeing him up and giving the pipe a twist, the edge glinting again. "And fed it to you, you son of a bitch!"

King shrugged like the threat was nothing. "So, Johnson put you up to this?" The man said nothing, but he took a pace towards King, mindful of the water on the floor and the spread of lathered soap suds. "What did he promise you?"

"Shut up and dance, mother fucker!" He swung the pipe and King dodged backwards, and to his annoyance he slipped on the wet, smooth concrete and nearly went down. The gorilla was faster than he looked and swiped the pipe a second time, slashing King across his bicep. King winced, and the man jeered. "How's that feel?"

King worked his way to his left, over the grate and to the dry concrete floor. He glanced at his arm, which was bleeding enough for a trip to A and E. The gorilla smiled and stepped around his two unconscious companions. He squinted through his one good eye, the eye-patch lending a comical pirate look, although the size and rage of the man could not be underestimated. King realised he was backed up against a row of sinks. He looked for something to use as a weapon, picked up a wet hand towel and caught hold of one corner. He spun it so that it twisted, then edged closer to his opponent.

"Ah, gee, I'm fucking scared now, punk," the gorilla sneered.

King whipped the towel out like it was locker-room high-jinks and it cracked on the tip of the man's chin. He howled and flinched, then came at King with a flurry of swipes with the pipe. King ducked and dived and whipped the towel again, this time cracking the man's nose. A half-inch gash opened up and started to bleed. He quickly followed it up as the man recoiled, the next flick catching him in his remaining good eyeball. The man screamed and dropped the pipe, falling to his knees and cupping his face with both hands. He was cursing and screaming, some of it incoherent. King picked up the pipe and stepped closer.

"That must smart a bit," he said. "You're not having the best day, are you? Well, it wasn't like I didn't warn you. Here, have some prison anaesthetic..." He swiped the pipe on the back of the man's head and he fell forwards onto the pile.

King put his orange jumpsuit back on and snatched his cleaned, but damp boxers off the hook. He bundled them up and tucked them under his arm as he left. The cavern looked large and ominous ahead of him. He glanced up at the guard, who did a double take when he saw King on his own. He looked uncertain what to do next, but King was already across the cave and up the steps. A backward glance as he left through the door showed the guard reaching for his radio.

He dutifully followed the yellow line and ahead of him his cell door opened. There were no instructions on the speaker, and he imagined that somewhere there was a very pissed off individual who had wanted him broken down and beaten in the most animalistic way possible. Sure, the guards could perform the beatings until they killed him, but they wouldn't have carried out the threat that the three prisoners had been willing to do. Somewhere, someone would be looking at a plan-B. But King was damned if he was going to give them the opportunity.

Chapter Twenty-Seven

King looked at the boxers on the floor. Damp, but clean. He could only assume that the camera was located in the ceiling rose of the single bulb high above his head. They would be watching him for sure. But he needed to remain calm. He had a chance now, but only if he could use it without drawing attention to it. He took off his shoes and placed them on top of the boxers, then pushed the pile under his bed while he peeled down the jumpsuit to his waist and used the damp towel that he had used against the gorilla to staunch the flow of blood to the slice on his shoulder. It was deep, but the bleeding had slowed. It was sore as hell, though. He looked up to the ceiling and pointed to the wound.

"Do you want me to bleed to death?" he shouted. He turned his attention back to the wound, but other than dabbing it, he had nothing to treat it with. "Get me some medical attention!"

Five minutes later and the cell door opened. A different procedure now. No cuffs, just three tough-looking guards with a shotgun each and a man in a white coat. The doctor who had searched him on arrival. The doctor scurried in and dropped a medical bag on the floor beside King. He opened it and set about taking out various packets. King watched him curiously, then looked over at the door as Johnson stepped in. He was still wearing his black suit with matching tie and white shirt. His resemblance to the actor Tommy-Lee Jones was uncanny. Perhaps the guy had watched the films, tried to replicate it as part of his persona.

"You're a tough son of a bitch, aren't you?"

King regarded him coldly as the doctor wiped the wound with antiseptic. "I am," he said. "Nature or nurture. I grew up tough. And then *they* made me tougher," he paused. "But I'm not sadistic. I can be violent when I have to be, but not purposely vicious. Whatever gets the job done." He felt the hypodermic needle going in and watched as the doctor took out a needle and thread, ready to suture. He turned back to Johnson. "But you're a vindictive shit. What you lined up down there for me was unnecessary," he said. "You've got to be a special kind of wanker to try and have that done to somebody."

"Needs must," Johnson said. "Time to let you know who's boss."

King nodded. "It was a good exercise, though." King watched the doctor perform the first suture. The aesthetic hadn't yet kicked in. The tip of the needle did not look sharp enough and it pushed the skin upwards before puncturing and being accepted by the pincers, the thread trailing behind, tugging its way through. The doctor tied it off and started the next stitch. King looked at the man's watch. A nice Omega on a leather strap. It was a date model with a few scratches on the crown. The sort of piece that was given as a twenty-first present and treasured ahead of fashion or whim. He noted the time and the date. It helped to take his mind off the pain.

"Really?"

"Yes," said King. "Because I got to see into your character."

"How so? Just because I got a couple of fags to soften you up? You think I give a shit about what happens to you?"

"No." King shook his head. "But it shows you don't have the balls or the strength to hurt me yourself. Sure, your stooges could beat me up..." He looked over to the three men. "But only if someone holds a gun on me, because believe me, they'd be dead before they finished flexing their steroid-induced muscles." He blew a kiss at the middle guard, then stopped the doctor short of the next stitch. "That'll do," he said and stood up, eye to eye with Johnson. "I'll do a deal with you. I have information regarding three separate terrorist attacks that will take place on US soil over the next month. I'll tell you about them, let you know everything I gleaned from my sources. But I'll tell you nothing if you try any deranged shit like that again. And I'll tell you in my own time. If you think torture will get you anywhere..." He pointed to the myriad of scars on his chest and torso. "Then you'll get to know just how far down in the amateur leagues you really are."

Johnson looked at the scars, then back at King's face. His expression told Johnson he was not to be doubted. "In return for what?" he asked.

"My freedom."

"Forget it."

"Three attacks."

"You're full of shit."

"And you're a sack of it."

"You'd better watch your mouth."

"Or you'll get someone to carry out your dirty work? Fuck it, maybe a gun on me won't help this time. Your pussies will just be in the line of fire."

Johnson shook his head and backed out the door. The guards followed, but they weren't happy about leaving with their hands clean. The doctor suddenly realised he should be leaving and was standing too close to the most dangerous man the prison had seen.

"Three attacks, Johnson! The third will be the worst!" King shouted. "Chicago is first! Got that? Chicago!" The cell door slammed closed, but King smiled knowing full well that Johnson had heard.

Chapter Twenty-Eight

"We stick to the plan. It's crucial."

"But we don't even know if he's still alive!" Ramsay retorted.

"And we never would," Rashid paused. "That was always the part of the plan that I thought was complete and utter bullshit!"

"And *I* am still here, Neil!" Caroline snapped from the backseat. She caught his eye in the rear-view mirror and he looked away uncomfortably.

"I'm sorry, Caroline. But I'm just stating facts, regardless of your relationship with Alex. And there's no going back, you know that?" Ramsay negotiated yet another junction and red light that turned instantly to green.

"And as I've said, that was always the plan," Rashid shook his head. "Bravo Team have done their work, we have to see it through."

"We're well out of diplomatic relations now. This is merely the next step to a plan that was good enough to start rolling out when we were back in London. Now King is wrapped up in it, we're not going to get cold feet!" Caroline snapped.

Ramsay sighed. "Alright," he said. "I suppose I never thought it would get this far. But this next stage is huge."

Caroline was pressed between the front seats, trying to look Ramsay in the eye, but she couldn't quite manage it. Ramsay glanced in the vanity mirror and flinched slightly when he saw how close she was to him. "So, Alex was what? Part of an ill-conceived plan with no legs? He would do his part, then we would fail at this stage?"

"No!" Ramsay snapped and twisted round in his seat to face her. "Look, it's just a big step, that's all. It's a prominent target with a lot of history."

"Bollocks to its history!" Rashid interjected. "Its history is commercialism and greed. Capitalism at its height. That's why it serves as a tourist attraction these days. No single business would have such a large headquarters nowadays."

"There are dozens of businesses based there now, Rashid. Restaurants, bars, offices..." Ramsay protested somewhat pedantically, given his audience.

"So, it's a good target. And that's what we need," said Caroline.

"Look, we're almost there now," Rashid said. "Let's move on and get this done."

"Christ Almighty," Ramsay said quietly looking up at the skyline and the buildings of varying height. They're huge…"

"And so is what is at stake," Caroline said quietly, although she knew what Ramsay meant. But Director Amherst had told them they needed a statement, and that was exactly what they were going to make.

They had driven into Chicago while Powell, Big Dave and Tattooed Mick had taken the train in from Roselle. Marnie and Adams had driven in on a different route from Bloomingdale, where they were staying at a large hotel in Indian Lakes. The three men would simply pose as tourists heading for Navy Pier where a rock concert was playing throughout the afternoon, along with an international beer festival. The train was full of teens and middle-aged hipsters who had started drinking early. By contrast, Adams and Marnie were driving to the south of the city where they would park and head downtown using a combination of taxis and Uber. They had downloaded the Uber app using a credit card issued through MI5's special operations wing that would terminate after settlement of the bill at the end of the month. Adams and Marnie would pose as a couple, and much to Rashid's consternation, Adams was insisting they were one of those couples who always put on a show of affection. 'Loved up' was what Caroline called it, encouraging the idea. Rashid thought they should be a couple who had recently argued and should both play it subdued. Adams liked the idea and floated the chances of make-up sex after they warmed to each other as the day wore on. Rashid had continued the briefing through gritted teeth but knew that to retaliate was to stand before the hounds in this group, where further banter and bad taste would be relentless. Marnie enjoyed Rashid's consternation. They hadn't been together long, playing the on/off game since they had first gotten together in South Africa on an assignment.

Tactically, they had covered the bases. Public transport, personal transport and a series of commercial vehicle drop-offs and pick-ups where Adams and Marnie would put at least a block between vehicles and zig-zag their way near the target and would walk the last two blocks. All three groups would enter the target building at staggered times and would not interact once inside. Each person had a specific task and a timeframe in which to perform it. Subsequent investigations would be hampered by the crowds of party-goers on their way through the city to Navy Pier and the beer festival and rock concert, and the routes in and out of Chicago were numerous, so numerous in fact that eight people entering by three different means would appear invisible. By the time any link could be made, they would be long gone.

Chapter Twenty-Nine

King stripped off and checked his arm. The sutures had held well, and the swelling was going down. He supposed if an infection was going to take hold then it would have happened by now. He bent down for the boxer shorts, still damp but he didn't have any drying options. He carefully unravelled them, used his back as best he could to block the overhead camera. He had snatched them from the loose hook, ripping the hook from the wall. He had ditched the hook beside the gorilla's unconscious body but had managed to keep two of the screws. He didn't have the luxury of pockets - the jumpsuit had been made without them. Guantanamo Bay surplus. King wondered what the clothing company's brochure said about the garment's uses and applications and whether they had depots in the Middle-East for ISIS to benefit from their marketing and commercialism. A dedicated beheading video issue range. The company selling to both sides of the conflicts. King put the suit back on and as he pulled on his plimsoles, he tucked a screw under each insole before pulling them on. He could feel them, but for the moment they did not protrude through the sole.

The alarm sounded, and the cell door opened. King waited at the threshold for the second alarm, then joined the line. One metre behind and one metre in front. They walked in unison through the cavern where only the day before three men who were too injured to stand upon command had been shot dead. Apart from bleach staining which had cleaned the grime off the rough concrete floor to a greater degree than normal, there was nothing to signify what had happened, and King knew that nobody in the outside world would ever know. The fate of every man here, himself included, relied upon support in dark political corners and shadowy intelligence agencies. When the prison became too hot politically, or the undercurrent changed, then he could only imagine the fate of the prisoners. As a man who had fought the worst of society, he wasn't sympathetic to the inmates, just incredulous to the prospect of the institution serving a significant purpose. Vladimir Zukovsky had been held here in secret. The Americans had wanted a high-value intelligence asset and after insisting they question the

Russian terrorist, had simply denied his existence. The British government and MI5 had been left with a dilemma – to go through the proper diplomatic and judiciary channels and to publicly fight the Americans would shed light on how close the United Kingdom had been to a nuclear weapon detonating in the heart of the country. The questions would be insurmountable, and Britain's security failings would be highlighted to other terrorist groups. Britain could let Zukovsky go, but considering the intelligence gleaned from an operation that MI5 were tasked with in the Arctic Circle earlier this year, and the threats of the Russian sponsored development of a global infecting virus for use as a first-strike weapon, MI5 needed information from Zukovsky. In short, the Americans had cornered themselves and cooperation would be zero.

The mess hall was an unpainted room, the walls and floors finished in rough concrete or exposed drilled rock. King stood in line. He could see the white supremacists watching him. The gorilla had both eyes bandaged and was being guided along by his own kind. He guessed the dynamic within that group would change soon. The wounded, older lion with younger, fitter lions ready to take his place. King kept his distance and took his tray over to an uncrowded bench, where he sat down and started to eat. He didn't care that it looked like vomit. He knew enough about calories and the importance of eating whatever he could, whenever he could. He did not subscribe to that at home, but when he was operating in the field he ate and slept as much as he could. The tray was piled high with the hardest scrambled egg he'd ever eaten and with each mouthful it threatened to break the plastic spoon. He figured it had once been powdered egg but was at a loss what the lumpy white sauce on top was, and nor why it came with a scone. It was only as he listened to the chatter around him that he realised it was biscuits and gravy. He decided it was singularly the worst meal he'd ever eaten, and he'd once been forced to make a cup of tea with his own piss before, so it was saying something.

He saw Zukovsky eating at a table on the other side of the hall. The man was with a group of tattooed, wiry men with Slavic features. King recognised the tattoos as Russian military and prison artwork. He knew that many tattoos had specific meanings, such as what crime they had committed to be incarcerated, how many men they had killed or what their gang ranking was. They looked to be tough men, and he knew that they would be aware that Zukovsky had previous history and bad feeling with the prison's latest arival. Perhaps they would act as his bodyguards. He spooned down the eggs and wallpaper paste and finished the biscuit. He washed it down with water and was sure he could keep the meal down if he tried not to think about it too much. He could kill for a cup of tea and looking around the room he was sure many of the men here had killed for far less. He kept checking behind him and using his peripheral vision to keep himself situationally aware. He busked his tray as everyone else did and he walked casually past Zukovsky, glancing at him and the men around him. Better to test the water now than be caught by a surprise attack later. The men watched him, but nothing was said. Zukovsky looked up, but quickly returned to his eggs and gravy. One of the men helped himself to Zukovsky's biscuit and King saw right there and then that the man had lost any dominance he may have had. These younger Russians were not subservient to him and as hard as it was to believe that a former KGB General with a lifetime's service had fallen so low, it gave King an insight to the man and his life inside this place. If a man like Zukovsky carried no clout, then this place could break anybody.

"You have beef with our friend?" one of the men asked as King passed by, forcing him to turn around.

"No."

"That's not what I hear."

"And I give a shit, because?"

The man stood up, still chewing on the biscuit. He took another bite as one would an apple and spoke through a cascade of crumbs. "You real tough guy, eh?" he asked in broken English with a heavy guttural accent. "If you want to survive in here, you need learn respect..."

"Thanks, I'll bear that in mind," King said. "When I eventually meet someone who deserves some respect, that is."

"You already fight with those fascists," the man smiled. "But they are soft faggots who eat too much burger and ice-cream in previous life and are only tough in big group..." His face fell, and he glared at King. "Watch your back, new boy."

King stepped up to him, his eyes colder, harder. They were kind to those he cared for, for others who looked into them, they looked like somewhere between purgatory and hell. The man swallowed, stepped back a pace. "And you watch your front, Ivan. Because I don't need to sneak up on people. Fuck with me and you'll eat the rest of your meals through a straw and shit in a bag..." He patted the Russian on his cheek and said, "And I don't think these hill-billy, trigger-happy guards will put up with your dead weight for long."

The rest of the men stood up in unison, the bench seats scraping on the ground beneath it. King saw that two guards had taken up position in an open window behind the Russian. Their M4 rifles were aimed. The men had noticed, too. They looked to change their mind and dutifully started to busk their empty trays. The Russian smiled and said, "I will remember this..." He turned and left, leaving his tray for his minions to clear away.

"That was dumb, even for you," said Zukovsky. He had finished his eggs, but King could see that even as an old hand, he had left the pale white gravy.

King sat down opposite him and said, "So, tell me about a virus that incapacitates people in a way only horror films would have you believe. Tell me about people reduced to a primal instinct that they only feed, like cannibals, and are unaware of anything else. You couldn't just stick with Anthrax or Novichok, could you?"

Zukovsky smiled. "Never in my lifetime would I have thought they could develop it."

"Well, they have."

"Then, we are done here." He stood up with his tray and looked down at King, a new fire in his eyes that had been lacking before. "And Russia will win."

"Win what? There'll be nothing worth having."

"We will clean up the mess. We will emerge the greatest nation," he paused, a thin smile on his lips. "As if there were any doubt."

"A nation of poverty and decadence, and nothing in between. A nation with nothing of value other than oil and gas. Where are your inventions, products or contributions to mankind and humanity? I've been everywhere and it's still the most miserable bloody nation on earth. And now, you get to spread some evil shit among the West. What for, to compensate for the misery our successes bring you? You feed off them, aspire to them. But where is your ingenuity? You make a bloody rifle and don't update it for sixty-years!"

"Because it was perfect the first time!"

"Debatable," King said. "It suited its user. It was simple, like them. It was rugged, like them. And it was repressed from evolving, like them. Nothing your country has ever made, apart from one cheaply constructed rifle, has made it anywhere else. And it's interesting that your most successful product in history was a weapon. A killing machine. You were second into the nuclear arms race. Second everywhere else, too."

"First into space."

"First, then last. Last in every other venture after that. You couldn't get vegetables to market, let alone men to the moon!"

"You are trying to provoke me?"

"No," King said. "I'm highlighting that your country has only given misery to the world. Repression of its people, and when communism failed, you repressed with money and wealth. Or a lack of it for all outside the party. You make chemical weapons, conventional weapons, small arms and specialise in obstinance. You already tried to kill millions of British citizens with a nuclear device. Why? Because this apocalyptic weapon wasn't deployable? You hate the West so much that you had to resort to a backup plan?"

"I despise the West!" he snapped, standing up suddenly.

"Sit down," King said. "Before I tell someone what you know about this virus project. I imagine they tortured you enough when they thought you had an inside line to nuclear weapons. I can see they did. You're a broken man," King paused. "The intensity has gone in your eyes. Sure, you had it a second ago when you thought of the misery your concept could unleash on the West, but it's gone now. That was as alive as you'll ever be in here. You look like a dead man walking. I doubt you could take another round of waterboarding and electric shocks. But they wouldn't care. They'll just kill you doing it and bury you out on the plains." King could see he'd touched a nerve.

The mention of torture had caused a flicker in the man's eyes. King had unnerved him. "But I have another way…"

"You can promise nothing," Zukovsky replied. Nevertheless, he returned to his seat. "You are here as a prisoner. Why? What did you do?"

"I shot at a Congressman."

"Good for you. I hope you hit him," he paused. "Why? To get in here?"

"Yes."

"You're crazy," he said incredulously.

"I think I must be."

Zukovsky wavered, then said, "How are you getting out?"

King smiled. "That's my business," he said coldly. "But will you be with me, or are you dying in here? MI5 want you, there's no denying that. But you're an old man. You'll get a comfortable safe house where you'll stay and drip information under house arrest. You know the score. It's tea and biscuits compared to this place and the NSA and CIA."

"Thanks, but I'll take my chances in here."

"Good luck," said King as he stood up. "You aren't in charge of anything or anyone, you look like shit and you only have a bullet and a shallow grave to look forward to. Well, as they say in these parts – have a nice day."

As King walked away, he looked up at the guards, who seemed to have relaxed. He walked out into the cavern and found a quiet corner, where he perched on a piece of rock jutting out from the wall and took some time to himself. He checked the guard's window and could see the man wasn't bothering to keep a look-out. King checked that the white supremacist bikers and the wiry Russians were nowhere near, and he dug one of the screws out of his shoe. He subtly placed the tip on the rock and worked it in long strokes. He then set about working the sides, his aim to flatten the edge into a flatheaded screwdriver, around the size of a household electrical type used for wiring plugs. He worked the metal, casually checked his progress. By the time the alarm sounded to return to the cells he estimated it was a quarter-way done. He slipped it back into his shoe and worked it under the sole. This time, he waited for Zukovsky to walk ahead of him, then fell in a few men behind.

Chapter Thirty

Caroline had paired off with Rashid and they posed as a couple in the line, which wound its way around the ground floor of the Willis Tower. She could see Marnie and Adams up ahead but did not look for the others. She knew Ramsay would arrive at the tower in another fifteen minutes. He would simply be on his own and take an interest in the Chicago tour guide he had purchased, as well as the information booklet he would buy at additional cost. People who attended such tourist spots alone tended to take great interest in where they were and learn as much as they could. Adams had his arm around Marnie's shoulder and Rashid was quietly seething.

"Let it go," Caroline whispered in his ear.

"He's just being a dick."

"He's being a pro," she said. "And they're a couple, for appearances sake. Nobody remembers the loved-up couple, but they will remember the couple who looked like they argued their way around the tallest building in the Western hemisphere. So, put your bloody arm around my waist and relax."

"Is it?"

"What?"

"The tallest building?"

"Yes, I think so. Sixteen-hundred and fifty-feet. And only relegated because the buildings in the Middle-East just slap on a bloody great antenna."

"Wow, you learn something every day."

"Once more with enthusiasm."

"And I thought we were just here for the view," Rashid chided.

"I think ninety-nine percent are here for the view," she smiled and put on a tour guide's impression. "You can see four states – Illinois, Wisconsin, Michigan and Indiana…"

Ahead of them, banks of monitors told different stories about how Sears built the building as their base and flagship store. There were narrations at certain points where the story of its construction would be told. Cardboard cut outs of celebrities and a chart of how many of them would make up the height gave photo opportunities for people.

They reached an escalator and travelled down forty-feet or so and re-joined a line, but this time they could see the ticket offices. Marnie and Adams had purchased their tickets and were joining a faster-moving line. Caroline caught sight of Big Dave who was reading a brochure and studying a timeline of the building's construction on the wall.

After Rashid and Caroline had purchased their tickets the queue moved quickly to the elevator bank. Among the fastest in the world, they could get from the basement level to the Skydeck viewing platform in forty-seconds. The elevators were crammed full and the sensation was one of tremendous speed as the car shot upwards and started its slowdown way before the top. As it glided to a halt, the mass of people disembarked, and Caroline caught sight of the bottom of the elevator shaft in the gap as she stepped through the doors. She had never been inside such a tall building and as she followed Rashid past a bank of windows, the height gave her a queasy feeling in her stomach and a leaden sensation in her legs.

"Are you alright?" Rashid asked.

"I think I have vertigo," she replied. "I feel really weird."

"Acrophobia," Rashid corrected her. "Vertigo is an imbalance in the ears, but Alfred Hitchcock's film hasn't helped to dispel the confusion."

Caroline looked at him as she forced herself to walk. "That couple who have argued scenario is getting pretty damned close," she replied scornfully. "Now, take my arm and help me."

"Seriously?"

"Yes!"

Rashid hooked his arm in hers and they passed the bank of windows and walked up a slope where gifts and sweets were on sale. She loosened up and by the time they had cleared the concessions, she was walking normally. She pulled her arm away and said, "Bloody hell! I've never had that before."

"Well, I wouldn't suggest the Perspex viewing boxes, then," Rashid said and patted her shoulder. "I've known skydivers who go to pieces on a cliff-edge," he paused. "Planes aren't a problem, but for some reason high places are different."

She smiled. "I think I'm okay now," she said. But she found she was breathing purposefully, calming herself down. "Or at least, I'll be okay in a minute."

Rashid nodded. "It's okay, we have plenty of time."

"I'll be alright here," she said. "You go and see what the viewing tower looks like."

"You're not coming?"

Caroline cocked her head and said somewhat sarcastically, "Er, no. I think I'll sit this one out." She watched Rashid go, then walked around the floor counter-clockwise keeping the wall on her left and forty-feet or so between herself and the windows, which had now become a constant wall of glass.

The lines had started for the viewing platforms. These were Perspex boxes allowing groups of up to ten people to walk out on and have the illusion of standing on thin air some fourteen-hundred feet above the ground. It was a selfie magnet, with many of the people concentrating on taking the perfect selfie for social media yet forgetting to take in the magnificence of the view or the sensation of walking on air. Many had turned the selfie into an artform, using large telescoping sticks to get the perfect angle and distance. Caroline wondered how many had stood before the world's most scenic views and taken away nothing but an upload to a social media page that showed their moronic pouting, yet nothing of the wonderment they had failed to truly see. She figured most of them.

Rashid returned having checked out what he had come to see. It was just a matter of timing now.

"Feeling better?" he asked.

"Feeling foolish," she replied.

He shrugged. "I'll let you into a secret if you promise not to tell Alex."

She smiled. "What's that?"

Rashid looked past her, caught sight of Powell and Tattooed Mick, and looked away. "I hate spiders," he said.

"Spiders?" she asked incredulously.

"Yes," he said sharply. "It's a pretty common fear!"

She laughed and walked further out from the wall. She was getting used to the height and found it better when she watched the horizon out over Lake Michigan, rather than looking down onto the distant streets of Chicago below.

Rashid shook his head. "Out in Iraq, Syria and Afghanistan they have camel spiders, they're as big as your hand! Sometimes bigger, and they have a nasty bite!"

Caroline rubbed his shoulder and smiled. "Oh, I'm so telling Alex about that…"

"Hey! I was trying to make you feel better!"

"Thanks," she said. "I do already."

Rashid looked at his watch. "It's close," he said.

"Do the sweep," Caroline said. "I have one in sight and I'll stick to that. I don't think I can get any closer to those windows. God! My legs feel drunk!"

"I'm on it," he said. I'll do a circuit, or at least as far as I can get, and check we're on." He checked his watch. "Five-minutes from my signal."

Rashid checked the viewing windows and stopped and looked out over the South of the city. He could see Tattooed Mick in position. He didn't signal, merely kept walking. Another twenty-five metres and he could see Big Dave studying a tourist map. He had bought something from the gift concession, a plastic bag with a souvenir. For a moment he thought it sloppy – something that tied him to the Willis Tower, but then he saw it was a chocolate model and realised it was probably just a snack he'd consume before the morning was out. He kept walking and Marnie and Adams were inside one of the viewing boxes. He wished he could have been in there with her. He felt a pang of jealousy, then saw the fire extinguisher to the left of the box. He realised they had timed it well. He saw Adams watching him but did not give the signal yet. Powell was near the elevators. He had purchased a Chicago Bears cap and was immersed in his phone, scrolling through. To all the world he would look like a man bored of queuing and waiting for his other half. He couldn't walk a complete circle, because the elevators running to take people back down formed the end of the line. Twenty-five thousand visitors a day queued to view from the Skydeck, so entering and exiting had to be a seamless affair.

Rashid made his way back to Caroline, walked past and caught sight of Ramsay. The man was taking in the view a little too intently but had found his mark. Rashid walked up to him and took in the view over Lake Michigan. "We're on," he said quietly and returned to Caroline. Everybody was in place. He sidled up to Caroline and whispered, "Go." Caroline checked the clock on her phone as he walked away. She felt a flutter of nerves and scrolled through and found the app Marnie had designed and installed to their phones back in England.

She thumbed it and edged closer to the fire extinguisher.

Rashid subtly nodded to Tattooed Mick and Big Dave as he passed. Adams and Marnie were out of the viewing box and Adams was scrolling through his phone. He looked up, caught Rashid's eye and thumbed open the app. Powell was last, but he already had his thumb hovering over the app. When he pressed the icon, a circle scrolled round and round. Rashid got to his post and opened the app. His was the final initiation of the circuit. The app finished swirling round and: *Synced 7/7* appeared on the screen. The timer had started and once the final circuit completed the counter adjusted to fifteen minutes.

Chapter Thirty-One

King had watched Vladimir Zukovsky enter his cell. He had taken a risk and bypassed his own, and when he made to turn around, he had been quickly overpowered by guards who had appeared from nowhere. He did not fight back. It didn't suit his plan and wouldn't pay to disrupt what he had started. As the guards had bundled him back into the cell, he felt a rifle butt strike his kidney and he sagged to his knees. He did not retaliate, but as he fell to the floor, he rolled and faced his attackers.

"Get Johnson!" he shouted. "I have something he'll want to know!" The nearest guard hesitated, his rifle butt raised ready to deliver another blow. "I mean it, that's where I was heading!"

The guards had backed away, the steel door slamming closed with a loud clang. King had waited, but Johnson did not show. He had passed the time tensing and flexing his muscles. He figured boredom was a contention with everybody locked up here and decided to openly perform press-ups and sit-ups until he was simply too exhausted to continue. The workout hurt his wound, but he put more weight on his left shoulder to compensate. He had given up counting the reps - as the mind was weak and would focus on a terminal number to stop - and started building a house in his mind. Foundations and footings, each course of blocks, the rendering, wiring, painting, flooring and furnishings. It amused him how quickly he could perform the tasks but realised he did not know as much as he thought he did about construction. He finally lay back on the floor, perspiring and panting with a roof to slate and a chimney he'd forgotten to put in when he'd started on the walls. And he'd forgotten about insulation as well. It had passed the time and he was surprised when the alarm sounded, and the cell door opened. He had eaten pork and beans again, and only noticed this time how the Muslim men picked through their meals. He imagined serving the chunks of pork in the beans was a form of degradation. He recognised the kind of men in here, so couldn't care less about their religious dietary requirements. He ate the pork and beans and had managed to take two chunks of bread. The first, he soaked into the beans and the other one he used to wipe the plate spotlessly clean. With a good workout behind him and a filling meal inside, he felt a little more human. He busked his tray and flimsy plastic spoon and helped himself to a plastic cup of water. He drank it down and refilled it three times. There was no access to water in his cell and he had felt in a permanent state of dehydration. He looked around the room and saw Zukovsky at a table flanked by two of the Russians. The white supremacist bikers were watching him intently, the gorilla still sporting two eye patches which looked pretty special. He wondered again how the man's dynamic would change in here, but found he couldn't care about him either, not a semblance of guilt in his mind. He scoured the canteen and saw the Russian he'd earlier had the run-in with perched on the edge of bench seat staring at him. He looked away when King caught his eye. King refilled the cup with water and made his way towards the exit.

He passed the Russian without a glance, but heard the sudden movement, sensed the rush behind him. He spun around, splashed the water at the man's feet and dropped the cup. The man had been lunging towards him and slipped, his feet sliding forwards and his head and body leaning backwards as he fought to regain his balance. King stepped in close, exercising a Judo move, and caught hold of him by his throat and slammed him down to the ground, helped by the man's own inertia, and hitting him with the biggest weapon of all. The earth. The back of the Russian's head cracked on the concrete floor and King didn't need to hang around to know he would not be getting up for a while, if at all. He looked up at the guard who had been looking the other way. King walked on and found his quiet spot on the rock, where he fished the screw out of his shoe and started to work it flat. He could hear the ruckus and see the prisoners gathering around the body of the Russian. He knew that no prisoner would willingly tell a guard what had happened, so would have to hope there was no CCTV that had picked it up. He hadn't noticed any such setup, but then again, he knew there was a hidden camera in his cell that he couldn't see, so it wasn't out of the question.

King estimated the screw was almost to the right specification. He continued to work it with slow, smooth strokes until the alarm sounded and the door to population buzzed open. He looked at the screw, then slipped it back into his shoe. He would be able to lie on his front and fine tune it on the wall beside him as he pretended to sleep under the coarse, hairy blanket. He would be ready to use it tomorrow, and the thought chilled him to his core. He had never taken such a risk.

Chapter Thirty-Two

When the timer got to three seconds Caroline dropped her hand and held the phone next to the fire extinguisher, the phone almost touching as she pressed the app icon a second time. She watched Adams do the same, Marnie hanging on his arm and posing for a selfie that caught the bay and Navy Pier behind them. She heard a single bleep come from the fire extinguisher beside her. She watched the crowds leaning into the windows, the perpetual poses and posturing in the two viewing boxes. The checking of images taken, the frowning, deleting and reposing. A young woman was pinching her own cheeks firmly to enhance the colour and glow. Caroline pitied her as she pocketed her phone and pulled the safety tag out of the fire extinguisher. She watched Adams subtly do the same, and as she made her way counter-clockwise around the Skydeck, she saw Big Dave and Tattooed Mick milling around at the back of the elevator queue. She stopped as Rashid joined her, wrapping his arm casually around her, wrapping his arm casually around her shoulder. She glanced behind her and saw Ramsay studying some fridge magnets at the gift concession. Ahead of her, Powell was getting into one of the elevators.

They did not ride the elevators down all at once, and after they had exited the gift shop on the ground floor Caroline and Rashid crossed over Franklyn and stood on the bridge, watching for Adams and Marnie to exit. They crossed over and took steps down to the river. They only had to wait a few minutes and as Ramsay exited and headed away to the car park, Marnie and Adams boarded a river boat that would take them down river to Navy Pier.

Powell came out next and after he disappeared for a moment behind some raised brick flower beds, Rashid saw him on the back of a pedal rickshaw, the cyclist pumping his legs to make the green light.

"Dave and Mick were ahead of us in the queue," Caroline said. "Time to make the call."

"I still don't see why it should be me," Rashid protested.

"We're not being racist, but you should be able to do the accent better than anybody else. The FBI would see through Ramsay in a second as he stammered and hesitated his way through and probably ended up finishing with *Cheerio*! at the end of the conversation." She handed him the pre-paid, cash-bought cell phone with the pre-set number already entered. What crime shows called a 'burner'.

Rashid shrugged and pressed the number. It rang for just two rings.

"Federal Bureau of Investigation, how may I direct your call?" a woman's voice, curt and business-like.

"We are going to remotely detonate explosive devices planted in the Willis Tower, Chicago..."

"One moment, please..."

Rashid dropped the phone down beside his leg and looked at Caroline. "I don't believe this, she cut me off and is directing my call!" He put it back to his ear. "Must be taking it seriously."

"Chicago office, Counter Terrorism..."

"We shall avenge our fallen brothers. The Great Satan shall feel the wrath of the Islamic State!"

"I understand you are calling in a bomb threat to the Willis Tower?"

Rashid ignored him. "We will strike at

America's heart, we will take down the Willis Tower, Sears' monument to greed and decadence, as our Al Qaeda brothers took down The Twin Towers on that glorious day of Nine-Eleven."

"Sir..."

"Do not interrupt me!" Rashid snapped, his accent thick and he rounded the R's and put emphasis on the M. He had been practising and was pleased he was sounding more Arab than *Goodness gracious me.* He was from Pakistani extraction, brought up in Birmingham. He had been annoyed that Ramsay had asked him to do it, and surprised that Caroline had agreed. But still, he was nailing this call. "Our fallen brothers will look down from Paradise and our bravery on this day will assure us worthiness to join them. We strike today, the first of three attacks that will thwart your efforts. Our last target will martyr us and open the gates to paradise. Glory will be Allah's! *Allahu Akbar!*" Rashid hung up and dropped the phone over the edge of the bridge and into the river. He watched it tumble and splash. He could see the boat carrying Marnie and Adams turn the corner near Trump Towers on its way to Navy Pier. "Now what?" he asked.

"We wait," Caroline said. "We're okay here. Let's see how seriously the FBI took you. We might have to up the ante."

In the distance sirens were already audible. The exits to the Willis Tower seemed to swell, more and more people spilled out onto the street. A couple of homeless men started milling around the crowd, experts on the day to day running of the landmark. No doubt they were saying they'd seen it all before, but they hadn't. A security guard started to wave the crowd out onto the street and urged them to get clear of the building, rather than simply congregate and become spectators.

The police department arrived first, and officers abandoned their Chevy SUVs and Dodge sedans and waved the people away from the building. A black SWAT van pulled to the kerb, and heavily armed and well-equipped officers took up positions, rifles aimed at nothing and everything. They had no idea what the threat would amount to, but better to be ready to shoot something.

Three black Escalades pulled in and the Feds had made it to the show. It was a good response time and no doubt more would be on the way. The FBI's own SWAT team followed, and the operators took up similar positions to their police counterparts. The circus was in town. The fire department sent everything it had, too. And then ambulance crews filled the streets and had to back up as a police officer attempted to affix a cordon. The windy city was living to its namesake and the tape wafted and bowed in the wind, the officer struggling to get it run out.

"This looks fun," Rashid said. He checked his phone. The clock was as accurate as it was possible to be, and all the phones were iPhones and synced perfectly. "I've got one minute."

Caroline looked at her phone. "Same."

"Shall we move?"

"No," Caroline replied. "I'll scream, you hug me, and we'll run like everybody else. Then we just keep running back to the car."

Rashid watched the FBI talk with the police and fire crews. They were getting a briefing from the tower's security chief when the first explosion blew out a window over fourteen-hundred feet above their heads. Six further explosions detonated in unison a second later, pouring vast quantities of acrid smoke out of the broken windows. The glass shattered and fell, smashing into dust on the ground below. The crowds that had failed to disperse had changed their minds and it was a mass scramble amid screams and shouts. Caroline had forgotten to scream, but plenty more people had, and Rashid put an arm around her shoulders, and they crossed the road and ran down the street towards the multi-storey car park, leaving a world of chaos behind them.

Chapter Thirty-Three

Ramsay had had the foresight to drive the SUV out of the multi-storey car park, ahead of a mad exodus. He parked it across the street, facing West, where they would pick up the freeway. He studied his rear-view mirror and had signalled Rashid and Caroline as they had drawn near. They each opened a door and slid in, Ramsay pulling away before their doors closed.

"Christ, I hope nobody was on that floor..." he trailed off, threading the vehicle through the traffic.

"Slow down, Neil," Caroline said beside him. "Nice and casual, stay under the limit."

"The first cannister to detonate was a sonic pulse. A lot of noise and directed towards the glass on the East-facing side. Enough to blow it out completely. The other six canisters were white phosphorus." Rashid settled back in his seat as a convoy of emergency vehicles came towards them, sirens blaring and lights flashing. "A hell of a lot of smoke and some big bangs as they initiated."

"But no smoke without fire," Ramsay said quietly. "God, I hope nobody was near."

"We all do, Neil," Rashid agreed. "But we called it in. We allowed enough time for security to be on the street, so I would assume that the public were nowhere near. We gave it every chance."

Caroline was scrolling through her phone. "CNN," she said. "Willis Tower hit by Islamic extremists claiming to be ISIS. Early reports are no casualties and a safe evacuation thanks to the rapid response and vigilant work of the Chicago FBI…"

"Love that!" Rashid jeered.

"Securing their future funding right there," Ramsay commented, a little cheerier than just moments before.

"… Extensive fire and smoke damage," she continued. "The building is yet to be searched by FBI and Chicago Police Department bomb disposal teams, as they are still planning the best course of action. It's thought that the IEDs failed to detonate properly, or that the terrorists planned to start a catastrophic fire, which has been contained by the building's state of the art sprinkler system."

"Well, that's something," said Ramsay.

"Let's get back to the hotel and regroup," Caroline said. "All that adrenalin has made me hungry."

Rashid pulled a card out of his pocket and reached it forward to her. "This is Chicago's best pizza place. Giordano's. They deliver to the hotel," he said. "The manager gave me their card when I checked in."

"What's so good about them?" Ramsay asked incredulously.

"It's more of a pie and they make it in reverse, so cheese then filling then tomato. It's unique to Chicago and meant to be amazing."

"I can't believe you two are hungry," Ramsay said flatly. "All that back there has made me feel sick to my stomach."

"It's the adrenalin rush," said Rashid. "It affects people in different ways."

Caroline looked at Rashid in her vanity mirror. "Call Marnie," she said. "She can get set up in her hotel room. That is, if she hasn't yet seen anything on her mobile phone."

Rashid nodded and took out his phone. Timing was everything, and the most difficult part of the operation was yet to come.

Chapter Thirty-Four

The door buzzed open and three guards bustled into the room and fanned out. Two aimed shotguns at him, the other held a pair of handcuffs and a baton. They had intended to shock him, and it had worked. King recognised the middle guard as the one who had inducted him and beaten him with the baton. He looked at the other two, concerned just how tight their fingers wrapped around the triggers of the Remington pump-action shotguns. Their entrance had been dramatic. Normal procedure was gone, but once King realised that they weren't going to shoot him there and then, he relaxed and went with it. As he suspected, the guard waited for him to be cuffed from behind, then dug the baton into his right kidney. King fell onto his knees and let out a gasp. The guard hit him again, but he was no real expert in administering pain. He struck the same spot, which was already numb, the pain receptors flooding the area with endorphins that were as good as anaesthetics. The repeated blow could cause damage for sure, but it only hurt about a third as much.

King wondered how this would play out, but he made a point of remembering the guard's face. He would teach him about pain if he got the chance.

The guard jabbed him again as they entered the interrogation room and Johnson looked up. King had dispelled with the Tommy-Lee moniker. He knew all he wanted to about Johnson, and what the man had been prepared to allow to happen. And not just to break King, but to teach him a lesson. Humiliate and degrade him. Johnson would not go unpunished for that.

"There's been a terrorist attack."

"So?"

The guard smashed his baton down on King's shoulder, forcing him to yell and sag in the chair. His cuffs stopped him from sliding onto the floor.

Johnson looked up at the guard. "Thank you, Brett. I'll take it from here."

King pushed himself back upright, still wincing from the blow. "See you, Brett." he said.

"What?" Brett lunged back into the room and came around on King, grabbing him by his collar.

"You heard, Brett." King grinned, his eyes unwavering and cold. Glacier cold, like an alpha wolf. "Take care now, Brett."

"You think I'm bothered you know my name?"

"Enough!" Johnson stood up, his fists splayed on the table. "Stand down!"

Brett looked at Johnson, then back at King. He released his grip, pushing King backwards. He shook his head as he left the cell.

"See ya, Brett!" King shouted, just before the cell door slammed closed.

"Finished?" Johnson asked.

"Not even getting started."

"The Russian is in a coma."

King shrugged. "I don't know any Russian."

"Word is you pile drove him into the concrete."

"You mean the one who slipped and fell on a spillage? Yeah, he took quite a tumble," King paused. "I doubt he'll be able to sue, though. What with no access to a lawyer and all."

"The other man's sight will probably be okay, though. In one eye, at least. The one you whipped with the towel isn't coming back anytime soon. It looks like the eye of a steamed sockeye trout."

King shrugged again like he wasn't bothered. And he wasn't. If you wanted to dance, you had to pay the band. He could have done far worse to him, considering.

"The other two guys lost some teeth. One has a fractured skull and the other has cracked cheek bones, but they're otherwise okay."

"With what they had planned for me, I could be sitting here having severed their cocks and choked them on them and I couldn't care any less." He smiled. "But tell me about the terrorist attack. Chicago, right. The Willis Tower? I must be clairvoyant, right? Jesus, I should do the lottery."

"What else do you know?"

"I know they are a bunch of fanatics. Your man missed them in New Jersey. Maybe they were lucky, but I know they'll get more proficient as they go along. Ultimately, they have their eyes on the President, and they'll get their man. I'm sure of that. They will sacrifice themselves, and that changes everything you know about security."

"Where or what is next?"

"Just like that?"

"I could torture you."

"No, you won't. You'll have someone else do it for you. Tell me, Johnson, do you even manage to do your own fucking? Or does someone do that for, too?" King laughed. "No, I bet you sit in the corner getting off on someone ploughing Mrs Johnson while you watch…"

"I'm going to break you," said Johnson. "I'll do it myself, and you'll regret that smart mouth of yours."

"And I'll tell you nothing," replied King. "I'll shut down and take the long, dark ride and I'll accept whatever awaits me at the end. The only way you're getting information about the other two attacks is to keep me alive and get me the hell out of here."

"Really?"

"Really. I want a comfortable cell, something to read and some decent food. A cup of tea, as well. What you insist on calling English breakfast tea. Like we just drink it at breakfast, for fuck's sake… And some biscuits, which you call cookies for some reason, and not those dry old scones at breakfast."

"And if I refuse?"

"Then no dice."

"We'll see."

"Just think about this, Johnson. Your pal Brett wants to teach me a lesson. What if he goes too far? That's anything I know which you can use to further, or perhaps even protect your career gone. I've made a few enemies in here as well. What if they get to me? The Russians, the white supremacists. Wave goodbye to your chances of keeping your employment if you could have halted major terrorist attacks from what information you could have easily obtained. Now, imagine if you obtained information that *saved* the President from an assassination plot? Imagine your career trajectory if that became a reality. No more low-rent version of *Men in Black*. No more being a part of a shit-pit, illegal operation like this. And what if this place ever became common knowledge? Hell, you'd be caught up in a shitstorm and all the brainless Bretts and Billy-Bobs in here will be pointing a finger at you like the foot soldiers did in Nazi Germany. So, take me back to my cell yourself, call off your dogs and get me a comfortable room before the day is out. Then we'll talk. Then I'll tell you what I know."

Chapter Thirty-Five

"That can't have been it!" Yates snapped. "We didn't train for that, so what the fuck was going on back there?"

Macintosh shook his head, kept his eyes on the receiver. Essentially a monitor with a pre-programmed map and an amber dot indicating the car in which Rashid, Ramsay and Caroline were travelling in. The other two vehicles they had planted tracking devices on were not in range. "I don't know," he said through gritted teeth. "Speed up or we're going to lose them as well."

"They'll be heading back to Indian Lakes, I'm not worried about losing them. I want to know what the hell they were doing at The Willis Tower, and why the place was attacked with IEDs."

"It'll be a diversion. Something for the heist. God knows what." He tossed the receiver into the footwell, amid family-sized packets of potato and corn chips and savoury snacks. The vehicle was a mass of kit and charging wires and sleeping gear. They were living in it. It smelled of damp, cigarettes and of body odour. "But I don't get why they would do it and not strike at something nearby." Macintosh picked up the receiver again and checked the screen. "I saw Big Dave going inside and I saw Adams leaving with that MI5 bird with the big tits. Looked like they were together, sticking it to the Paki with any luck."

"It'll be a play," Yates corrected him. "They're not shagging each other, you can bet they all played parts. My bet is they came in on different modes of transport, so that they could disperse and disappear. The beer festival and rock concert would be a good place to disappear and take another vehicle or taxi elsewhere. You can bet your arse they'll all meet up again at the hotel in Indian Lakes."

"Yeah, looks like they're heading that way."

"So, we head back there, park up and wait?"

"I don't see what else we can do," Macintosh paused, studying the screen. "But when they move again, we'll be ready."

Chapter Thirty-Six

The room was still only an eight by eight, but it contained a single bed with a mattress and sheets instead of the heavy woollen blanket. It had a toilet and a sink, a polished metal sheet above the sink instead of a mirror, in which he stared in shock at the gaunt, hollow face staring back at him. On the sink was a bar of soap, a toothbrush and toothpaste and a safety razor. There was even a hand towel hanging from a loop and toilet paper on a holder. It was probably more in line with a regular prison cell and by no means was it to be thought of as luxury. There was a hell of a long way to go before it came up to a particularly tired *Motel 6*. A stack of paperbacks rested at the foot of the bed. They weren't King's first choice, but he couldn't afford to be choosy. He couldn't remember the last time he had read, let alone painted. He had had less and less time for his usual creative outlets lately. But he vowed if he ever got out of here, he would take a well-earned break.

Johnson had escorted him straight here. King was glad he had secreted the screws into his shoes. Having stripped and taken a full-body stand-up flannel wash at the sink, he had shaved and brushed his teeth twice. Unlike in his former cell, he had running water and had practically drank the tap dry over the next hour, but this was as much to mask the finetuning he did to the screw on the rough concrete wall, as to slake his thirst under the tap. After another hour a guard King hadn't seen before showed up and placed a tray on the floor. He said nothing as he closed the door and left King alone. The tray had contained a burger wrapped in greaseproof paper and a cardboard cup of fries. A home-cooked imitation of a drive-thru meal. There was a cup with a lid and some cookies, too. King ripped off the lid and took a sip of his first cup of tea in over two-weeks. It was strong and tepid, and he savoured every mouthful. Afterwards, he devoured the burger and fries, the grease feeling good on his tongue and the tangy sauce giving him a mild sugar rush. He washed his hands in the sink and took another swig from the tap. He reckoned he was about there with the screw. He hoped it would work and that he hadn't worn too much away, but he had the spare screw in his other shoe. After that, he would be out of options. But by then, he would be out of time as well. He took a deep breath and closed his eyes. He pictured Caroline, but curiously, his mind flicked to images of his first wife, Jane. He could see her on their wedding day. Long brunette hair, the warmest brown eyes he had ever known, and her smile. Pearl white and ever-so-slightly crooked. Just enough imperfection to make her perfect in his mind. They had a summer wedding and a tan had shown up her freckles. He felt a pang of delight, as he no longer found himself able to picture her when he tried. And then his mind, cruel and relentless, pictured her on the bed. Frail and thin, but peaceful after such a savage illness. The note in his hand, he fell to his knees beside her, sobbing and knowing that life would never have joy in it for him again. But he had been wrong, and he pictured Caroline again. Dirty-blonde hair simply pulled back in a ponytail and sporty-looking. Her eyes were clear and full of energy and he pictured her on a Cornish beach in winter, wrapped in a coat and scarf and pulling him towards the surging shore break as she laughed. She had brought him peace after five-years of hurt. He opened his eyes and stared at the floor. He wasn't sure he could do this. He had never had self-doubt before. He needed to know there would be a chance of seeing her again. And if he stuck to the plan, there was always the chance he wouldn't.

King took another breath, closed his eyes and tried to make sense of the situation. His mind taunted him again. He pictured his mentor, Peter Stewart. A tough Scotsman who started the day with a dram of Scotch and ended it the same way. A man who once killed a man and then ended up using his body as a pillow until morning. He looked younger in his mind, because they were in Africa and around two-hundred men were hunting them through the bush armed with machetes and AK47 rifles. They had butchered the rest of the team, and in a show of force they had eaten parts of them as King and Stewart had awaited their fate. When it was their turn to be led from the cages, the two had overpowered the men and fled through the bush. They had been hunted for days, surrounded. King had wanted to get to the river and swim, chancing the giant crocodiles, where if they survived long enough, they could build a makeshift raft and flow with the Congo river until they found civilisation. Stewart had told King their only way out was to fight. To take the battle to them because they would not expect it and that way, they had a chance of seeing their objective through. Their training and tactics would eventually win out. King knew what his memory would bring back to him. Knew it before he heard the words in his mind.

"We're pretty much dead already," Stewart had pressed. *"So, let's fight like hell and see if we can beat the odds and get out of this mess…"*

King opened his eyes. He looked into the polished steel mirror, his eyes hard and cruel and cold. Sometimes, he scared himself with the intensity his reflection could return. He was going to finish what he had started. He palmed the screw, then picked up one of the paperbacks and laid down on the bed, resting on his stomach, his back to any potential camera in the ceiling. He opened the book and pretended to read. He took a deep breath and dug the flat, shaped tip of the screw into his right upper molar and started to work the tip into the slot of the metal filling. His hands shook a little, because of the enormity of what he was about to do next. He checked himself, breathed steadily and found a good fit. He eased counter-clockwise, surprised at how stiff and secure the fixing was. Slowly it began to turn. He twisted and twisted, and the cap dropped out. He could feel cold on his tooth. He dug into the cavity with the screw and a capsule dropped out and into his mouth. He carefully retrieved the capsule and set about replacing the cap back in the hole and getting it to secure into the threads. After a few attempts he worked the cap clockwise with the screw and felt it tighten. He was nearly there.

King had visited the dentist on five occasions in preparation for the operation. Twice, a good tooth had been drilled and hollowed out and a threaded filling put into the cavity. A cavity within a cavity. The cavities had been packed with rice paper and sealed. Two weeks later, the cavities had been opened and the rice paper removed. Both pieces were bone dry. Both cavities were filled and re-sealed. In this instance, the cavity had been filled with a gelatine capsule containing a powerful cocktail of adenosine, verapamil and cocaine. It was all in the timing now. Because timing would be the difference between life and death.

Twenty-minutes later and the cell door opened.

"Get up, Johnson wants to see you," said the guard.

"No cuffs?"

"There's more of us outside, you won't get very far."

King got off the bed and followed the guard. Brett was outside, but he barely glanced at King. King followed the guard, expected a jab to his kidney at any moment, but it never came. The guard opened the door and Johnson was seated behind the table with two cups on the table. King conceded it wouldn't get any better than this and coughed, put his hand to his mouth and took the capsule to the back of his throat. He sat down, and the guard remained, but Brett and the other two left and closed the door.

"I got you some tea," Johnson said.

"Great," he said as he sat down and reached for the cup. He drank the capsule down and placed the cup back on the table.

It was done.

There was no going back.

Chapter Thirty-Seven

"You said that Chicago would be first," Johnson said. He sipped his coffee, a more relaxed manner to his questioning. He had clearly thought over King's words, maybe he had plans of being the hero. In fact, King was certain of it. "It's clearly not a coincidence, so tell me what you know."

"You haven't had a report yet?"

"It's fluid. The investigation is in full flow, but we naturally have access to it."

"Naturally," King commented flatly, then asked, "What is today's date?"

Johnson looked at him sceptically. "Why?"

"I'm not sure how long I've been here," he replied.

"But you must have a clue. There would have been a date for the attack on Chicago."

King rubbed the perspiration off his brow. He was getting hot. He took a sip of tea. "Do you have any water?" he asked.

"You okay?"

"No," he said. "I'm really hot…"

Johnson looked up at the guard. "Get him a glass of water."

"But…" the guard went to protest.

"Oh, Mister King is not going to do anything stupid." He looked at King. "Is he?" King wiped his brow again, then placed his right hand over the left side of his chest. He felt as if he were having an outrageous bout of indigestion, but he knew it was so much more than that. He coughed, felt the pain ease, but it came back as quickly and more acutely. "Are you okay?"

"The date…" King said. "What is the date?" His arms ached, and he started to pant for breath.

"The eighteenth," Johnson said, watching King, who had turned ashen and swayed in his chair. He looked up at the guard. "Get the doctor!"

The guard bolted out of the door and slammed it shut behind him. Johnson was wary of King, didn't rush to his aid, but he could see that he couldn't put on the colour or the perspiration. He sidled around the table and touched King's brow. It was cold and clammy despite the perspiration. He snatched up King's wrist and checked his pulse. King was having difficulty sitting up unaided. He lolled to one side and slipped off the chair, Johnson just breaking his fall enough by still holding onto his wrist.

The doctor burst into the room, followed by the guard. He was carrying a compact defibrillator and his old leather medical bag. He dropped both down beside King and took a pen torch out from his top pocket. He checked King's pupils, holding his lolling eyelids open. Then he pressed his fingers deep into King's neck, found the carotid artery and checked his watch. He didn't count for long. King started to shudder and almost as suddenly, he went still.

"Don't fucking lose him!" Johnson shouted.

The doctor started to unpack the defibrillator and snapped at Johnson, "Get him unzipped, I need to get to his chest!" Johnson unzipped the orange jumpsuit and pulled it open. "Check his airway!" Johnson did so and looked back at the doctor. "Tilt his chin back, he may have swallowed his tongue!"

Johnson tilted King's chin backwards. He looked back at the doctor and said, "I think he's okay…"

"Clearly…" the doctor snapped. "Start chest compressions!"

Johnson recalled doing this in his early training, he found the spot and started to rock on his heels. He continued as the doctor pinched King's nose and breathed steadily. He checked King's pulse again, then frowned and picked up the defibrillator. He opened the lid and peeled off an adhesive pad. He secured it against King's chest, then peeled off another pad, struggling with the wires which had twisted. He untangled it and fixed it on King's left side, just under his ribcage. The machine ran a quick assessment and the red light illuminated on the box.

"Stand back," he told Johnson and pressed the button. The amber bulb on the machine flashed and the doctor started performing chest compressions. He pumped thirty times, then breathed twice for King, before repeating. He checked King's pulse, then looked at Johnson and shook his head. "I think we've lost him…"

"Don't fucking tell me that!" Johnson raged. "Do it again!"

"But…"

"Do it!"

The doctor pressed a button on the box and the unit processed the information of the

ECG. The red button illuminated again, and he said, "Stand back..." the machine shocked. There was no dramatic arc, judging by King's reaction it wasn't even clear the machine had shocked him. The doctor watched Johnson perform another thirty compressions, then when he stopped the doctor breathed for King twice more. He checked the pulse.

"Again!" Johnson shouted.

The doctor allowed the defibrillator to perform another shock. He checked King's pulse, frowned. He dug into his medical back and brought out a syringe. "He has a pulse..." he said. "It's faint, but there's sign of life." He found a vein in King's well-muscled arm and administered the drug. "Bretylium," the doctor said to Johnson. "Outlawed now, but my budget is fuck-all and there's no traceability of this stuff." He looked up at the guard and said, "Get a trolley and a couple of medics!" He turned back to Johnson. "He'll need to go to the infirmary. And he'll be there for a day or two at least."

Chapter Thirty-Eight

The beacon that had been installed in the second molar on the other side of King's jaw used the metal lining of the cavity as both an electrical conductor and an aerial. Installed in an inert state, making it undetectable to scanners and x-rays, it had enough power in its lithium battery to emit a high-frequency pulse signal for one week. All it needed was over seven-hundred volts of electricity to kick-start it. King's height, weight and physical condition, combined with the severity of the cardiac arrest induced by the cocktail of drugs in the capsule he had taken, meant that anybody using a defibrillator would be unlikely to dial in any less than eight-hundred volts. It had taken a great deal of analysing, especially as the average defibrillator could be dialled in between two-hundred and fifteen-hundred volts. The drug had been concocted by a team of chemists and a cardiothoracic specialist tasked with stopping King's heart without causing permanent damage and leaving his heart in a receptive state after unconsciousness and organ failure. A derivative of drugs used to stop a patient's heart for rhythmic irregularities, it was a procedure that in theory would work so long as facilities for resuscitation were readily available. The rest had been down to King. It was imperative he kept his weight within the parameters, and that before he took the capsule, he would be over-hydrated. In short, he was to drink water until it became physically impossible to drink any more. Even so, he had still drunk down the tea that Johnson had offered him. The hydration would keep his organs in a healthier state once his heart had stopped, and the excess fluids ensured the electric charge from the defibrillator would maintain a good contact.

Somewhere between three-thousand and fifteen-thousand miles above the earth, three orbiting communication satellites piggy-backed by GCHQ triangulated the signal emitted once every thirty seconds from the beacon inside the molar in the back of King's mouth. The signal co-ordinates were sent directly to GCHQ in Cheltenham via the Echelon system, where an algorithm detected the coded signal and forwarded it directly to Simon Mereweather's computer inside MI5 headquarters at Thames House and straight to Marnie's smartphone. Upon receiving notification that the beacon was live, Marnie fired up her laptop and connected to the internet. She found the dedicated webpage that had been created without metatags and keywords. A webpage that nobody would stumble across unless they had the direct coded web address. She signed in, clicked on the icon and found the coordinates.

The three vehicles were on the move within fifteen-minutes. Ramsay, Caroline, Rashid and Marnie formed the head of the convoy, with Marnie's laptop plugged in and monitoring the signal through a wireless dongle working on 3G and 4G. Powell and Adams followed, with Big Dave and Tattooed Mick bringing up the rear. Everybody's phone had the coordinates punched into Google Maps. This was their secondary location. Their primary objective now was to get to a staging post. Ramsay studied the map and for logistical reasons and anonymity, chose a town in the Black Hills called Custer, over one-thousand miles away.

Chapter Thirty-Nine

King woke, his head thumping, his mouth dry. He had tubes in his nose which ran down the back of his throat and a canular fitted to his wrist. He followed the tube and saw the drip beside him hanging from a trolley stand. He was hooked up to a monitor with various sticky sensor pads stuck to his chest. He could see his blood pressure reading. It was a little high. His pulse was seventy-seven. He rested at around sixty, so it was high and in line with his blood pressure. Not altogether surprising considering what he had been through.

The room was completely clad in plastic and the floor linoleum ended a foot up the wall. King supposed it was for heavy sluicing and cleaning. There were three other beds, all of them empty. Either the Russian and the two supremacists had returned to their cells, or this was one of multiple rooms. King could see medical equipment on the counter tops, alcohol wash and paper towels beside the sink. He went to move, but heard the clang, felt the restriction and realised he was cuffed by his right hand to the bed. He was thirsty. There was a jug of water on the table beside him, but he couldn't reach it.

The door opened, and the doctor walked through breezily. "You're awake, then," he stated.

"Could I have a drink?" King asked.

The doctor nodded. He was around thirty, dark skinned, slim and preppy-looking. He poured the water into a plastic cup and passed it to King. "Who are you?" King drank the water down, held the cup out for a refill, but the doctor shook his head. "No, you'll be sick. Give it thirty-minutes. I asked, who are you?"

"I've already done the interrogation with Tommy-Lee Jones."

"Funny," the doctor said. He looked at the monitor, picked up the records at the foot of the bed and frowned. "I've taken bloods," he said. "Johnson, or *Tommy-Lee*, can be told they're clear, or he can be told you took a cocktail of drugs that induced a heart infarction, leading to cardiac arrest."

"I'd prefer if he was told they're clear."

"That's what I thought."

"So, who *are* you?"

"That was my question."

King shifted in the bed. He felt as if he'd been thrown off a tall building. He tried and failed to get comfortable. "That you offer two options to the blood tests infers that you are not what you seem, either."

"It's not right," the doctor said. "What goes on here." King was cautious. He knew that the doctor could be working as a stooge. The discovery of the drugs in his blood could have led to the opportunity for a different approach to questioning. He waited for the doctor to speak again. Sometimes the best way to get someone to speak was simply to remain silent and allow them to fill the void. "People are killed when they are no longer of use. I'm not saying these people aren't bad, Lord no. But like in Guantanamo, there are a few scooped up. Wrong time, wrong place. They might have thought it a good idea to fight with ISIS, but a few weeks and they'd be high-tailing it back to Uncle Sam, swearing allegiance and never talking about their mistake again. Bravado and ideals are easily worn out on the battlefield. I know we need to be tough, but..."

"It's a tough world," said King. "The fight against terrorism is hampered by legal constraints." He knew this all too well. Had it not been for Simon Mereweather's predecessor, Charles Forrester, then King would not have been drawn into working for MI5. The then deputy director of the Security Service had tired of fighting a constant battle through the courts against an Islamic extremist and prominent Imam who recruited for ISIS. Forrester needed to sever the link with extremism and was willing to fight dirty. The same Imam had secured a nuclear device through the very man King was here to break out. Vladimir Zukovsky. Full circle. Only now, what information Zukovsky had would counter a threat every bit as lethal as his stolen nuclear device. In the long term, even more so.

"I'm a doctor," he said. "I built up a great deal of debt during my medical training. And then I made a stupid mistake, tried to take a shortcut. That bit me in the ass, because it allowed me to be pressured. Before I knew it, I was working here. I get leave and great pay, but my life is not my own. I know they keep tabs on me when I'm at home. My parents think I work in a research facility in the Arctic. That's what they told me to say. God only knows how I wish that was really the case." He hung the notes back up at the foot of the bed. King could see he was stressed, his mannerisms. A twitchiness to him, erratic. He had seen junior doctors look the same way, but this guy would be a few years past that stage. "Are you a reporter?" he asked.

"Quid pro quo," King said.

"You want something first? I get that," the doctor said. "Name it."

King smiled. "I will," he said. "But not yet."

"You don't trust me?"

"No."

"I saved your life!"

"Thanks."

"I'll go to Johnson."

"And say what?"

"I'll tell him your bloods were full of…"

"Oh, cut the crap!" King snapped. "I already know you got into debt, you did something dumb and they used that against you. I know both your parents are alive and well and think you work in the Arctic. You take leave and they keep tabs on you." King shifted, winced. His rib cage had most likely been cracked in a few places with the CPR. "If any of that is true, then I can tell Johnson. I can elaborate the shit out of that as well. Hell, you could be my inside man by the time I'm finished."

"So, what? We have a standoff until we know we're both on the level?"

King shrugged, regretted it almost at once. "I worked for my government," he said. "I killed people. I then went freelance. That's how I ended up in here."

"So, what about the drugs you took? I performed a thorough search on you when you were admitted. Scan and x-ray in the doorway, and a body cavity search."

"I remember the last one well. I've been waiting for flowers."

The doctor failed to find his sense of humour. "How did you bring it in?"

"You've got short fingers." King said. "Which was a blessed relief."

"I can see I'm going to have to go all in."

"Like hell you will."

"I mean with this... standoff we have. Like a game of cards, I have to go all in with my stake." The doctor checked his watch. King caught sight of it but had lost track of whether it was morning or night. He'd been unconscious and had no way of knowing how long for. "I don't want out," he said. "They'll kill me. Or my parents. But if somebody was to get out, blow the whistle…"

"You'd take the rap."

"I am confident I can plead entrapment."

"That thing you did will come to light."

"Maybe that's for the best?" the doctor paused. "You can't escape the past. Perhaps it's time for me to accept the consequences of my actions."

"You can get me out?" King asked, bemused. "There's a lot of security here, isn't there?"

The doctor shrugged. "Sure. But I can get you out. I can't arrange any help on the outside, though. You'll need help to get away. A car, money, the ability to stay ahead of a search. Can you get help? Do you have help nearby?"

King watched the man's eyes. He'd seen enough. Maybe it was because of the magnitude of the treachery, or maybe he was under pressure from Johnson to trap King, but the signs were there. The man was perspiring, his eyes darted downwards, and he couldn't leave his face alone, especially his lips. King knew the tells to spot a liar. He'd been taught the best tactics to avoid detection himself. But King had been played before. He didn't play cards or gamble for fun. He gambled with his own life and occasionally with others. "I have nobody," he said decisively. "Nobody knows where I am, and there's nobody I can call on for help." He may well have scuppered his chances of having an ally in his escape, but he'd take that chance. Time would soon tell if this pathetic man standing in front of him was on the level.

Chapter Forty

They had driven through the night but were spent. Even taking shifts the drive through Illinois, Wisconsin, Minnesota and into South Dakota was a long haul. The I-90 switched from two lane to single and back again, depending how far you were from a town. They had crossed the Mississippi and caught sight of the wide body of water over two-thousand miles from where it emptied into the Gulf of Mexico. Caroline was surprised just how wide and full it looked, so far from its ultimate destination, but she didn't voice it. That was something she would have talked about with King and the thought depressed her further.

A long pull through mountains and they were high above sea level and drove the continuous plateau to the Great Plains. The sun broke above the distant horizon behind them, a golden hue giving way to pitch darkness ahead of them. When the dawn overtook the darkness and daylight slowly enveloped them, they found themselves in an ocean of grassland. Green as far as they could see in every direction.

"I need breakfast," Rashid said.

"I'm surprised you're not still full from that bloody pizza," Ramsay commented flatly.

"I could go something to eat, too," Marnie said sleepily. "And a bathroom break."

"Very American of you," Ramsay commented.

"Okay, then," Marnie said tiresomely. "A bloody great pee..."

"Me too," said Caroline. "I'm sure the others are hungry as well. Let's pull off at the next exit."

The road was much the same as the rest of America. And being a well-travelled and long route, the exits did not simply lead to fuel stations and fast-food outlets, but to clusters of independent and chain motels. Although at no time did the road feel busy. They had driven miles without seeing another vehicle and had spent hours with a car behind their convoy and another up ahead without change. The seventy-five mile-per-hour speed limit allowed for swift progress, and being almost completely traffic free, their progress had certainly been swift. The miles were simply sailing by in a way one would never achieve in Britain, despite the faster, more erratic drivers. The sedate pace of the I-90, utterly free from congestion and bottlenecks, made the overall journey faster than a German autobahn.

Ahead of them a sign indicated a mile to the next layoff. Ramsay slowed down and took it, he slowed down further, the slip road was little more than a track. There was a diner next to the fuel station. Ramsay parked up and the other two SUVs swung around in the parking area and parked nose outwards.

"Time for scran!" Big Dave shouted through their closed windows and didn't wait for them as he marched off into the diner.

The other men stretched, and Powell lit up a cigarette. "Ah, get us a coffee and a Danish and I'll be there in a minute." He stretched his neck and paced around the front of the diner smoking as if it were the last cigarette he'd ever have.

The booths and tables were in twos and fours and the men spread themselves out while Rashid and Marnie took a four and motioned for Caroline to join them. Ramsay checked his phone, then slid in beside Caroline. Marnie checked her phone, looked up at Caroline. "Still there," she said. "Just to let you know."

"Thanks," Caroline replied. She was tapping the edge of the table with her fingertips

Her apprehension had been building since they had left Chicago. She had been unable to nap in the car. She sighed loudly, shook her head. "I'm so nervous," she said. "It just doesn't seem real. I'm so close to getting him back, but it's such a risk, the odds seem ridiculous."

"We'll get him back," Rashid said emphatically.

"I know," Caroline replied, but she did not sound confident.

The waitress came over and they gave their orders. Another waitress was doing the rounds with coffee. They all loaded up on the caffeine, nipped off independently to the lavatories. The windows on the east side of the building had turned golden and the diner brightened as the sun rose high above the sea of green.

Outside a group of bikers pulled up and revved their engines. They were big, chrome and loud. Indian Chiefs and Harley Davidsons. Most of the men were overweight, but not merely fat, and tattoos featured heavily. Those who were not overweight were sinewy and muscled. They were all in their late middle age, to sixties and beyond and all of them wore cut-off denim vests and sported mahogany-coloured arms. Another band of bikes came in. There were a few Ducati Monsters and Triumphs, but mainly it was American-made muscle. There were a few women, too. Some of the bikes towed trailers and there was an array of add-ons like drink holders, GPS and sound systems. The noise of the bikes shook the windows of the diner.

"Could be trouble," said Ramsay, watching another group of bikes.

Big Dave got up and took a piece of French toast with him as he headed for the door. He walked up to a group of bikers and started chatting and pointing to various parts and nodded.

"We'll soon see," said Rashid.

Big Dave got on one of the bikes and took a selfie with his phone. One of the bikers got into the frame with him and they laughed. Adams had joined him and was like an eager child waiting for his turn on a one-pound mechanical ride outside a supermarket.

"I think it's safe to say we're in the clear," said Marnie.

The bikers made their way in and the diner was starting to buzz. Their food came, and Big Dave returned to his table just in time for his twenty-ounce T-Bone and hash browns. The steak was an inch thick and bloody and the hash browns were piled high.

"Christ, that man can eat," said Ramsay. "The expenses are taking a bloody hit."

The other three shared a look and Caroline tucked into her eggs Benedict and smiled. "Steak's cheap in these parts. We'll hit your mini-bar later."

"You bloody well won't!"

When they travelled, Ramsay often directed meetings in his own hotel room, where the rest of the team would generally use up his complimentary coffee, tea and biscuits, then empty his mini-bar. It had become standard operating procedure to enrage the man who held the purse strings.

The diner was full to capacity now. Big Dave got up and dropped his paper napkin onto his empty plate. A single gnawed bone was all that was left. He stepped near their table and said, "I'll be outside checking out the metal," he said. "If that's okay?"

Ramsay nodded and asked, "What's with all the bikers?"

"It's Sturgis," he said. "It's a motorcycle rally here in South Dakota. Half a million bikers will attend in the ten days it runs for. There's rock groups and circus acts, a stunt show and the US equivalent to the Red Arrows are putting on a show."

"Sounds cool," said Rashid. "And these guys are heading there?"

Adams joined them and smiled. "They are. Half these guys are dentists and bankers," he said. "This has been a dream of mine since I first got a bike. I'd love to do Route sixty-six, just me, my hog and the road. I ride a sports-bike at home, but out here a Harley really works. Some of these rides cost over fifty-grand. Most of them are between ten and twenty."

"Just old bikers looking to feel young again," said Marnie.

"If you could say that any louder?" Ramsay said. "There are certainly enough of them within earshot not to upset them."

Marnie shrugged and finished her pancakes and blueberries. "I bet there are lawyers here, too. The vibe is okay, Neil. I don't think this will be like one of those old Clint Eastwood films where he beats up all the Hell's Angels."

"The one with the monkey!" Caroline said, excitedly, clearly a moment of relief.

"Clyde," said Rashid. "And he was an orangutan. And the bikers were called The Black Widows…"

"I have no idea what you are all on about," Ramsay said, getting up and taking out his wallet. He thumbed through a stack of fifties and looked for the pay station. "Let's get going."

Rashid looked at the bikes out of his window, then turned to Caroline and said, "You know what? This has given me an idea…"

Chapter Forty-One

"I'm bloody starving!"

"Eat some crisps."

"I can't eat bloody crisps for breakfast," Yates complained. "I need a full English."

"Good luck. The bacon out here is shit and they fry their eggs dry. All crispy on the bottom and cold yolks."

"You can ask for them over-easy."

Macintosh shook his head. "You want to try their scrambled egg. Hard as nails."

"Stop talking about food!"

Macintosh pointed at the fuel station and diner. "That's them, parked up."

Yates switched on the receiver device and nodded. "All three vehicles. The bastards are eating breakfast."

"This road is straight and goes on for at least a couple of hundred miles before any major turn-offs. There are more restaurant stops up ahead. We'll shoot on, take a piss-stop and get some breakfast. We'll let them pass us, then follow them like we have since Chicago. This road is a dream and the trackers are holding up well. How much longer will they last?"

"About two days," Yates replied.

"That should be enough. I'm figuring we could be on the West coast by then, but I don't reckon they're heading that far."

"Look! There's an off-ramp and a bridge over the road. There's a burger joint and petrol station on the other side of the carriageway."

"That'll do," said Macintosh. "And they won't see us on the other side of the road."

"We're close now. I can feel it. Whatever is going down, it's near. We're near the Black Hills. There are new gold mining concerns starting up here again. They thought all the gold was gone, but some Canadian firms have bought up permits to mine and a company mining gold in Alaska has secured land after extensive drill tests."

"You an expert all of a sudden?"

"Wikipedia," Yates said. "But this has to be it. They are hitting the gold mine at clean-up time, and that bloke King is on the inside. That's why Rashid wants non-lethal rounds used."

"So, what's the angle?" Macintosh asked, scratching his head as he swung the SUV into the car park. "You were convinced the desk guy and the women were 'Box. So why are they hitting a mine? Funds?"

"Has to be. Getting money together for black-ops operations," Yates paused. "Or, they have simply come up with a scam and the taxpayer is footing the bill."

"Well, we'll soon find out," the Scotsman switched off the engine, took in the peace and quiet, the huge expanse of grassland in front of them. "But either way, we waste the fucking lot of them…"

Chapter Forty-Two

King opened his eyes, waking suddenly from the deepest sleep he'd had in over two-weeks. He looked up at the man standing over him. Strong features and black skin, which highlighted the whites of his eyes. He felt uncomfortable, knowing the man Johnson had referred to as Cole must have been watching him for some time, King oblivious as he slept.

"I could have killed you," he said.

King raised his right arm and the handcuff clinked against the metal bars of the bed. "That would have been big of you. All tied up and all."

"I could have pinned your arm and strangled you."

"Don't be so sure," said King. "It hasn't panned out that way for anyone yet."

"Me neither. Or anyone else on the planet, when you think about it. So, lying in your bed, all tough-guy and stuff means nothing."

King shrugged. "But not everybody has had our life, have they?"

"I guess not."

"Nice place you've got here."

"It's not mine."

"Johnson's then."

Cole smiled. "There are a lot of Johnsons," he said. "This isn't his place. Not exclusively, at least. Many agencies send a Johnson out here to interrogate, or occasionally disappear an inmate."

"Well, whoever runs it, it's a shithole."

"It serves a purpose," Cole said. "We put all the shit nobody wants in here."

"Thanks."

"You're welcome."

"If I were you, I'd be in a quandary," said King.

"You would?"

"Absolutely."

"Well, I guess I ain't you."

King shrugged. "What's Johnson got planned for me?"

Cole smiled. "Tell me about Chicago."

King shook his head. "Got any kids, a wife?"

"I don't see what business it is of yours."

"Just answer me," King said. "Humour me, at least."

Cole relented. "A wife and son."

"You're welcome."

Cole looked at him and shrugged. "Where are the rest of your team?"

"Don't have one."

"You're lying."

King shrugged. "Prove it."

"That psycho Scottish guy is out there, isn't he?"

"He's dead."

"I'm sorry," he said. "Okay, King. You saved my ass. I'll acknowledge that."

King shook his head. "You have a wife and child, you son of a bitch! You'll do more than fucking acknowledge it! You found love, had a child. However all of that worked out for you, it wouldn't have happened without me."

Cole shook his head. "It can't change a thing," he said.

"Bullshit! I saw you with Johnson and I thought it was a sign," said King. "If ever there were a higher being, it was then. That was it. A secret prison in a country of over a quarter of a billion people and in walks a guy I saved from being beheaded. At best. What are the chances of that?" King shifted up the bed, the handcuff hampering him. "You and another SEAL and the helicopter pilot. You remember?"

"Of course I remember!" Cole snapped.

"Good. For a moment I thought you'd forgotten that I saved your arse and could sit by and watch me incarcerated, perhaps worse. Not when you saw what happened to the two French soldiers I didn't get there soon enough to help. One burned to death in a cage, the other spilt down the middle with a fucking shovel! From groin to head, Cole. You remember that, don't you? Watching, pissing your pants and crying your fucking eyes out?"

"Look…"

"No, you look!" King retorted. "Look at what's happening here. Do you want to be involved in this when it gets discovered?"

"It ain't ever being discovered, brother."

"*I* found it!"

"By chance!" Cole paced around the bottom of the bed and stood on King's right side. "Whatever you're involved in, it caught up with you. They've sent you here, and there's nothing I can do about it!" He moved again, shuffled closer.

"Are you actually trying to flank me?" King asked incredulously.

Cole moved quickly as King twisted and rolled onto his right side. The cuff pulled tight and Cole seized his chance. He put a hand over King's mouth and pinched his nose and clamped King's left wrist with his right hand. King tried to fight with his right hand, but it strained against the cuff and did nothing.

"I'm sorry," Cole said. "It's better for you this way…"

King struggled, but Cole's right arm was a match for his left. He tried to press the man's arm upwards, but Cole had his own body weight and used all of it, and gravity, to his advantage. He could also breathe, which gave him more strength while King's own strength was ebbing with every second.

Cole looked away from King's eyes and said, "I want to thank you for saving me. You and that crazy fucking Scotsman. But Johnson will have you tortured and shot, and there's no shortage of vindictive volunteers in this place to shoot you up a bit first."

King could barely hear the man now, his own pulse thudding in his ears. He felt drunk, drowsy. The pressure building up in his ears from the lack of air was unbearable. He knew he didn't have much time left.

Cole pressed down harder. "Give into it,"

he said quietly, his teeth gritted. "It'll soon be over…"

King felt the first wave of darkness wash over him. The fight was leaving him. He pictured Caroline, a fleeting image of Jane. He was back with Caroline. A distant shore, her white bikini. She was smiling at him. King saw red spots through the darkness. He was back at Jane's bedside. Her body was still. It was how he had found her. Gone. He held onto her hand, could see her tiny, frail hand in his own. She sits bolt upright, her eyes wild and she screams, "Fight! Fight Alex, Fight!" King opened his eyes, snapping back. Cole, shocked at his stamina and will, slipped momentarily and King managed a precious gulp of air. He pressed his weight down into his feet and rose off the bed, lifting the man into the air. He dropped down and did it again. Cole shifted his weight and King thrust himself high, but when he dropped, he lifted his left leg up, got the sheet free and wrapped his knee around Cole's head. He forced his leg downwards and Cole lost his positioning. King got his right leg up and scissor-wrapped them together around the man's neck, locking his ankles tightly. Cole's grip on King's mouth and nose slipped, then was gone altogether as he grabbed King's legs with both hands. King squeezed for all he was worth, rolled onto his side and caught hold of his right ankle with his left hand, which tightened the grip and locked it off, his forearm pressing the back of Cole's neck and with it - his throat into the vice-like grip of King's Ju-Jitsu hold. The contortion burned his cracked ribs, and his chest ached with the exertion. But he could breathe now, and with each breath he put more strength into his grip. The man was straining, wheezing. King could see the whites of his eyes turning red and bloodshot. He was seeing the dots, too. There was spittle at his mouth and King could see the life leaving his eyes.

"Your turn to give into it, you bastard! Think about your child, Cole," King said. "Think about the day he was born, his birthdays. The love you gave him, and he returned with smiles and hugs and pictures he drew for you, songs he made up and sang for you..." King's legs were shaking, but there was still more in his tank, he wasn't spent yet, and he gripped as tightly as he could, watching the man whose life he had once saved. "I *gave* you that. I saved you and gave that life to you. And you try to kill me?" He took a deep, calming breath and adjusted his knee for one final squeeze. Cole only had mere seconds left, and the man knew it. He'd been around the block, and he knew he was done.

The door crashed opened and rocked back on its hinges, and two guards entered ahead of Johnson and the doctor. King looked up, then gave the squeeze everything he had. He hadn't even registered that one of the guards was Brett, who charged in and drove the butt of his shotgun into King's face. The blow made a sickening crunch, and King dropped back on the bed, Cole falling from between King's knees and crashing onto the floor and taking with him the drip, ripping the canula out of King's forearm. King was smarting after the blow but did not see the second one coming. And he remembered nothing more after that.

Chapter Forty-Three

100 miles north of Rapid City, South Dakota

The signal emitted its pulse just twenty-miles West of the Cheyenne River reservation. They had separated into groups, with Big Dave and Powell taking a route in from the East. Adams and Tattooed Mick had driven Northwards and aimed to turn around and come in from the Northwest. Caroline, Rashid and Marnie headed in from the South. They had checked into a motel in a town called Custer, in the Black Hills, near the Mount Rushmore national monument park. The town was a hive of activity with motorcyclists cruising the main drag and the mountain roads to other towns. The Sturgis motorcycle festival had brought half a million bikers to South Dakota and the Black Hills, and at times if felt like it. The roads were still quiet, though – such was the vastness of South Dakota. However, every town they had driven through was awash with leather, denim, tattoos and chrome. The men and women spent well, and they had seen no signs of trouble. These were just people with an expensive hobby out to express their freedom. In a way, a hark back in time to the cowboys who roamed the range. Many of the bikes resembled tacked-up horses, and some even sported rifles or shotguns in Western-style rifle holsters tied to the bike's saddles, complete with western saddlebags.

Rashid and Big Dave had looked around while the rest had taken some rest and eaten burgers in a nearby barbeque and smokehouse. The two men had met up with the others in the smokehouse and after they had eaten, and Big Dave had finished two mains and three sides, Rashid and Big Dave had disappeared again for a few hours and returned to the motel ready to go on their recce. Caroline had watched the two men return but hadn't asked where they had been. Sometimes it was better not knowing. The need to know mantra also meant you had plausible and culpable deniability.

Ramsay had taken a different route. After the others had left in the cars, he had typed out and emailed a report for Simon Mereweather, who would forward it to Director Amherst only if he thought it necessary. Again, deniability. He had used the time to call his wife and hear about his daughter's preparations for university and his son's recent trip to the dentist after chipping a tooth falling off his bike. An all too brief moment of the wonderfully mundane. A semblance of normality in the craziness of maintaining his country's security.

After the long drive, it had been nice to unwind with a coffee and the sensation of constant moving had gradually worn off. The others had a long drive ahead of them and he could afford a couple of hours to himself. Refreshed, he had taken a taxi around five miles towards Mount Rushmore, where he had chartered a helicopter. Having noticed the company operating three helicopters on the side of the road on the way into Custer. He had negotiated a rate of one-thousand dollars with the tour operator and the pilot had been grateful for the chance of a longer flight and a break from flying groups of tourists to Crazy Horse – the little-known rock carving of the Indian chief and the same size as the faces of the presidents on Mount Rushmore. No such charter existed for Mount Rushmore, but the route did allow for glimpses at the iconic attraction from afar. Today, though, they would be flying North and away from the tourists.

"So, what are you, a wildlife photographer?" the pilot asked, glancing at the photographic equipment in Ramsay's lap.

"I am," he replied.

"What are you hoping to see?"

"Plains buffalo, or bison," Ramsay hesitated, remembering what he had previously Googled on his smartphone. "Mountain goats, deer, cougars."

"Antelope, you might call them pronghorn," the pilot said. "I can show you some on the way to the reservation."

"Thanks," Ramsay took out a sheet of note paper and passed it to the pilot. "Do you work for the company, or own it?"

The pilot frowned at the paper, then said hesitantly, "I work there."

"Good," Ramsay took out a stack of fifty-dollar bills, still bound with the paper band. "There's a thousand dollars bonus to fly over, or as near to those coordinates as you can."

The pilot glanced at the wedge of money, then looked fleetingly at Ramsay before checking his attitude and altitude. He corrected his height with both the cyclic and collective. It was a tidy sum for a bonus, and nobody would be telling the IRS. "Hey, buddy, what is this about?"

"Curiosity," Ramsay replied. "Do you

know of any reason why we shouldn't fly over there?"

The pilot carried on flying straight and level, although it always felt as if the helicopter wanted to flip over. The pilot worked both rudder pedals, the yoke and the collective near-constantly to keep the craft under control. "There ain't nothing out there but grassland," he paused. "But it's restricted airspace. You can't hunt there, either."

"Why?"

The pilot shrugged. "There was talk of sensitive flora and fauna, the US Fish and Wildlife Service sent literature out to the residents, but there's nothing there for miles and the reservation has its own laws and law enforcement, so nobody tends to go out that way anyway. You can hunt on the reservation, or at least the Cheyenne Indians can. And if you ain't a native American, or more specially a Cheyenne, then it ain't worth your while."

"Why?"

"Them boys are real protective of their rights. They'll as likely shoot you if you turn up to hunt of their land. There are few jobs, little money and they get real protective of their land

and their rights. And they have the right to protect their land, with their own marshals and deputies as law enforcement. Local cops can't go out there either, only the FBI."

"Sounds like a political and law enforcement minefield."

The pilot shrugged. "Doesn't affect you if you don't go there. I figure we took enough off those guys a hundred-and-fifty-years ago. They can do what the hell they want."

"But the land those coordinates are on is not part of the reservation?"

"No. Close, but no."

"Are you willing to chance a fly-by?"

"I don't see what harm it can do, it's not like there's anybody living there or anything," he paused. "But why are you willing to part with a thousand bucks?"

"I'm interested, that's all," said Ramsay. "I work for The World Wildlife Fund and I'm hearing that hunters are going in there, flouting the law and taking advantage of the growing numbers of animals. There're reports of buffalo being shot and butchered for a mass-market. If that's the case, then the fish and wildlife boys have a lot to answer for. They're not doing their job."

"Right," the pilot said, and nodded. "World Wildlife Fund? Well, that accounts for the accent. Australian?"

"You guessed it, er, *mate*," Ramsay said. He was as typically middle-class English as it gets and did not have an accent, but almost every American he'd met had thought he was Australian. It didn't hurt to add a little subterfuge. Anything to create false trails.

"How low do you want to go?"

"I'll leave that to you," said Ramsay. "Low and slow, I suppose."

"Suits me fine," the pilot said. "We can skim the daisies! Just like back in the 'Stan. Except out there it was opium poppies and every man, and his brother was shooting at us! Damn, I miss that shit!"

Chapter Forty-Four

King awoke, water pouring into his lungs, his senses coming back to life all at once, amid confusion and fear. He coughed and spluttered as he tried to clear his lungs, the water had been little more than a trickle down his throat, but the lungs couldn't handle the merest quantity, and he was retching uncontrollably. He was aware of people in the room, chatter and breathing, but could not yet focus.

His arms were searing, the pain burning his joints and tearing at his muscles. The shoulder that had been dislocated back in Washington DC was threatening to pop loose at any moment. He squinted against the light, could see the guard he knew as Brett staring at him, two guards behind him edging their way forwards. Johnson was seated at a stainless-steel table looking through a report with Cole sitting beside him. The man's demeanour was low, not helped by the neck brace he was wearing and the redness of his eyes. King stared at him, but the man looked away.

They had strung him up. He was naked and soaked from the bucket of water that one of the men had thrown into his face. His hands were cuffed, and a length of rope had been looped through them and hung to a hook in the ceiling. King dangled limply, his feet a foot or so off the ground.

Brett stepped forwards and punched King in the stomach. King wheezed and was rocked backwards a foot or so. He swung inertly, starting to spin counter-clockwise, which suited Brett because he followed up with another punch to King's kidney. King forced himself not to cry out, but it was no use. He breathed hard, tried to get himself under control. The guards were sniggering, and as King twisted back around to face them, he could see the delight on their faces. He caught sight of Cole, who had averted his eyes and made no attempt to look at him.

"Why did you attack my man, here?" Johnson asked without looking up from the report. "There was no way in hell you were going to get away. Which kind of leads me to suspect you are a psychopath. In which case, there would be little point me taking anything else you say seriously. I think it may be about time for that nine-millimetre and shallow grave we talked about."

"After you," King groaned.

Brett stepped forwards but was knocked off balance by the other two who were eagerly making their way towards King for their turn. One of the men was knocked aside and fell onto the ground, landing like a child on his hands and knees and pulling a face of annoyance. Brett and the other guard lost concentration and were about to get back to King when Johnson shouted for them to stop.

King chuckled as the man got back to his feet. "Fair game," he said. "But does it have to be these three pricks? On second thoughts, go for it. I could probably take them all down with my hands behind my back, anyway."

Brett tore at King, swinging wildly with left and right hooks. King was sent into a spin and Brett waited for him to slow down and turn back towards him. Johnson's shouts fell upon deaf ears, and when King slowed and was facing him again, he kicked out and caught Brett in the groin with a hard snapping front kick that sounded wet when it made contact. The man went down fast, but King snapped out another kick that landed under the man's jaw. It helped him on his way, and he landed in a heap, cracking the back of his head on the edge of the metal table. One of the guards took Brett's place, punching King but guarding his groin with his other leg. It made for a poor stance and he was pulling back a poorly-landed punch, when King's foot drove up under his chin. King had pulled his bare toes backwards, driving the front part of the sole of his foot into his throat.

"Enough!" Johnson leapt out of his chair and marched forwards. He glared at the remaining guard and snapped, "Get the doctor!" The guard did as he was ordered, and Johnson stood in front of King, a good and handy metre away. "What the hell is it with you?"

King was spinning once more. He waited to slow down, when he could eye Johnson he said, "You want me to hang here and take a beating? Fuck you!"

Johnson looked down at the two guards. Brett wasn't moving a muscle and the other guard was rasping for breath. He had started to turn a tinge of blue, clutching his throat and twisting from side to side. Johnson ignored him and looked back at King. "Why did you attack Cole? You couldn't have hoped to get away."

King could see Cole looking at him for the first time. He thought he detected a slight shake of his head. The man's eyes were bloodshot, but there was an intensity behind them. A throw of the dice. He didn't understand why the ex-SEAL would look at him that way. "I guess I didn't think it through," he said. "I saw an opportunity and went for it."

Johnson stared at King for a moment, then returned to his folder and opened it. The doctor and the other guard bustled in and the doctor bent down and started ABCs on the two men. The guard shadowed the door.

"I think you've played me. I think you have a reason to be here and an exit strategy. I'll be damned if I'll let you get away with it. I think you're a dangerous man to have around," said Johnson. "Too dangerous."

The doctor stood up and shook his head. "They're both dead," he said, not looking at King.

"And that would confirm it," he said. He turned to Cole and said, "You and I need a talk."

"What about the attacks?" King shouted. "I gave you Chicago, there will be others!"

"And I'll let the Secret Service know and increase the threat level on POTUS. There's always the chance of a plot and an attack, and the Secret Service will have to deal with it. It's what they do." He looked back at King, eyeing him up and down with contempt. "And you had your chance. You *were* warned."

Chapter Forty-Five

"We're twenty-miles from the signal," Marnie said, her eyes not leaving the laptop balancing on her thighs.

Caroline noticeably shivered, despite the balmy temperature. She was a bag of nerves. If she wasn't working, and if the situation had been different, she could have done with a drink. Or six. She craned her neck to see the screen, taking some comfort that she was just twenty-miles away from the man she loved. With every mile they had driven she had taken solace in closing the gap. Only now, the closer she became, the more impossible the task seemed.

"This road looks more like a private track," said Rashid. He looked out across the seemingly endless expanse of grass. "We'll be in the shit if it takes us directly there."

"It doesn't," said Marnie. She was seated in the front seat and twisted the screen so that Rashid could see. "There are smaller tracks intersecting. But the more I study the map, the more it looks like the area around the signal has no roads at all. Not even a track."

Caroline leaned forwards from the rear seat. "Why is that area blurred?"

Marnie reverse pinched the touchscreen with her thumb and forefinger and nodded. "All I can assume is the Pentagon has deemed the area a no-go zone, without labelling it. Google Earth doesn't record imagery that is politically sensitive," she said. She switched to another tab and tutted. "Nothing to show, yet. But Ramsay has requested a fly-over. Re-tasking a satellite is a big deal, but GCHQ are piggy-backing a network of satellites and Simon Mereweather is convinced the boys and girls in Cheltenham can get us what we need, soon."

"And what will that give us?" Caroline asked indifferently.

"Now that we have the signal, then a full and detailed picture of where he is. We can use that as a background map, much like we are using now."

"This terrain looks okay to go off-road," Rashid commented. "There's more agricultural wire fencing than I imagined, but most of it looks decades old and I've got a wire-cutter in my kit."

There was a distant mountain range North-West of them and the Black Hills behind them. Other than that, the grassland stretched on for hundreds of miles back along South Dakota to their right and Wyoming to their left. The sky was an azure blue, almost completely cloudless. The land and sky contrast reminded Caroline of being at sea, out of sight of land. Big skies. She looked back at the signal and frowned. "Is it me, or is it bleeping slower than before?"

Marnie studied the screen. She turned and looked at Caroline. "I'm sorry, but I think we have to face the fact that the signal is weakening."

"Why?" Caroline retorted. "That's not good enough!" She shook her head in frustration, but also because she realised how maniacal she had sounded.

"I'm sorry, but I suppose the battery is running out." She took a screenshot of the map and saved it to the desktop. "Look, we have this signal and coordinates saved and we're only twenty-miles away."

"But this is a reconnaissance!" Caroline snapped. "We're a hundred miles from Custer on a shitty road and the signal is dying! We need to scope the place out, return to confer, plan what to do and return! It's so damned remote, we're miles away from anywhere!" She flung herself back in the seat and rubbed her temples. "Oh, God!"

Marnie turned around in her seat and reached a hand back to her. She squeezed Caroline's knee and said, "Then we'll forget the recce and go in."

"Excuse me?" Rashid said. He looked at her like she was mad. "That's what a reconnaissance is for – to plan. If we go in blind, we risk being killed. It's almost a certainty."

"We risk being killed, anyway," said Marnie.

"Have you ever even fired a gun?"

"No, well, my brother's air rifle when we were kids."

"Then please, keep quiet."

"Excuse me?" she glared. "A – don't *ever* speak to me like that again. And B – Caroline has a point. If the signal dies, then Alex will be lost forever. Face it, this is the United States and they aren't exactly the land of the free, anymore. Not with prisons that fall outside of Miranda rights and the judicial system. And the objective all along was to snatch Vladimir Zukovsky to ascertain what he knows about the virus. Without King and the signal, we won't get him out."

"We can still get to Zukovsky…"

"Rashid!" Marnie snapped.

"King knew the risks," he said. "I tried several times to talk him out of it. Zukovsky is the target, King was the stalking horse to get into the place."

"Was?" Caroline leaned forwards between them. "You've written him off already?"

Rashid slammed on the brakes and Caroline had to press against the two seats to stop herself going through the gap. The SUV slewed to a halt on the deserted track. He turned and glared at her. "The objective is Zukovsky. Just in case you've forgotten what we saw on those files in Lapland! King is an operative and he knew the risks. But believe me, if we go into this secret prison without a recce, then there will be deaths on our hands. Big Dave, Powell, Adams and Mick. Marnie and myself. Ramsay, wherever the hell he is. He'll be waiting for us back at the motel with intel he's collected. And from a chopper, he may well get us vital information. And then, you. So close to King, but you could get killed at the last hurdle. We'll walk into a fight we can't win. We need subterfuge, an infiltration plan, an exit strategy.

And that's assuming King can locate Zukovsky. We have one chance of that."

"And we need that bloody signal! Not just to locate him, but for the second phase... getting Zukovsky out!"

"We won't need a second phase if we go in blind!" Rashid drummed his fingers on the steering wheel. "Fuck it!" He took out his phone and got out of the car, slamming the door closed so hard it rocked the two-tonne behemoth on its wheels.

"We've got the satellite footage," Marnie said. "It's decoding right now."

Caroline leaned forwards and looked at the screen. Marnie turned it towards her, shielding it from the sunlight with her hand. The decoding finished, and the screen pixilated, then rested on an image. The image cleared, and Marnie clicked on an icon and brought the magnification up.

"So, what are we looking at?" Caroline asked. "Grass?"

"Pretty much," Marnie replied. "And a hangar. It's covered with turf, but you can make out the size, like a knoll." She increased the image. "And there's a communication tower, and an airstrip." She pointed to the corner of the screen. "There's a large military-style helicopter, laid up just outside the hangar."

"But no roads," Caroline commented. "So, everything, or everyone, comes in by air."

Marnie nodded, looked out the tinted window at Rashid, who was talking animatedly on his mobile. "Who's he calling?"

Caroline smiled. "I imagine he's re-routing the SAS boys. I think we wore him down," she said.

Marnie laughed. "Always…"

Chapter Forty-Six

There was no hood this time. Johnson didn't care what King saw from now on. He was loaded into the front seat of a civilian Jeep Wrangler. The convertible model. It had been painted a dull olive colour and had a spare wheel fixed to the bonnet and another on the rear door. There were snow shovels strapped to each front panel and snow chains coiled and bolted to the roll bars. The guard who had been present while King had been strung up drove, and he looked pissed off. He had lost two buddies and he was looking forward to taking out some payback on King. He had placed a long-handled shovel and a pick behind the front seat and let King know what they were for. Cole sat in the rear seat, a .40 calibre Sig Sauer pistol in his hand.

King couldn't see a way out of his cuffs, his hands behind his back and his ribs and stomach still aching from the beating. His shoulder was on the cusp of dislocating, and the slightest movement emitted a sickening twinge. Some physio would sort it, but it didn't look to be on the cards now. He always hedged his bets, but it wasn't looking good. The guard had keys on his belt, next to his own set of cuffs. They would be common to this unit, but they might as well have been at the bottom of the ocean. Getting to them couldn't be any more difficult.

They drove for twenty-minutes over a variety of tracks which looked to have been made by animals, before the guard took the vehicle off road and out across what looked like well-grazed grassland. After another twenty-minutes the guard slowed the vehicle and pulled a lazy circle.

"Here's about right," the guard said. He stopped the vehicle and switched off the engine. "Time to get digging."

Cole got out of the rear, leaping over the side and onto the grass. He winced, rubbed the side of his neck through the neck-brace. The guard walked around the Jeep and pulled King out of the open door. He pushed him back against the side of the vehicle. Cole covered King with the pistol.

"Who's digging?" asked the guard.

"Well, I sure as hell ain't," said Cole.

"Looks like it's you, shithead," the guard said to King. He fumbled for his keys, then spun King around and undid the cuffs. He pulled King back around and pressed him back against the Jeep. "Time to dig your own grave." He reached into the Jeep and pulled out the shovel, thrusting the handle into King's chest.

King gripped the shovel with both hands, then thrust it downwards into the guard's foot. It sliced through the soft desert boot and cut deeply into the man's instep, breaking the leader bones in his foot. The man howled, but King shoulder-barged him towards Cole, blocking his aim. King swung the shovel and had it scything in the air, missing the top of the falling guard's head, but embedding the blade into Cole's shoulder as he struggled to aim the pistol without a clear shot. The gun went off as Cole started to spin, but King was already adjusting his aim on his backward swing, which caught Cole's right arm and forced him to drop the pistol.

Although in great pain, the guard was already countering his balance to attack when King sent the shovel into the side of his head. The blade of the shovel caught against his shattered skull, and the handle was pulled from his clasp as the man started to fall. King was closer to the pistol than Cole, and he picked it up as Cole made a last-ditch attempt and dived closer. King merely stepped backwards, and

Cole thudded onto his stomach. He shot the moaning guard in the head without emotion or ceremony, then turned the pistol back to Cole.

"I'll say it once," said King. "Don't move a muscle."

"I'm not going anywhere."

"That look you gave me in the interrogation cell, what the hell was that about?"

Cole hesitated, but then he was desperately unsure about moving. He slowly looked up at King, straight into the muzzle of a .40. "I was going to let you go," he said. "On account of what I did, or at least, tried to do to you."

"You mean murder the man who saved you and your two buddies from the hands of ISIS?"

Cole winced at the memory. "Yeah, I guess. I couldn't see a way out for you, and I knew things were going to get worse. Look, I don't know what shit you're trying to pull here, but the reports came back from the FBI. The devices planted in the Willis Tower were incendiary. Low fuel. A lot of smoke and no chance of any lasting, or catastrophic damage. Risk to life, low. Johnson went apeshit. He knew it was a ploy, and in that case, something to buy you some time. However you're doing it, it's clear you have a plan with outside help."

"So, why didn't you save me just now?"

"Man, you just moved too fast!"

King shrugged. "Too much at stake, got to take the opportunities when they're there."

"So, we're cool?" Cole asked, starting to get up.

King fired the pistol and a sod of grassy earth blew up into Cole's face. The ex-SEAL froze, shaking his head as King laughed. "No, we are not cool," he said, bending down and retrieving the handcuffs. He tossed them in front of Cole's face. "It would have been great, but unfortunately I'll never know. It could be the sort of crap that someone who tries to kill the man who saved his life says when he's neck-deep in shit. Now, cuff one hand, then roll back onto your stomach and put your hands behind your back. And stay still while I cuff the other hand, or your brains will be fertiliser."

"Seriously? What the hell are you going to do to me?"

"Nothing," said King. "But you're going to sit right beside me when we drive back into that place."

"You're going back?" Cole asked incredulously. "What the hell for?"

"To finish my job," King said quietly. "To finish my bloody job."

Chapter Forty-Seven

"I don't understand that." The pilot pulled back on the yoke and collective, increasing the power and pitch and the helicopter climbed steeply. "There's a considerable sized runway down there, and enough hangar space to house several aircraft."

Ramsay found himself grabbing hold of the door handle grab-strap. The helicopter entered a tight turn to the left and the pilot made another run towards the area.

"And there are no airports listed here?"

"No." The pilot levelled out the helicopter and said, "Now's your chance with the camera. If this is a protected zone, then someone is going to want to know there's a God damned airstrip in the middle of it."

Ramsay took some pictures but struggled to release his grip on the handle. "No roads," he said. "No way in or out except by air."

"Or cross country," the pilot replied, then added, "But that sure as hell ain't happening in the winter. The snow's three-feet deep for six months of the year out here."

Ramsay looked down on the area. He hadn't expected to see as much, and in truth, he hadn't expected the pilot to fly directly over the area until it was too late. It was happening, and Ramsay prayed that the people down there didn't know they'd been overflown. The helicopter banked to the right.

"Seen enough, or do you want me to put down?"

"Oh God, no!" Ramsay snapped. "Let's get out of here, I've got enough shots and a film of our last pass." He could see some movement below. "What's that?"

The ground seemed to slowly bulge and split in a perfect square. The two halves of the square dropped back on flaps, hinged and fitted perfectly. Something protruded, rising from the middle. Ramsay squinted against the sunlight shining through the hot plexiglass of the canopy. The object started to turn towards them, like a compass needle getting a bearing.

"Oh shit! No, no, no!" The pilot heaved on the yoke and the helicopter turned sharply to the left. The speed increased with the whine of the engine, and they dropped twenty-feet in altitude. "That's a SAM!"

"A Sam?"

"Fuck! Shit!" the pilot screamed and hammered the aircraft to the right, increasing to what could only have sounded to be full throttle. "A missile! A fucking surface to air missile!"

There was an audible bang and whoosh and seconds later, the helicopter heaved left and dropped and the missile shot past them and snaked its way across the sky. Both men watched the missile paint a white streak across the pale blue sky, then turn around and head back towards them. The pilot reached under his seat and took out a flare gun. He tossed it into Ramsay's lap and brought the helicopter into a steep climb. Ramsay fumbled with the pistol. He looked at it blankly.

"Open your window!" the pilot shouted. "Cock back the hammer like on a regular pistol and fire out of the window when I say so!"

Ramsay thought back to the range. He had used a Glock. A hammerless weapon. He had seen enough westerns to know what the pilot meant though, but even still he struggled to pull the hammer back, his hands soaked in perspiration. He slid the plexiglass panel in his window forwards, and when he looked up, he saw the missile heading directly at them.

The pilot dropped the craft into a steep dive, putting on the power, the ground racing towards them. "Steady..." There was little height left and the helicopter came up from its dive mere feet from the ground. "Fire!"

Ramsay squeezed the trigger, but it was stiff. He squeezed harder and the flare gun kicked in his hand. He hadn't compensated enough, and the weapon rose as the flare shot out and hit the rotor-blades above them. The flare ricocheted off the propellers and kicked up into the sky before exploding like a firework finale. The missile streaked away from them and started to climb, detonating on the white-hot pieces of phosphorus that had starburst into the clear sky.

"Yes!" screamed Ramsay. He looked at the pilot, but the man remained silent. He was fighting the yoke and rudders and it was only then that Ramsay noticed the smoke above them.

"You've blown one of the rotor-blades off!" He struggled to correct their height, but it was too late, the tail thudded into the ground and the entire aircraft bucked back up into the air, this time with the cockpit low and the tail high. "Brace! Brace! Bra..."

The helicopter smashed into the ground and pivoted forwards. The damaged rotor-blade sliced into the ground first, its alignment was off and as it dug in, the rest of the blades smashed into the ground and were ripped out of the rotor. The noise was deafening, and the plexiglass buckled and cracked into spider's webs. The pilot had had the presence of mind to let go of the collective and the revs had died, but momentum was doing the rest, the helicopter, now free of its blades, tumbled and rolled and came to a stop some fifty-metres from where the tail had first hit the ground.

"Get out!" the pilot screamed, piercing the silence which had briefly enveloped them. "These things burn up fast!" He struggled with his harness, then started to scream. "My legs, I can't feel my legs!"

Ramsay snapped back. He got off his own seat harness and slid into the Perspex canopy. His equilibrium was off kilter, the helicopter was on its right side – the pilot's side – and almost inverted. Ramsay kicked at his own door, then remembered the safety briefing and removed the pin. He kicked again, and the door spun off and slid down the frame. He got the pilot's harness undone and pulled. The pilot screamed and did so for the five-minutes it took Ramsay to get him out. The smell of fuel was nauseating and there were electrical sparks coming from the control panel.

"My gun," the pilot said weakly. "There, in the cubby space." He pointed. "Anybody who would shoot us down will be coming to finish the job," he said. "Just like in the 'Stan…'" He winced as Ramsay laid him down on the ground and ducked back in for the gun. He returned with a semi-automatic pistol. "It's locked and loaded. Ready to go," the pilot said. "God dammit! It's one thing getting shot down by the fucking ragheads, but in my home state?" He struggled to get to his feet but fell back on the ground.

Ramsay could see that both of the man's legs were broken. He secured him under his armpits and said, "Hold on, this will hurt. But I want to get clear of this thing!" He lifted and dragged him, the screams of pain almost making him stop.

The pilot panted and wiped his brow with his sleeve. "We've got to get out of here. Whoever launched that thing will be here any minute."

Ramsay looked out across the plains. No roads, no houses. He couldn't even see the hangar or the runway. He had no idea which way to head. "How can we get away?"

"You'll have to leave me," the pilot said through gritted teeth. The pain was immense, but he carried on. "That way is East. That's the reservation. There will be people there who can let you use a phone…"

"Oh, shit! My phone!" Ramsay tore at his pocket and took out his iPhone. His heart lifted when he saw a two-bar signal. He started to dial.

"That ain't no good unless you can call the Marines and get them to send an entire unit."

"I'm not calling the Marines," Ramsay said with renewed confidence. "I've got something even better."

Chapter Forty-Eight

"Well, that takes care of that, then," said Cole. He was seated in the front seat of the Jeep, his hands cuffed behind his back.

King, seated behind the steering wheel and dressed in the dead guard's clothes, had paused to watch the aerobatic display some five-miles distant. The two men had watched the SAM cut swathes of white trails across the sky. The helicopter had dropped below a series of knolls, and the SAM had followed. The explosion had lit up the clear blue sky like lightning, yellow and white, then nothing but white smoke. Within a minute the smoke had dispersed and there was no trace of what had happened. There had been no further sign of the helicopter, but the explosion would have made anybody presume the worse.

"That chopper will be missed," King paused. "Within the hour, would be my bet. Look's like your world is going to come tumbling down."

Cole laughed. "Don't bet on it. There will already be a team dispatched to pick over that mess and Johnson will have it filed as a tragic accident with the FAA before it's even on the news," he paused. "Hold that, it probably won't even get on local radio."

"He has that power?"

"You're kidding, right? The guys behind this place don't answer to anyone. But the whole of the United States answers to them. They own the CIA, the FBI... hell, they even have the President in their pockets. How else do you think a secret prison like this can even exist?"

King put the Jeep back into gear and sped off across the grass. "But it's not a secret anymore," he corrected him. "I know about it, and so will the people I work for."

Cole scoffed and shook his head. "Well, if you're going back inside, I don't think you'll be taking your secret anywhere in a hurry."

"But you'll be with me," King said. "And I have a feeling there will be a lot of interest in that downed chopper. And that will mean less boots on the ground."

"Perhaps," said Cole. "But you still need to get inside. And I won't be helping you."

"No?"

"No."

King hit the brakes and as the Jeep nosed

to a stop, Cole was thrown forwards, when he came back towards his seat, the back of his head butted up against the barrel of the .40 Sig Sauer pistol held tightly in King's right hand. "Picture your son," he said. "And your wife. Got them?"

"Wait!" Cole tilted his head forwards, trying to get away from the cold steel. "Just wait!"

"I'm not playing games here," said King. "I couldn't give a shit about that trailer park piece of trash back there, I couldn't care less about the two guards this morning. And after what you tried in the hospital, I couldn't give a crap about you. So, here's the deal. One time only. Get me back in to finish my job, and I'll let you live. Deny me that, and I'll kill you. Plain and simple. And I'll let you know something before you make your decision, before you think about playing me and double-crossing me. Navy SEAL training, British SAS training, whatever you want to set out as the gold standard of the military elite – it doesn't even compare to what I've learned, perfected and been through. You won't get the drop on me. You won't beat me in a fight. I can out-shoot you. And I won't quit. Not ever. You'll be thinking about ringing the quitting bell while I'm planning how to use it to beat my enemy's head in. So, don't try anything, do as I say, and you'll see your wife and child again."

Cole pressed his head back against the pistol in defiance. "I hear a lot of talk," he said. "I've bled my own and taken my fair share of people's blood in Afghanistan, Iraq, Syria... we went to the same holiday resorts. I've served with men far tougher than myself. So, if I help you, it's because you saved me once, and not because I'm scared of you or your talk."

King laughed and tucked the pistol back in the utility belt. The guard's uniform had been a decent enough fit. "Well, I guess we will just have to wait and see," he said. "But I had you circling the drain with broken ribs and one hand chained to the bed. So, I guess we both really know who the bigger dog is, and who needs to bark in order to save face."

Chapter Forty-Nine

The bullet skimmed past them with a crack and struck the wreckage of the helicopter behind them. The gunshot roared a full second later. Ramsay ducked down, but too late. He scrambled for the pilot's pistol and checked the breech like Caroline had shown him. He took aim, sighting on the vehicle and the figure who was taking aim.

"Forget it, they're too far away!" the pilot snapped. "Get down!" Ramsay ducked down, and another shot zinged overhead. The gunshot followed a second later. Then half a dozen more shots fired, and clumps of earth flicked up around them. The pilot rolled onto his side and started to crawl, but his horribly broken legs didn't follow neatly, and he screamed and shouted in agony. "Get out of here!" he shouted, waving a hand at Ramsay. "Stick to the low ground," he panted. "Try to keep the knolls and depressions between you and these bastards!"

"I won't leave you," Ramsay said, as he crawled over and caught hold of the man's lapels. He heaved and struggled, and the man screamed, but Ramsay found the strength and got him onto his shoulder. He picked up the gun and squat-pressed himself and the man upright. He wobbled as he ran, gunshots behind him. He tucked the pistol into his pocket and fumbled out his phone. He was panting hard. He looked at the message, then thumb-swiped and opened the compass app. It paused for a moment, then spun and he found East and changed direction.

"Put me down," the pilot said weakly. "You've got next to no chance on your own, but none at all with me."

Ramsay could hear a vehicle behind him. Thankfully, there were no more gunshots, but he had visions of being run down by a huge American truck that would likely carry on without feeling them under the wheels. He checked the compass again, kept on his heading. The ground was undulating, and the truck would have to go around. He deviated and headed for two hills that made a shallow valley between them. They were no more than eighty-feet high, but they would provide them with cover. Another gunshot rang out and a clump of grass channelled out a sizeable divot near Ramsay's right foot. He dared not look behind him, but the powerful V8 motor was gaining rapidly. Another three gunshots rang out, this time the divots happened in real time to the gunshots and Ramsay knew they were closing in on them. He pressed on, but as he started down the gradient of a wide depression, he stumbled and fell. The pilot screamed, and Ramsay sprawled, dropping the phone and the pistol springing from his pocket. He went for the pistol, but a bullet struck near. He turned and saw two men barely thirty-metres from him, both holding automatic weapons. Ramsay went for his phone, but a well-placed shot destroyed it. He was still two-paces from the gun. He hesitated and watched one of the men take aim. The man fired and the pilot's head split like a watermelon. Ramsay turned and ran, leaving the pistol and zig-zagging towards the vee between the two hills. There were no more shots, but he could hear both men laughing. He sprinted, forgetting to breathe, his eyes welled with tears. The pilot had known what was going to happen. There had been a look of acceptance on his face a split second before the inevitable, and Ramsay felt ashamed that he had experienced a moment of relief that it was not himself who had been shot when the man's head had puffed a crimson mist into the air. If he lived through this, Ramsay knew he would never forget the man's expression, the sight of what followed.

He could feel his heart pounding, kept forgetting to breathe as he fled towards the vee between the two hillocks. The men were fitter than he was, and they did not have the sheer terror of being hunted hampering their efforts. He couldn't rely on his phone now and had to use dead-reckoning as he headed into the shade afforded by the higher ground. Another gunshot rang out and more earth sprayed up into Ramsay's legs. One of the men shouted, but his heart thudded so heavily that he could not hear what was being said. It wouldn't have been good, though and he was almost out of their line of sight.

Both men stopped and took aim as Ramsay darted into the lee of the first hillock and disappeared from view. They both smiled and looked at each other then followed their quarry into what would become their killing ground, but the smiles would have told any observer that they planned to have some fun with their prey first.

In the distance a loud V8 rumbled and the vehicle rutted and bounced over uneven terrain. Ramsay ran into the vee of the lower ground, hearing the sound of the vehicle cutting off his escape. There were boulders stacked in piles and he realised they were probably Indian burial monuments. Whatever they were, they would only give him cover if he was armed, and he had dropped the pilot's pistol. Without a weapon, they were just places for him to wait for his pursuers to catch up with him. Another shot rang out, the sound enhanced by the enclosed sides of the two hills.

"Stop running!" one of the men shouted. "It's over!"

"Put your hands on your head!" the other man shouted.

Ramsay's heart sank, and he turned and saw both men in the entrance to the vee. He had nowhere to go, nowhere to hide. He stopped, his lungs burning, heart pounding. His legs suddenly felt leaden and he realised he had lost control of them. He doubted he could turn and run and frustratingly, as the men drew near, he knew he wouldn't. For the first time he understood why so many people went to their deaths with no fight or resistance. The body and mind knows when it is beaten and merely shuts down in order to avoid trauma and pain.

Both men walked slowly and confidently. One had lowered his assault rifle, the other was aiming at Ramsay, the same way he had just before he shot the pilot. Sunlight hit their faces as the sun edged above the ridge above them. Ramsay could see the sadistic expressions they had, their intentions clear.

The gunshots came rapidly, but unlike the short, sharp report of the 5.56mm assault rifles the men carried, these sounded like cannon-fire. Ramsay ducked down as portions of the men were blown off in chunks the size of oven-ready chickens. Ten shots in all and what was left of both men had fallen and lay twitching in two crumpled and bloody heaps.

Ramsay was shaking, but he managed to look up the side of the slope nearest him and shielded his eyes against the sun. The figure slid down the grassy slope and as they dropped into the shade, Ramsay saw Rashid, his expression impassive.

"Thank God for that..." Ramsay said, trying to regain composure, but failing. He was so happy that he realised he didn't care.

Rashid looked around the vee and turned his attention back to Ramsay. "A decent killing ground," he said. "Better if you hadn't left the gun out there."

"You saw that?" Ramsay asked, incredulously.

"Sure did."

"Why didn't you shoot them then?"

Rashid held up the shotgun. "Too far away," he replied matter-of-factly. "Had to wait until they were drawn in."

Ramsay sat down on the grass and his shoulders sagged. "I thought that was it, for sure."

Rashid said nothing as he walked over to the two corpses and picked up both M4 rifles. He slung them over his shoulder on their straps and checked the bodies for spare magazines. Two were damaged from the buckshot and were a twisted, bloody mess. But he managed to pull two more magazines clear and pocketed them. He didn't bother with the magazines that were excessively bloody; he'd used them before in Syria and Afghanistan, and they clogged up as soon as the blood started to clot. It simply wasn't worth the trouble. The magazines would need taking apart, and the entire weapon stripped down and cleaned thoroughly. He pulled out the pilot's pistol from one of the body's waistband and held it out for Ramsay. "Come on," he said. "Let's get out of here."

Ramsay followed Rashid up the slope. As he crested the summit, some eighty- feet above the flat plain, he saw Caroline aiming one of the bulky BR99 shotguns at a man on his knees. They were in front of a Dodge Ram pick-up truck, its driver's door still open and the engine running.

"I'm so glad you found me," Ramsay said. "I thought that was it. Thank you."

"Don't mention it," Rashid said, stopping to look at him. "I mean it. We're a team, it's what we do."

"The crash was frightening enough. Thank God I got hold of you. You can't get a mobile signal when you go down to Cornwall for the weekend, but out here in the Great Plains with a hundred miles between towns, I've got at least two bars."

"I wouldn't mind betting that's got something to do with the communication tower near that air strip. They must have a thing going with the cell phone companies."

"What about the bodies?"

"Let 'em rot."

"But the pilot!"

Rashid nodded. "Shit."

"The guy was okay, he was a veteran. He flew in Afghanistan."

"You're right," he said. "But we have to prioritise. We can drop a line to the sheriff or police department later. But right now, getting Zukovsky is the mission."

"And King," Ramsay added.

"Of course, goes without saying," he replied. "But Zukovsky is the priority. We want what he knows and right now, we have next to no time before we are compromised. There will be people looking for these guys when they don't report in. Marnie is contacting the others, we're going in as soon as we can regroup."

They slid their way down the hillside and Rashid strode up to Caroline. "Good work," he said.

"And yourself," she replied, looking at Ramsay. "Hi, Neil."

"Hello," said Ramsay. "You guys got here just in time."

Caroline smiled and turned to Rashid. "What are we going to do with this chap?"

"Is he clean?"

"He is now. He was carrying a Beretta, a well-used M9," she said. "Which is now in my pocket."

Rashid nodded. The M9 was designated US military issue, what was sold elsewhere by the Italian manufacturer as a 92FS. Which meant the weapon was US government issue. He looked at the man and said, "If we were to try to get into that prison, would we stand a better chance with you?"

"What prison?"

Rashid shrugged. He lunged forwards and jabbed the muzzle of the BR99 into the man's sternum. He went down and made next to no noise, but that was because he couldn't breathe. It seemed he never would again, but eventually he managed a lungful of air through gritted teeth. He moaned and rolled on the grass. Rashid looked up to see a black GMC bouncing towards them over the grass. He looked back at the man on the ground. "My colleagues will be here in a minute. There'll be no shortage of men willing to slice out your throat for an easier life, especially when they find out you guys killed a veteran pilot."

"I didn't kill anybody!" he growled. "I'm just the driver."

Rashid shrugged. "Yes or no. Can you help us inside?"

"And if I do?"

"I'll knock you out and leave you outside while we do what we've come here to do."

"And if I don't?"

"You're a big boy, I shouldn't have to spell it out. Your buddies are in bits." He turned and walked to the SUV, which had pulled to a stop with Big Dave getting out and striding towards him. He made the massive BR99 shotgun in his hand look like a toy. Rashid felt like a child when the man reached him.

"Did you see the bloody chopper go down?"

"No," said Rashid. "But I guess you can say Neil did…"

"King's signal has configured as six-miles Northwest of the prison," Marnie said, pushing her way between them. She held the laptop out to allow them to see.

"So, he's out?" Rashid asked, somewhat incredulously, straining to see the screen clearly in the sunlight.

"He is, but he's heading back. He's less than half a mile from the hangar and travelling at thirty-miles-per-hour."

"Do you think he escaped and has been recaptured?" Big Dave asked, frowning at the screen. "That airstrip is about five miles Southwest from here, we'll never make it before he gets there, not going by the rate of that flashing dot."

"We've got to go in!" exclaimed Marnie.

Rashid glared at her. "Thanks for your tactical advice," he snapped. "But we're not going in yet."

"Too right!" Adams joined them, peeked at the laptop and said, "We can't go into that place in daylight. There's no cover from high ground. It's suicide!"

Big Dave nodded. "We need the cover of darkness. We also need to take down that communications tower. I doubt there would be a mobile signal out here without it. And it will black-out their radio comms, too." He looked at his watch and said, "We've got around three-hours before darkness. I say, we use it to plan and evaluate."

Caroline backed up towards them, the shotgun still on the man. The man still on his knees. She said, "I don't like the fact Alex has gone back. What can that mean?"

Marnie walked over to one of the SUVs and put the laptop on the bonnet. It was almost shoulder height, but she fiddled with the touch screen and wound back the image. She typed something, and the image changed. "This is the helicopter going down," she said. "And over here..." She moved the screen along and increased the focus. "This must be King, in the Jeep. It's the only vehicle in the area. So, it *has* to be him." She took the focus up, then typed on the keys and the image cleaned up. It's a no brainer," she said. "The other guy in the passenger seat is black. That must be King in the driver's seat."

"But he's in a uniform!" Caroline said. She had taken her eyes off the prisoner and he bolted towards the truck. "Shit!"

"On it!" Big Dave took off after the man, who had made it to the open door of the big pick-up.

The man was fumbling with the ignition when Big Dave got to him. He went for the door and Big Dave didn't hesitate, punching through the glass and into the man's face. He leaned inside, caught hold of him by the hair and his collar and heaved him out through the window. The man was screaming and struggling, but he couldn't hope to contend with the big man's strength. He bounced on the ground and started to get to his feet when he caught Adams' boot in his face. He went down hard and lay still.

"Hey, I said I was on it!" Big Dave protested.

Adams grinned and said, "But we need him alive, big man…" He looked at the man laying crumpled on the ground, his face bloody and already bruising. He looked back up at Big Dave. "My bad. He isn't looking great," he said.

"Well, he isn't going anywhere in a hurry," Big Dave replied. He bent down and caught hold of the man's belt, lifted him clear of the ground and carried him over with one hand to the rear of the pick-up and swung him into the loading bed. "There's some rope there, I'll truss him up."

"We have a problem," Ramsay said to the group when Adams and Big Dave had finished tying the man up. Powell and Tattooed Mick had joined them and were updated by Caroline and Marnie. The three SUVs were pulled into a sort of semi-circle, much like wagons on the range almost two-hundred years ago. "From what we can ascertain from the satellite footage, King got out."

"Escaped?" asked Big Dave.

Ramsay shook his head. "We've got real-time of King driving back with somebody in the passenger seat."

"I followed the indentations in the grass, made by the Jeep's massive tyres. The grass has folded over, and before it springs back you get a good trace. It's hard to follow, but it goes all the way back around five miles to a sort of clearing in the grassland." She had captured the imagery into a short film. The men huddled around the screen.

"Wait! There's a body!" Powell said, his Geordie drawl difficult to decipher at best, let alone understand when he spoke quickly. "Aye, he's in nowt but his kacks, man!"

Everyone frowned but seemed to get the gist of what the Geordie was saying. The guard lay dead, dressed only in socks and white boxer shorts.

"All I can assume is that the body and the man in the passenger seat drove him out there, an altercation took place and King is now heading back to the prison to finish what he started. It looks as though he has the other man prisoner. Judging by the position of his hands. Nobody rides in a car with their hands behind their back."

"Go back to the body and magnify the image," said Adams. He studied the screen, a little closer to Marnie than Rashid would have liked, his shoulder brushing up against hers, but it was difficult for everybody to huddle around. He shrugged it off, telling himself he was being ridiculous. "There!" Adams said, pointing to patches of deeper colour, greener than the grass around them. The grass a little longer, perhaps covered with clover. "I've seen that in Kosovo," he said. "When I worked with the UN searching for mass graves. The soil has a higher nutrient content. Like fertiliser. Those patches are grave-sized, because I'd bet every penny that I'm earning on this job that there are bodies buried there."

"Oh, God!" Caroline said. "But if they were driving Alex out there…"

"He's turned the tables on them," Rashid said. "He's gone back for Zukovsky. He's getting him out on his own."

"Bugger me," said Big Dave. "The guy's got fucking balls of steel!"

"We've got to go in now," said Caroline.

"We won't stand a chance!" Adams argued. "We need a plan, darkness at the very least."

Rashid shook his head and made his way back to his truck. He started to reload the BR99. "I'm going," he said. "Who's with me?"

Caroline followed, the shotgun in her hands looked almost as long as she was tall. "We'll need a diversion at the very least," she said.

"We need to take down their comms," said Big Dave. He was heading for the Dodge Ram. "Seeing as we haven't got any ordnance, I'll have to find another way."

"You're joking, right?" Adams said. "It can't be done!"

"Rashid! You all have comms, right?" Marnie asked, juggling her laptop and heading for the SUV.

"Of course. Two-way, short range."

Marnie looked at Ramsay. "Get on the phone to GCHQ and get something over that location right now. A reverse thrust, slow pass should allow me to be their eyes. We could have up to five minutes overview, and I can spot any hostiles."

"I'm on it," Ramsay said. "But I lost my phone." Caroline tossed him her own and he started to dial. He wasn't going to mess around and was dialling Director Amherst's private number.

"Eh, fuck it..." Tattooed Mick tossed his cigarette and tightened his belt. "I'll take one of those captured M4s. It'll make a decent support weapon. I'll lay down three-hundred metres out and take out as many as I can." He picked it up and waited for Rashid to toss him a spare magazine. He caught it and checked both magazines and the weapon over. The sight was decent enough and had a magnification of four. It wasn't a sniper's tool, but it would be good enough if he got down in the longer grass at the fringe of the runway.

"Seriously?" Adams shook his head. "What about the assault?"

"I'll have some of that," said Powell. He shrugged and made for one of the Yukons. "Shit, lad. It's what we've been paid to do."

"We don't need all of the vehicles," Rashid said. "But if you're bugging out, I'd appreciate your weapon and ammo."

"I'm not bugging out!" Adams snapped. "We just need a plan, that's all."

Caroline turned around and said, "Things changed, this is as good as it gets. You don't have to come with us, but I'd appreciate you stop wasting time and either load up or ship out."

Adams shook his head and took off his utility vest. He picked up his shotgun from where he'd leaned it against the vehicle and walked it over to Rashid's vehicle. "Sorry, but you guys are committing suicide." He tossed them into the vehicle and made for the last Yukon. He got behind the wheel, drumming it impatiently with his fingers as he watched the two GMCs and the Dodge pickup truck turn and head Southwest.

Chapter Fifty

King waited for the three trucks to tear across the runway before heading across the apron and pulling up in the lee of the hangar. He had tensed when he saw them drive erratically out from the hangar, was amazed they had not seen him. They made directly for the direction of the downed helicopter. Two of the vehicles were open-topped Jeeps, both crammed full of bodies with rifle barrels poking out in every direction. The third vehicle had been a Ford F-150 with a growling V8 engine. There had been at least six men in the bed, another three or four in the double cab.

"You're a lucky son-of-a-bitch," Cole commented. "But even the best of the best big dog couldn't take on a small army like that with just a pistol," he said incredulously.

"Not going to let it go, are you?" King said. He switched off the engine and pocketed the keys. He had the guard's 9mm Beretta in the belt holster he was now wearing, and the .40 Sig in his hand. "Get out," he said coldly.

"I can't use the finger ID pad with my hands behind my back."

"Got a pocket knife?"

"No." Cole frowned.

King shrugged. "Want the big dog to chew off your index finger?"

"Of course not."

"Then, when I uncuff you, you'd better behave."

"You really are one to hold a grudge, aren't you?"

"Like you wouldn't believe," replied King. "Especially when people I've risked my life to save try to suffocate me."

"I told you why."

"And yet, here I am. Still alive, despite both yours and Johnson's efforts." He stepped out of the Jeep, walked around and pulled Cole out of the vehicle. He used the guard's key to unlock the handcuffs, shoved Cole forwards and took a step backwards. By the time Cole regained his balance and turned, King was six-feet away with the pistol aimed at the man's torso. "Do what you have to do," he said. He watched as Cole pressed his finger against a pad on the wall. The great doors started to part. King kept the pistol on him, got back in the Jeep and pulled it forwards, parking it directly over the roller gutter in the doorway. The vehicle was completely in between the doors when they started to close. He got out and could already see two men approaching behind Cole.

"What are you doing, man?" one of the men shouted. "You know you can't park that there!"

Cole didn't turn around, but he shook his head at King. King raised the pistol and fired twice one side of Cole's face, lifted the pistol and settled on the second man, who was reaching for his own pistol. King fired twice more. Both men were down and still.

"Bastard!" Cole spat at him.

King shrugged. He had a narrow window; the three vehicles had taken a lot of men out to the crash-site. He could hear the doors butting up against the Jeep behind him. The motors whining under the strain. He swapped the pistols over. He preferred the lighter recoil of the 9mm, and the Beretta had more rounds in it. He gave Cole a wide berth. "Is your finger getting me in there?" He nodded to the main entrance across the hangar space. "Still attached to your hand, that is?"

"Yes." Cole was subdued. He had protested but showed no sign of chancing a move. Not yet, at least.

"After you, then."

The hangar housed a helicopter and a light aircraft. King recognised the helicopter as a Bell and the plane as a Piper twin-prop. He wasn't expert enough in aviation to know the model numbers. He followed Cole across the smooth concrete floor and towards the first locked door he had encountered. He wondered who was watching him on the CCTV. But there weren't masses of guards yet, so he figured he was in the clear until the three vehicles returned.

Cole pressed his index finger against the pad and the door clicked open. No fancy sliding doors with a Star Trek whoosh, just a simple click and Cole pushed the door inwards.

And that's when the world erupted.

Chapter Fifty-One

The antenna towered over one hundred and fifty-feet into the air and a concrete block building about eight-feet by ten-feet and eight-feet high was attached to one side. This housed the electrical output, generator and receiver unit. The antenna itself was a complex construction of woven carbon fibre, fibre-optic cables and woven steel wire. It started out about the radius of a football at its base and tapered to a fine tip. It was enclosed in a metal grid and held from moving in the wind against the sides of the grid by a series of welded loops.

Big Dave stepped out of the Dodge and shouldered the BR99. He checked on the unconscious man tethered in the bed of the pickup, then made his way across the open ground twenty-metres to the building. The building appeared unguarded but looks could always be deceptive. The building did not have any windows, but as he drew just a few steps away, he noticed the CCTV cameras on each corner. He hesitated, listened for movement. He took another pace and the door opened inwards, a rifle barrel protruding. He dodged to his left, the angle more acute, forcing the gunman to show himself if he was to fire. Big Dave fired at the doorway, cursed as he saw the effects of rock salt on the half-opened metal door and doorframe. A burst of white dust puffed into the air. The gunman ducked out and knelt low as he aimed using the corner of the building as cover. The next round in the BR99's magazine stack was a solid rubber slug and it took the gunman clean off his feet and he sprawled in the doorway. Big Dave charged forwards with the weapon aimed at the man and the doorway. He fired two rounds inside the building, the first round was rock salt and the second was another ballistic gel slug. He could hear it bouncing around the confines of the building, then heard a solid thud and a scream. As he swung into the doorway, he kicked the downed gunman with a solid boot to his gut, then fired at a stumbling figure who was holding his head with both hands beside a bank of switches and monitors. The man dropped and groaned. He'd taken the alternated round of rock salt in the chest and it had torn through his jacket and shirt and he was bleeding from thirty or so individual holes. The salt hadn't penetrated deeply, and no doubt stung like a million bees, but he'd live. Big Dave slung the weapon over his shoulder on its webbing sling and took out a roll of duct tape. He wasted no time trussing both men's wrists and ankles, then helped himself to spare magazines and both M4 rifles.

"Sorry, chaps," he said quietly. "But it's a hell of a lot better than lead."

There were mutual grunts on the floor, but neither man was fully coherent. They were bound tightly and going nowhere. Big Dave studied the array of switches, buttons and monitors. He shouldered one of the M4s and emptied the thirty-round magazine into everything with an electrical circuit. He changed the magazine over and peered outside before making his way back to the Dodge pick-up. He dropped the captured weapons onto the passenger seat and studied the antenna, before looking at the rear of the substantial truck. He shrugged. It wasn't much of a plan, but it was more than he'd had a few minutes ago. The Dodge started with a growl, its Hemi V8 roaring with almost four-hundred horsepower on tap. He swung around and lined up the rear with the antenna. There was a heavy-duty tow-hitch back there and it was almost four-feet off the ground. Big Dave selected reverse, kept his foot on the footbrake and allowed the revs to build. The automatic gearbox held for a while, the rear wheels starting to squirm. When he finally released the brake and mashed the throttle, the heavy beast shot backwards, the engine and twin three-inch exhaust pipes snarling. Big Dave had a sudden realisation that he'd forgotten to put on the seatbelt and move his prisoner out of the bed, but he was too invested now, and hoped the force would simply send him into his own seatback. He wasn't entirely convinced the guy in the back was going to have a comfy ride.

The vehicle struck the antenna at an indeterminable speed, but it was considerable, and the big pick-up rose in the air as momentum drove through the structure. Big Dave was at first pushed into his seat, but the Dodge powered into the air and came down hard on top of the fallen antenna. The rear wheels caught up in the steel frame and bit in hard. There was an audible crunch and the rear axle gave under the stress and smoke billowed out from underneath the vehicle. Big Dave had lifted out of his seat and came down on his stomach across the two seats, his chest taking the impact against the gear-shift. He groaned and struggled to get out of the cab, falling onto his backside as he got out. He grimaced, knowing he'd cracked a rib or two in the impact. He was about to try to get to his feet again when he heard the familiar 'click' and 'zing' of gunfire. He ducked down, and a few bullets struck the vehicle. He rolled onto his stomach, howled at the pain, then shuffled his bulky frame underneath the pick-up truck. He looked back over his shoulder and could see two men rushing towards him, both semi-shouldering their rifles and covering the ground quickly. He turned back and heard some more bullets striking the bodywork and glass. He got his Beretta out of its holster. He'd loaded the BR99 with non-lethal rounds, but he hadn't bothered with the pistol. He'd figured if he had to use a pistol, then he would be in the shit deep enough already. He rolled out of the other side and twisted around in time to see the first man's legs and waist, his body out of view as the truck covered him. Big Dave aimed and fired three shots. The man's legs buckled, and he fell. Another shot split his head like a watermelon, and Big Dave pushed himself backwards and pressed his back against the wheel and front panel. He listened, tried to take in the noise around him over his pounding heart. He could hear distant gunfire, but as he tried to rationale the noises of this, the ticking engine of the truck and the sound of fluids leaking from underneath the chassis, he heard someone behind the vehicle taking cover behind the twisted wreckage of the antenna and tripod. He closed his eyes, the loss of one sense highlighting another. He could hear a scrape and some metal on metal. He slinked down onto his stomach and opened his eyes, started to crawl on knees and elbows on the grass. He made next to no noise, but could hear someone moving, could picture the man in his mind – impatient, scared – uncertain of what had happened and why they had been drawn into a fight.

Big Dave could hear the person moving again. A creep and peep. No doubt they could see the body of their colleague and that would change their perception, challenge their guile and resolve. They would be under more pressure because they had caught a glimpse of their fate if they did not win. Big Dave estimated the distance. He knew how long the tripod was, how long the vehicle was and what cover the person could hope to be afforded from the twisted metal. He took a breath, decided to make his move. He was a tall man, but he was a big man and big men made easier targets. He rose up fast, saw the man curled up against the twisted metal, and fired a double-tap. He knew he'd missed, and the man had time to return a volley, but Big Dave was already sprinting, bent over almost double, he lurched out from behind the truck and kept running for fifteen to twenty-metres before stopping and squaring up for another shot. The man had rested his weapon amongst the metal to aid accuracy and in the instant Big Dave had fired, he had seen the fundamental mistake. Big Dave aimed and fired, and the man was unable to bring his weapon around on him as he attempted to counter. The rifle struck a length of metal rod and went nowhere. Big Dave fired three shots into the man's back, and the man had known a fraction before he'd been hit that he was going down. The grimace was enough to say it all – he had been out-manoeuvred, and it had cost him everything. The three bullets struck in a close group and the man slumped forwards.

Big Dave sat down on the grass and clutched his ribs. He could see the tethered man's body, impaled high up in the metal grid. He shrugged it off, but the adrenalin that had spurred him onwards was subsiding and his legs were turning to jelly. He was a tough and battle-hardened solider, but he was human, too. He took his canteen out and downed the water, then fought his own instincts to get back to his feet. He wanted to lie down and sleep. But he had heard gunfire and that could only mean one thing – his team were in trouble and he would do something about it.

Or die trying.

Chapter Fifty-Two

The gunfire was heavy and sustained. King had dodged back behind the doorway and the bullets ricocheted off the steel doorframe and bounced their way around the cavernous space of the hangar. He didn't have a target, but he could see two separate muzzle flashes – one each side of the corridor. Two doors were open, and a man had taken up position in each room, laying prone on the floor.

King turned to his right. He looked past the two remaining Jeeps and saw shelves of tools, oil cans and fuel cans. He glanced at Cole, the pistol turning on him with his stare behind the sights. "Get a can of petrol," he said, then clarified with, "Gas, get me a can of gas!"

"No... you can't..."

"Get it!" King fired, and the shot tore past Cole's head and ricocheted around the cavern. The man flinched, but he was resolute.

"I'm not letting you burn those guys up," he said. "They're just doing their job!"

"So am I," said King and shrugged as he shot Cole in the thigh. The man howled and fell forwards, his leg taken out from under him like a bowling pin. King turned around and headed for the shelving and grabbed a fuel can and opened the lid. It was petrol, or gas in these parts. He left the cap off and picked up a screwdriver. He returned to the doorway and fired a couple of rounds down the corridor. It had the required effect and the two men sent a considerable volley of gunfire back his way as he ducked aside. He glanced at Cole, who had rolled onto his back and was attempting to sit up. He was clutching the entry wound, and tentatively searching for an exit. King could see that the femoral artery had not been nicked. There was a coffee cup quantity of blood on the floor and Cole seemed to be applying the right sort of pressure. He looked daggers back at King.

King stabbed the can with the screw driver and bowled it down the corridor. It stopped short of the doorways but was leaking from a half a dozen holes and the open neck. King fired the rest of the magazine and tossed the Beretta aside. He took out the .40 Sig and fired another two shots. The reply came with another burst of gunfire from both doorways and the muzzle flashes did the rest. The petrol ignited with a bang as loud as a gunshot, and a whoosh that filled the corridor with flames and heat and light. Both men screamed. One door closed, and the other man chanced the corridor for his escape from the fumes and heat. King fired once, and the man went down. He entered the corridor, the flames already dying for lack of a flammable surface. The smoke and stench of fuel was intense, but he skirted the dying flames and could already see that the man was dead. He would be at a disadvantage entering the other room, so decided to pick up the man's rifle and kept moving. He checked the magazine inspection holes and the weapon's action. Twenty-two rounds. The corridor wound around to the left, and King eased through the corner. There was movement ahead – just the glimpse of someone closing a door. The cells would be locked automatically, so it would have had to be an office, interrogation room or a storage room of some description. King kept the weapon aimed, but as he drew up on the cell that he knew to be Zukovsky's, he paused and studied the lock. There was a single tumbler lock that enabled the guards to manually open each door, but he knew the doors to be automatically opened also. Which meant that there would be a control panel someplace. He turned around and made his way back to the dead guard. He rolled the body over with his foot, saw a bunch of keys on his belt and snapped them off the loop. He glanced up at the entrance, saw movement and ducked backwards. There was a burst of gunfire that chiselled rock off the corridor. King dropped onto one knee and returned three shots but could already see that numbers were massing behind the door jamb. He walked backwards, firing single shots at the doorway. Men were getting brave, and by the time he reached the bend in the corridor, there were several muzzles blasting away, and the ricocheting high-velocity rounds were pinging off down the corridor, threatening to hit him. He kept close to the inside of the curve and fired a couple of rounds into the wall, hoping they would bounce their way towards the men in the cavern. He took a breath, checked the weapon again, then turned around and walked into a burst of gunfire from the opposite end of the corridor. The bullets peppered the rock walls, chipped off stone and dust and ricocheted around the tunnel. King recoiled and stepped backwards to the sound of gunfire opening-up behind him. He darted forwards and squatted on his haunches, his back tight against the rough stone wall. He had a sanctuary, out of the line of sight of both points of gunfire. A space of about a metre to contemplate his fate, and his next move.

Chapter Fifty-Three

He hadn't wanted it to be like this. He wasn't scared. He'd done more for his country than anybody should have been asked to, seen more than anybody should have seen. He had fought in battles and skirmishes all over the world, although politics dictated this should largely be in the Middle-East. But what the team from MI5 wanted from him was suicide. And he wouldn't go to certain death for fifty-grand. He would have done it once for queen and country, but he had no idea of the ramifications of this job, the agenda MI5 had from their actions. He would have hit the base with a proper and well-devised plan. But for that they would need the cover of darkness, a diversion, and an exit strategy. What they had was nothing more than bravado and hopeful intentions. And now that the quiet man with the cold, grey-blue eyes was in trouble, they all seemed willing to risk their lives and pay no thought to the men they had recruited. But they were a tight unit, and he was a hired gun. It was their sacrifice to make, not his. Guys like Big Dave just wanted to fight. He would have been a gladiator in another life. Powell was too old to care, too world-weary to break the chain of command and status quo. Adams suspected the man needed the money more than everybody else. He had taken some seriously dubious close protection jobs with little in the way of security and certainly no liaison or back-up with allied forces. He had taken one-on-one bodyguard jobs with scrappy businessmen out to make money from the Wild West era of Iraq and Afghanistan. Adams was surprised the man had made it this far, and he knew from what conversations he had with the man that some of his charges had not.

Adams had cranked up the stereo. The classic rock music drowned out his thoughts. He was no coward, but he couldn't help thinking that is exactly what the others would think of him. *Fuck them!* He thought. He had some of the bounty in his bank and he was alive, and he rather liked it that way. He doubted the rest of the Sass-men would be alive by the morning. And he was certain the MI5 team would be gone before them.

He watched the vehicle grow closer to him on the horizon. He had found the track, one of myriads around the base, and had decided it headed in the right direction. He knew he'd pick up larger roads to the south, some intersecting so laterally that he would never miss them. The vehicle loomed closer, a dust cloud behind it like the wake of a boat in this sea of green. The track was barely wide enough for one, let alone two, so Adams slowed and kept as far to the right as the road would allow. He contemplated going off road, but the ground was rockier – most likely waste from the construction of the track – and he did not want to chance a puncture out here. The SUV ahead slowed, though maintained its position. Adams wondered whether it was an unmarked police vehicle, then started to worry he'd be questioned about being out here this near to the base.

He slowed down, but habit and a life spent in the worst places already had him reaching for the Beretta. He tucked it under his thigh and selected the sport setting on the automatic gear shift. It would make acceleration sharper if he needed it. His fingers tensed on the wheel, and he could make out two men in the front. The SUV wasn't as large as the GMC Yukon he was driving, but this was America and it was still up there with a Range Rover Sport. Adams indicated right and eased his tyres slowly onto the gravel and chipping surface. He looked back at the approaching car – now only a few car-lengths away – and still could not see the faces of the two men. Both sun visors were down, despite the sun being far off to his right. There were only a few hours of daylight remaining and the golden hue that comes with a setting sun over a huge vista was starting to soften and flood the distant horizon.

Adams could see the driver's window lower. He had no doubt that the mid-west was the friendliest place he'd ever been, so he thought nothing of the possibility of a *'how ya'll doing?'* coming from the driver. But still, the Beretta under his thigh reminded him of who he was and why he had been here.

Adams was crawling, the other vehicle was crawling too. And that's when he saw a flash of ginger hair ducking below the sun visor and a blur of black as the barrel of a long weapon pushed past the driver and towards him. He dropped low across the seat as the blast took out his window and showered him with thousands of tiny squares of glass like cut diamonds. His foot slipped off the accelerator and he found himself near-stationary, heard the rack of the pump-action as the shooter prepared for another shot. He fumbled for the pistol and reached it behind him, squeezing off three shots as he jammed his other hand on the accelerator and pressed it to the floor. The V8 surged into life and the car lurched forwards as the second blast took out the rear passenger window. Adams shook away the ringing in his ears and bounced on the seats as the GMC slewed and squirmed across the track, across the loose stones and onto the grass. He got back behind the wheel and checked his mirrors for the other vehicle.

He was in no doubt that the gunman had been the surly Scotsman, Macintosh. He could see the SUV turning around for another pass. But this time, he was ready. He changed the pistol to his left hand and gripped the wheel tightly with his right. The SUV had turned a wide circle and was closing in on him. He could see Yates behind the wheel, the sun visors dispensed with as they got on with the task.

Shock and awe was a technique used to break a regime. And it was the same at grass-roots level with a simple shooting. It had been the last thing Adams had expected, and now his mind was whirling when it should have been planning. How could Yates and Macintosh be here? And why were they shooting at him? Had they come to help and merely mistaken him? Adams shook his head, tried to gather his thoughts. The SUV was closing in, and this time Macintosh had positioned himself out of his own window, and Yates had driven the vehicle to compensate. Adams swung the wheel wide and closed the angle. Macintosh was already struggling to get the shotgun on target, and he fired a shot which largely sent buckshot over the Yukon, scattering a few pellets on the roof. It sounded like a heavy shower of hail, and Adams ducked down despite the unlikelihood of the pellets penetrating the steel bodywork at this range. The range was closing, though and Adams tightened the angle, Macintosh now unable to get off another shot before the two vehicles closed on each other. The vehicles were going to pass. Adams had a good shot and took it with a double-tap. Yates was already hunkered down, but one of the 9mm bullets struck his shoulder and the man arched his back and winced and Macintosh went for the wheel. Adams could see the panic on the two men's faces. He swung the wheel and hit the brakes and the Yukon shuddered to a halt. Adams cursed the vehicle's traction control, its lack of ability to drive evasively. All vehicles were getting that way now, and when he worked close protection detail, he usually took the vehicle he would be using to a garage to have many of the features temporarily disabled so he could power slide, handbrake turn and J-turn.

Either Yates was not badly wounded, or Macintosh had taken over the wheel, because the SUV was back on it and heading for Adams before he could line up a better position. He did not have a good angle for a shot and did not want to waste precious rounds shooting through the windscreen. He stamped on the brakes, selected reverse and powered away from the oncoming vehicle. The rear passenger window lowered, and the shotgun poked out, Macintosh having thrown himself over the front seat and into the rear seats. He had a good shot at Adams, and he flinched as he swung the wheel to change the angle. Macintosh fired, and the front tyre blew out. Another shot and the rear tyre gave way and the big vehicle sagged on its suspension. Adams could hear multiple hits on the bodywork and the roar of the shotgun as

Macintosh found his groove. He returned fire, this time through the windscreen. He punched out the shattered glass, adjusted his aim and fired a volley, but the SUV was getting some distance between them. Adams ejected the spent magazine and reloaded, but only had the ballistic gel rounds left. Better than nothing. He floored the accelerator, but nothing happened. He worked the ignition, but again, there was no sound. The SUV was several hundred metres away now and posed no threat as Adams got out and walked around to the front of the car. He could see where the solid slugs had punched straight through the wing and into the engine bay. He could smell hot water and antifreeze and oil. The smell of a ruined engine. The tyres did not matter anymore; the Yukon was going nowhere.

They had known it had been him. There was no disputing or doubting that. The follow-up attacks, the close encounter as both cars had passed like medieval jousters. The two misfits had been out to kill him. He watched the SUV become a speck on the horizon and then disappear. Adams walked around to the rear of the vehicle and took out his kit. He had a knife, water flask and a jacket. He knew the temperature dropped on the plains at night. He stashed what he needed into his small rucksack and took out his phone. He called Rashid, but there was no answer. He knew the score. It would all be going down at the base. He tried Ramsay's number, but again, no answer. He could have called everyone, but he knew the story would be the same. He took out the flask and drank down half before replacing it and strapping the sack over his shoulders. He estimated seven or eight miles. He checked his watch and took one bearing from the sun to find North, before breaking into a trot, which increased in pace over the next three-hundred metres as his muscles warmed and he settled into his pace.

Chapter Fifty-Four

"I could do with that extra pair of eyes we spoke about Marnie," Rashid said into his mouthpiece. "Anytime ten minutes ago, would help."

"I'm on it!"

Rashid had the BR99 resting tight into his shoulder, tracking an armed man through the tactical scope around the side of the hangar. He had been ready to take the man out with the ballistic gel slug, but upon hearing the muffled gunfire within the hangar, and the distant sound of a battle over at the antenna, he had swapped over to a magazine of solid slugs. He had removed the ballistic gel slug from the breech – a difficult task to do quietly – and was now stalking the man from one-hundred metres away, tucked up in a mound of grass in the lee of the building. He had seen the trucks return from the airstrip, and he knew that the battle taking place inside – now trailing off to pot-shots – could only involve King. What worried Rashid most, was the ebb in battle. It usually signalled the end; either of ammunition or resolve.

"Anytime!"

"Wait... I have it. Right, ahead of you, one man..."

"Got him."

"*Three-hundred metres out, parked in a depression, it looks like Tattooed Mick and Powell are setting out.*"

"*We are,*" came the gruff, Geordie growl of Powell. "*No tangoes in our location. Eyes on two at the hangar door.*"

"*Have that. Outside the main entrance, two men are rigging up a vehicle with chains. Looks like they're going to tow something... I can't see what...*" Marnie added.

"Armed?"

"Yes. And there are three vehicles parked in front of the doors. Open-topped, no sign of the men."

"I suspect they're inside," Rashid said. "Gunfire still audible."

"*I'm South-bound. Just put down two hostiles, have two more winded and tied up, and the antenna is down,*" Big Dave puffed. It was evident he was running. "*Oh, and the prisoner didn't make it and the truck's out of action, I'll need a lift,*" he paused. "*The control panel and electronics are ruined, too. Their comms are down.*"

"Good work," Rashid said. He sighted on the man who was guarding the rear. He fired, and the man went down and rolled backwards. He rested still. Rashid was up and moving forwards. "The guard's down, I'm heading for the entrance…"

Rashid ran down the edge of the mound that constituted the building. It was mounded with earth and grass had grown creating something from the set of *Teletubbies*, but on an epic scale. As he reached the end of the mound, he could see Big Dave running across the flat ground, one-hundred metres out. Rashid looked at the man, his eyes white and appearing frenzied, highlighted by his black face. The man was near enough now, and Rashid turned the corner, could see one of the men Marnie had warned him about. There was no time for a warning, no chance of the non-lethal ammunition coming into play now that there had been so much gunfire from inside the building. He raised the shotgun and stopped running. The man sensed movement, turned and Rashid fired. A click. A sudden rush in heartbeat as Rashid took a knee and cleared the misfire from the breech. His heart was hammering his chest and his limbs flooded with lactic acid as he tried to clear the massive shell. The man fired, but at the same time as Big Dave blasted away with four or five rounds. The man dropped and skidded on the concrete, the ground already soaked in blood. Rashid cleared the cartridge and re-cocked the weapon. He changed the magazine over to be safe, just in case it was a feed issue. He didn't check the live shell which was rolling across the concrete.

Big Dave was changing over to a new magazine. He nodded towards the doors. "Another man in there!" he shouted, taking up cover behind the mangled Jeep that had jammed in the electric doors. "But all these vehicles mean there's going to be a reception committee waiting for us!"

Rashid nodded. He picked up the dead man's weapon and helped himself to two spare magazines. Once bitten, twice shy and he was done with the massive shotgun. He dropped it on the ground and shouldered the M4. The hangar was almost three-hundred metres across, and the M4 would do just fine. "Stay on my six!" he shouted. "I'll take point."

Big Dave nodded, glancing in the direction Rashid had come. "Mick and Powell are thirty-seconds out."

"They'll have to catch up!" Rashid snapped and climbed over the Jeep, sliding over the bonnet and keeping the front of the vehicle as cover.

There were men checking weapons, reloading and regrouping at the far end of the hangar. They looked up at Rashid, then back at the open doorway that a few of the men were aiming through. Rashid hesitated, then realised he'd been given a gift. He waited for Big Dave to climb over, then saw the other two SAS men arrive, red-faced and short on breath. Both men adjusted their kit, subconsciously checked the magazine fit and eased the closed breech back a touch to see the shell.

"They think we're their mates," Rashid said quietly.

"Let's take the fuckers down, then!" Big Dave said gleefully, and was off, running across the three-hundred metres or so towards at least a dozen men.

"Shit!" Rashid shouted as he watched the big man take-off. "On me! On me!"

Rashid sprinted out from cover and Tattooed Mick and Powell climbed over the Jeep and fell in behind. A few of the men watched, but still they turned back to the fight, which was sporadic, with what sounded like a few mere pot-shots being returned at them. Confidence was growing, and the men took cover less, stood confidently in the doorway and unleashed a full magazine into the corridor. They reloaded casually and waited their turn to fire. They looked like they had all but beaten their enemy into submission.

Chapter Fifty-Five

King checked the Sig Sauer. He had five rounds remaining. He had emptied the assault rifle and had admitted to himself that he was out of options. But five bullets meant he could take five more before they got to him. But they would have to come to him, now. He wasn't going to fire until he had a target. He would never have contemplated using a bullet on himself. MI6 had issued him with cyanide pills at one stage, but he had never carried them. He would always take a chance and see how fate played out.

He eased around the corner on the downward side. A shot rang out and he ducked back into his sanctuary. As he suspected, only a couple of armed men at most. And from the return of fire, he guessed they were as low on ammunition as himself. They had certainly lit up the corridor and pumped a lot of lead his way. At one moment, he had merely three-feet of space that gave him sanctuary from both directions, but it would seem now that the men were communicating with each other, because the last few times he had fired, the men in the opposite direction had opened-up a volley, hoping to catch him with ricochets.

"Give it up, King!" King smirked upon hearing Johnson's voice echoing from down the tunnel. "There's a lot of firepower heading down your way in a minute. My boys are getting ready to launch an assault!"

"Thanks for the heads-up," King said quietly, not caring that Johnson hadn't heard him. Maybe the *Men in Black* wannabe would come and check things out for himself. King had five reasons why he'd like that scenario. He cupped a hand and shouted, "I'll give *you* the chance to surrender, Johnson! Just throw out your weapon and walk up to me!"

"Still a funny guy, eh? Well, that will change in a minute!"

King heard another barrage of gunfire, and then the rate and ferocity increased, but no bullets came down the tunnel towards him. He could hear the shouts and cries of battle, and with that, he edged up the tunnel and peeked out from the corner. The battle was taking place in the hangar. And that gave King an idea.

Chapter Fifty-Six

Big Dave had made it half-way across the floorspace before Rashid had caught up, cursed him and overtaken him. He fumbled out one of the spare magazines and kept it in his hand as he slowed and dived onto his stomach, taking up aim with the rifle. He started to fire single, aimed shots at the men and they fell one-by-one. Big Dave dropped to one knee and started to fire. He was on double-oh-buckshot and each time he squeezed the trigger, nine 8mm balls left the barrel at five-hundred-and-fifty feet per second. Slow compared to the three-thousand or so from the 5.56mm M4 rifle in Rashid's hands, but this was like comparing a spiked club to a surgeon's scalpel. The job was getting done.

Tattooed Mick and Powell were now laying prone and taking up fire, both men using alternated stacks in their magazines. Buckshot and solid rifled slugs taking casualties as the men returned fire. The surprise had worked, the shotguns and their devastating spread of shot taking the men down with impunity. Rashid's aimed shots were working at one-shot-one-kill, and it wasn't long before a few of the remaining men were tentatively holding up their hands, still unsure whether to go all in and actually commit to dropping their weapons. It was a difficult thing to do, survival instinct always telling you that there was still a chance, when rationality said chance had left the building long ago.

"Cease fire!" Rashid yelled. "Cease fire!"

The gunfire slowed, then stopped altogether. All the men waiting for the other to start firing again, and the men in their sights to make a wrong move.

"Drop your weapons and place your hands on your heads!" Rashid shouted. The men glanced at one another, their eyes lowering to survey the grisly scene of the dead and wounded on the ground. "Do it now!"

The first of the guns clattered to the ground, and a few more followed suit. Four in total. The men placed their hands on their heads with fingers linked. They looked like prisoners of war everywhere – subdued and unable to comprehend how it hadn't gone their way. There were nine men on the ground and six of them were not going anywhere. Only time would tell with the other three.

There was the sound of shouts from the

corridor, a gunshot, then nothing else. Rashid got up and walked forwards. He kicked the AR rifles backwards, where Powell kicked them further into the hangar. "Stay here," he said to Powell. "Keep them covered but let them tend to their mates' injuries. There's still a threat from in there, we need to keep up momentum."

Powell nodded, then swung his weapon towards a door that was opening tentatively. The doctor stepped out, his hands raised in front of him, his medical bag in his right hand. He looked at the men on the ground, shook his head in dismay.

"Who are you?" Rashid asked, taking the bag off him and opening it. He pushed the bag back across the floor to him.

"Simpson," he replied. "I'm the doctor."

"Well, get busy, then. Your men will help you, but rest assured, if anyone tries anything stupid, my man here will finish what we started."

The doctor looked at Rashid with disgust and said, "I have no doubt about that."

"Yeah? Well, you're not all that, either," Rashid said, changing over the magazine to his weapon. "Otherwise you'd be in a nice hospital in an affluent area with your own parking space and a nurse on speed-dial for a fuck-buddy." He turned to Big Dave and Tattooed Mick and said, "Right, lads. On me."

Chapter Fifty-Seven

King had acted as soon as the gunfire had died down. He had perfected his generic American accent for the first part of his infiltration, and he reverted easily enough, casting his voice down the passageway and shouting that the prisoner was dead and the corridor secure. He waited, the Sig held firmly and aimed at the edge of the bend.

Two men showed themselves and King shot the first man between the eyes, held the weapon steady on the second. "Drop it!"

Johnson hesitated for a second, then dropped the Glock on the ground, raised his hands cautiously, looking down at the man dying at his feet. "Bastard..." he said quietly.

King shrugged. "Big boy's games, big boy's rules."

"What the hell do you want here?"

"Former General Vladimir Zukovsky. Ex-KGB and FSB."

"Not one of mine."

"But you know him?"

"Yes."

"Whose is he?"

"CIA."

"Well, he's MI5's now," King paused. "Again."

"So, that's it?"

"Get him out."

"And you walk away?" Johnson scoffed. "You'll start a war between our two nations, and we won't win until lunchtime the same day."

"Your grasp of history leaves a lot to be desired. America's wars are far from quick, and don't always lead to victory," King paused. "And we'd never go to war. Not over something like this. A few dead, a few injured. You guys killed more of our troops in Iraq with friendly fire."

Johnson shrugged. "And you're claiming back your asset and walking away?"

"That's about the size of it."

Johnson shook his head. "You don't know what you've started."

"Finished," King corrected him. "Your lot started it when they took advantage of our good nature. But no, you had to be top-dog. Take him out the country, whisk him away to your secret prison."

"Not so secret now," Johnson said. "And nor will what's happened here be. You Limey assholes have dug your own graves."

"Plenty of room in a grave for two," King quipped and pushed him backwards. "Now, release my prisoner, or join your buddy down there." He nodded to the corpse which had stopped twitching and bleeding. "Now, or I swear I'll do it."

Johnson nodded and turned away. He led King down the corridor to a door, just before the main body of cells. He opened the door, the muzzle of the pistol pressed firmly into the back of his neck. "Okay, you win. I won't try anything."

The room was about ten by twenty with chairs and a table, coffee machine and some magazines and paperbacks piled high. There were batons and handcuffs on a set of shelves and a panel of Tasers and two-way radios on charge. One wall housed a bank of CCTV monitors and a control panel with numbered switches. King could see Rashid and two others edging down the corridor on one of the monitors. A door opened, and the men fired. The sound resonated down the corridor to them a second later. The door was the one King had thrown the petrol can to, and the man who had shut himself in had chosen the wrong time to play peekaboo. Rashid was crouched beside the door and the big black man was readying himself for a kick. King could see the empty mess hall, the cavernous rec-room and the shower block. The thought of what Johnson had planned for him down there at the hands of the white supremacists filled him with bile and a flutter to his stomach.

Johnson found the cell and opened the door. King could see Zukovsky stand and look at the door. The man was hesitant, scared even. A shadow of his former self. And King liked that. The man was pure evil and would have delighted in killing millions in his failed attempt to detonate old Soviet-stock plutonium secreted in Britain during the Cold War. And what he had been part of, perhaps even masterminding, all those years ago and now near-perfected in a secret facility near the Finnish border in Russia, showed his pure and unadulterated hate of the West. King would never allow him to succeed.

"Let's go," said King and pushed Johnson ahead of him. He paused by the shelves and took two sets of handcuffs and a set of keys. He held out a pair of cuffs and said, "You know the score."

Johnson scowled as he put the first bracelet on, then King spun him around and cuffed the other behind the man's back. He pushed him onwards and they walked the fifty-metres or so to Zukovsky's cell, where the man stood in the doorway, peering out.

"You?" he said, bewilderment giving way to incredulity.

"Who else?" King tossed him the other set of cuffs. Zukovsky started to put them on, but King pushed Johnson aside and reemed the bracelet on tightly and spun the Russian around, before trussing him up like Johnson. "Now move! Out and to the left!"

Both men walked ahead of King out of the cell and into the corridor. King checked right, then followed his two prisoners. When they reached the control room, King gripped Zukovsky's shoulder and pushed him down onto his knees. "Take a break," he said. The Russian dropped down and looked up at him. He seemed to accept the inevitable, but his eyes never left the pistol in King's hand. King knew that the man thought the end had come, and he didn't see the need to assuage his fears. He held the pistol on Johnson and said, "Kneel."

"No… don't…"

King shoved him into the wall, gripped

the back of the man's neck and pressed him down to the floor. "Stay still."

King stepped into the control room. He glanced at the bank of monitors and could see Rashid and the two SAS men starting down the corridor. It looked as if they had subdued and secured the man with duct-tape. King picked up a chair, a baton and another set of handcuffs, then returned to the two men waiting outside. He slung the chair towards Johnson and said, "Take a seat." The old agent got off the floor, his knee clicking in protest. He sat down on the chair, wearing an expression of bewilderment. King secured the cuffs around the chair and locked the other bracelet around the handcuffs securing his wrists. He wasn't going anywhere. King dropped the baton beside his feet.

"What are you doing?" he protested.

King stepped back inside the control room and flicked a switch on the board marked 'All Cells'. There was the sound of locks opening in unison, doors opening automatically. King stepped back out into the corridor and said, "Just letting some of your friends out to play."

"No!" Johnson rocked on the chair. He shook his head, pleading with King. "It wasn't personal! I have a job to do. Not just me, but others too! This isn't my place! The CIA, FBI and Secret Service all have a stake here, as well as us!"

King nodded. "Well, this *is* personal," he said. "But I'd prefer you to get what's coming to you from the scum in here rather than me waste a bullet on you."

Zukovsky was smiling, clearly enjoying witnessing the man's fate. King pulled him up and pushed him down the corridor. He didn't look back, despite Johnson's protests. He could hear shouts behind him, the sound of a group of men with hate in their hearts and an opportunity too good to miss. Johnson screamed, but King did not care. He shouted ahead of him, warning Rashid he was coming toward them. "Rashid, it's King, don't shoot! I have the asset with me!"

King eased around the bend, saw three muzzles at head level. They lowered one-by-one. Rashid stepped forwards and hugged King.

"I was worried I wouldn't see you again," he said, then glanced at Zukovsky before looking back at King. "Fuck me, I can't believe we did it."

"We're not done yet," said King, breaking away and nodding at the other two men. "Let's get the hell out of here."

"Clear down there?" Rashid asked, nodding in the direction of the screams.

"Nothing to worry about down there, mate," said King. "Just cleaning house, that's all."

Chapter Fifty-Eight

"I want to get into the fight!" Caroline snapped.

Ramsay shook his head. "How many times?" he asked. "Just wait!"

Caroline carried the BR99, holding it in both hands. It was a large weapon for someone her size. She wore one of the tactical vests and it was a little loose on her. She watched Marnie as she worked on the laptop and studied the screen.

She said into the mouthpiece, "The satellite has completed its pass. There's no more real-time footage, but I'm getting the last of the static images now... we have two men on foot, not far from our position. A vehicle East of here. I didn't notice it before. It's parked up, judging from the tyre tracks on the grass."

"Might be a good time for you to check on these two men," Ramsay said to Caroline.

Caroline nodded, checked the screen. She got a surprise at just how close they were. She spun around, saw movement in a bank of long grass. The gunshot came before she could find a target.

"Down!" she screamed behind her.

Ramsay ducked down beside the wheel of the Yukon and Marnie flung herself inside. Caroline sent a volley of five rounds into the grass, then backed up behind the bonnet of the large SUV and fired five more. There was a scream and a return of fire. Caroline reloaded the weapon, struggling with the weight and clunky magazine change. The cocking lever held back after the last shot, but like the AR it was based on, she hit the button on the other side of the frame with her palm and the bolt dropped and chambered the cartridge. She took aim again, this time she had loaded up with solid slugs. She could see a figure in the grass through the x4 scope and fired two shots. Both hit, and once she had recovered from the savage recoil, she re-aimed and could see the damage done in the scope. She did not dwell on it, merely searched for the other target. "I can't see anyone," she said to Ramsay. "Get up and get the vehicle running. We need to get out of here!" A volley of shots hit the windscreen and tore into the seats. "Marnie!" Caroline ducked back, saw Marnie lying in the footwell.

"I'm okay..." she replied quietly. She was covered in padding that had puffed out of the headrests. "I can hear Rashid talking on the net… they've got Alex!"

"Then let's get out of here," said Caroline decisively. She aimed at the knoll and fired single shots, the recoil knocking her sharply backwards with every shot. She got into the passenger seat and adjusted her aim out of the window, firing slowly as Ramsay started the vehicle and they pulled away. The gunman fired a volley and bullets struck the rear of the Yukon. Caroline changed over to a magazine of buckshot and within seconds had sent over eighty steel balls back in his direction. She dropped the magazine and replaced it with her last one loaded with solid slugs. She willed Ramsay to drive faster, but all she could do was breathe deeply to steady her nerves and anticipation. She was so close to Alex now, she just wanted to grab him and flee. Get away from danger and have nothing stand in their way.

Chapter Fifty-Nine

"Bugger me!" Macintosh smiled wryly. "There's Sporty, Tits and Fop..."

"Where?"

The signals on the Yukons had died an hour ago. But the last they had seen, the vehicle Adams had been driving was stationary and eight miles out when the signal died, but that may well have been the range limit. The vehicle carrying Tattooed Mick and Powell was parked in a grassy depression three-hundred metres from the hangar. That left the MI5 team, who they figured were together after they had watched Big Dave and Rashid storm the hangar and the other two SAS men arrive a few minutes later.

"Right there," Macintosh paused. He pointed towards the hangar, where Ramsay had driven directly to and was parking in the lee of the building. Macintosh replaced the binoculars to his tired eyes and focused them closer. "Sporty's tooled up with a shotgun and the Fop is getting out. He has a pistol and is holding it like it's scalding hot!"

"And Tits?" Yates asked. He adjusted his

own field glasses and watched. "Looks like she's staying put."

"Right. On me, then. Let's shut this thing down and get what's inside."

"Going in strong?"

"As strong as it gets," Macintosh grinned. "No witnesses. No chance of any comebacks."

Chapter Sixty

The Americans were tending to their wounded, the doctor working on the casualties from gurneys that had been pulled in and extended and arranged in a makeshift triage. There were drips and saline packs giving precious fluids, and packaging from dressings littered the floor. King looked around but could not see Cole among the dead or walking wounded. He wasn't on a gurney either.

"Looking for someone?" Rashid asked.

"A black guy," King said. "Tough looking, five-eight or five-nine, well-muscled."

"Fucking hell," said Rashid. "Two weeks and you're prison gay already?"

"Idiot," King replied impatiently. "He's an ex-SEAL and he's an assassin-come-clean-up man for the NSA agent who put me in here."

"Is he a good guy?"

"I thought he was, but he proved me wrong. Then he wavered, got on the fence. But I don't trust him now," King shook his head. "No, he's dangerous. And he's wounded."

"Which makes him even more dangerous," Rashid commented.

King saw the trail of blood. He snatched Rashid's Beretta out of the holster on his tactical vest and followed the blood. A drip here, a smear there. Cole had gotten the bleeding under control, but there was still a trail. King moved as quickly as he could across the hangar space. Every muscle ached and throbbed, and the bruising to his face and ribs was coming out, making breathing through his nose painful, and as he breathed harder and worked his lungs, the ribs ached even more. He reached the Jeep he had jammed the doors with. There were two men down. King bent down and examined one of the men's kit. He saw the magazine in the pouch and took it out. A regular M9/92F. He put it in his pocket. It then dawned on him he was wearing the dead guard's uniform and that he would look for all intents and purposes, like the enemy to the rest of the team. The thought of walking right into friendly fire slowed his progress, and he hesitated as he squinted in the setting sun. A vehicle was high-tailing it across the apron. He squinted in the sunlight, noting it was a large, black SUV similar to those he had seen at the camp in Virginia. He wasn't too familiar with American cars, didn't know the make merely by its grille badge. He waited, but it was heading straight for him. The headlights flashed, and King resisted the temptation to bring the pistol up to aim. The SUV swerved and hit the brakes. The driver flashed the lights again and the passenger door opened. He recognised the SAS operative. The cockney one, Yates, he thought. He nodded, and the man looked relieved. The driver's door opened, and the other man got out. King couldn't remember his name. Scotch, he thought.

"Aye, Jimmy lad!" Macintosh greeted him loudly. "You'll ride with us."

King nodded. He tucked the pistol into the holster and climbed over the Jeep. He walked to them, smiled. Yates stood back and allowed him to go first, but as King passed him, he snatched out his pistol, shoved him in the back and took a step backwards.

"What the...?" King caught himself before falling, turned around.

Yates had the pistol aimed at him and Macintosh had retrieved his pump-action shotgun from his seat. "Tide's turned on you," Yates said, somewhat pleased with himself that he had the jump on him. "Where's the Paki?"

"Fuck you," said King.

"What the hell is this place?" Macintosh asked, he jacked the pump-action and aimed it at King's waist. "We thought it might be a goldmine. But there's no machinery."

"It's a prison," said King quietly. There was a burst of gunfire and King smiled. He guessed the prisoners had made it to the end of the corridor. "Run by all of America's intelligence agencies."

"What?" Yates turned and stared at Macintosh. "What the hell have you got us into?"

"Put the guns down and I'll arrange for a comfy cell for you both," King smirked. "You two fuckwits have played a duff hand."

"Aye, but at least we have a hand to play," Macintosh growled. "Get in the fucking truck."

"No."

Yates stepped forward and pushed the pistol into King's face. "It wasn't a question, it was an order!"

"Put the gun down!"

The men looked up, but Yates remembered his prisoner in time and turned back to King. Caroline had her shotgun aimed at

Macintosh, but he had his aimed at her. There was twenty-metres separating them. No way out for either if they fired.

"Do what she said!" King shouted.

"Shut up!" snapped Yates. "Mac, I've got a gun on him. Tell the bitch to put hers down, or I'll waste her boyfriend!"

"Aye, bitch. Like he said, put down the gun or lover-boy gets it."

Caroline shook her head. She had her finger resting on the trigger, the barrel aimed at the Scotsman's midriff. "Put yours down!" she yelled.

"I've got a gun on you, too!" Ramsay stepped out of the lee of the building, holding a Beretta.

"You've got the right end, eh?" Macintosh laughed, but it was a nervous one at that.

"You'll find out if you don't do what we say," Ramsay said coldly. Despite his inexperience and the seriousness of their situation, the weapon in his hands was unwavering. "Put the gun down."

"You're the only one without a gun on them!" Macintosh shouted to Yates. "Waste that fucker, I can take these two!"

"Don't bet on it!" Adams stepped out from behind the GMC. He was heaving for breath, but he had a pistol in his hand, and he was aiming it at Yates. It was loaded with ballistic gel, but nobody knew that. And they were close enough to go down hard. "That's it, Mac! You're outnumbered!"

Macintosh grinned, red hair, yellow teeth and dark eyes made him look like a troll, or something from a picture book that would scare children. Adults, too. "Aye, outnumbered, but not outclassed…"

Caroline didn't allow him to finish his sentence. She dodged and fired, but so did he. She caught some of the shot in her stomach and went down. Macintosh caught the blast in his hip and spun like a top. Caroline dropped her weapon, but Macintosh grimaced and pumped the action. Ramsay fired but missed and he was moving to cover when he fired again.

King slapped Yates' wrist aside and the weapon discharged into the truck. He already had his other hand moving and when it finished its arc, the magazine he'd had in his pocket was imbedded in the man's skull. King smashed the man's gun hand with his forearm and the pistol clattered to the floor. He drove his hand back up and grabbed the side of Yates' face for extra purchase, drilling the magazine and its sharp neck, that held the bullets in place, further into the man's temple. The man, shocked at the initial impact and rendered close to unconsciousness, had no fight in him as he dropped to his knees and King twisted the magazine into his brain. The light went out in the man's eyes and King let go, the body falling to the ground, snatching the magazine out of King's hand and taking it with him.

Adams darted around the back of the truck and fired at Macintosh. The man's adrenalin was flared, and he barely felt the two 9mm bullets against his tactical vest as he spun around in the direction of the gunshots and fired the .12 gauge. He didn't have time to aim, but at that range the spread pattern did all the work for him and Adams went down.

Ramsay fired a volley and Macintosh grimaced as some of the bullets found their mark. Some hit the trauma plates in the tactical vest, and some tore through the stitching and went right through him. He was still moving, even managed to pump another shell into the action. He was bringing the weapon back on

Ramsay when Caroline fired. She was laying on her back, the barrel of the BR99 resting on the toes of her right foot. A full ounce of lead and zinc found its mark at five-hundred and fifty feet per second and Macintosh went down. She fired again, and he slid a foot backwards on the dry concrete. She dropped the shotgun and fell back on the ground.

King picked up the Beretta and ran around the bonnet of the Yukon. He could see Adams but knew there was nothing that could be done for him. He passed Macintosh, didn't check whether he was alive or dead as he put a bullet through the man's head, then reached Caroline and dropped onto his knees beside her. There was blood, and she was shaking. Ramsay stood over them and Marnie was standing behind him, her look aghast.

"Caroline..." King said softly. He dropped the pistol and held her hand tightly, stroking her cheek. She went to get up, but he stopped her. "Wait..." He let go of her and checked her stomach. He unzipped the tactical vest and she winced. He looked up at Ramsay and said, "Get inside, there's a doctor in there. Go and get Rashid to bring him out here..."

Chapter Sixty-One

"You've got about an hour," Doctor Simpson said. "There are fail safes, protocols in place. They have not been adhered to, so the local FBI and their SWAT unit make the first move, but they have the Air Force Special Operations Command over at Ellsworth Air Force Base on speed-dial. You haven't got long before Blackhawks full of special forces soldiers and helicopter gunships come in and take the place."

"Why are you telling me this?" King asked, watching the doctor clear the last of the steel balls from Caroline's midriff.

"I don't want further bloodshed," he said. "That person you came for... he's worth all of this?"

King nodded. He had been squeezing Caroline's hand, just the touch of her filled him with emotion. He thought he'd lost her. "What he knows is worth a thousand times more." King looked at Adams' body on the gurney. They couldn't take him with them, and he never liked to leave a man behind. It was a mess, but that was what happened when the people who ran things couldn't talk it out and get things done. "Your government screwed ours, now we're screwing you. Trust me, when we get around to caring and sharing again, your lot will be thanking ours forever more."

The doctor dropped the lead ball in a kidney dish and started to perform his tenth cross-thread suture. The tactical vest was made from a core of woven Kevlar, and Caroline had taken some of the birdshot through the seams. The force of the blast had taken her off her feet, possibly broken a couple of ribs and winded her terribly, but ten BBs a centimetre deep in her flesh was getting off extremely lightly.

Caroline looked up at King and smiled. Her cheeks were wet with tears, and she had flecks of blood over her, a lot of grime as well, but she was alive and would walk out of here. She shook her head and said, "I thought I'd lost you. I thought we'd come so far, and that bastard was going to kill you because he was the only one without a gun on him. And then Adams came back. Thank God that he did, for us, that is. Oh, shit, it's a mess!"

King nodded. He wanted to hug her, to hold her and never let go. But he knew that the FBI were on the way, that they could get a force of special forces to secure the place and he eased her off the gurney and nodded to Ramsay and

Rashid, who were loitering impatiently in the background. "There's a lot to talk about," he said. "But we have to hit the road." She nodded and winced, the local anaesthetic starting to wear off. As she got unsteadily to her feet, he hugged her close and said, "I love you."

She smiled. He never said it often and for some reason, it surprised her. "I love you, too," she said. "Like you'll never know."

Chapter Sixty-Two

"We need to ditch this and get another vehicle," said King. "People have seen these Yukons. And there's bloody bullet holes in them both."

"Tell me about it," Rashid said, bobbing his head so he could see through the spiderwebs of cracks. The holes let in enough air to blow his hair into a quiff.

"What's up, Elvis?" Caroline said from the rear. She was propped up on kitbags and some sheets.

"I've seen him look worse," Marnie quipped. "Bleached blond was quite a look."

"You mean orange, don't you?" Caroline chided. She grimaced as the vehicle rutted over some rough ground and finally the track became a road. Of sorts.

They were over an hour from the prison and every mile they gained opened-up the search area to hundreds of square miles. Ramsay rode in the Yukon behind them, with Big Dave driving and both Powell and Tattooed Mick either side of Zukovsky, who was handcuffed and thoroughly subdued. He had not said a word since he had left his cell. But King had known that his mind would be working overtime. He would be planning his story, working the angles and countering hypothetical questions. He had not made it this far without outsmarting the opposition, and he was not finished yet.

"What's the exfil?" King asked.

Rashid smiled. "A stroke of genius, really."

"Now you surprise me," said King.

Rashid frowned. "I haven't let you down yet."

King shrugged. "By the way this operation has gone, I'm just ready for something simple."

"Ah, well I can't do simple," Rashid paused. "But I can do effective."

"Such as?"

"Well, Big Dave and I secured a van. A big job, with a big engine."

"Like the A-Team?" Marnie asked. "This just gets better…"

"No, not like the bloody A-Team," Rashid said irritably. "Why do you all gang up on me?"

"Because Ramsay's not here, and you're the default," Caroline chided. She shifted and winced. "It's what we do."

"You need some humour, mate," said King. "Otherwise you'd crack up in this business."

"I just can't stop thinking about Adams," Marnie said quietly. "It's a relief to keep talking and have a joke or two."

Rashid nodded. He remembered feeling annoyed at how Adams had wound him up about Marnie back in Chicago. He felt foolish now. He'd been over-protective and proud. He wished he could have taken those feelings back. The man had wanted out, the plan too ill-conceived. That was his prerogative, he was here for the money and had no clue as to Zukovsky's importance. Merely that the government who had cut him free from his career in a round of austerity lay-offs had needed his services once more. Rashid thought that Adams and the rest of the men would have found a perverse satisfaction in that. Perhaps that had been their motivation – to be useful once more. But no matter what Adams had thought, he had returned to help. They had passed the destroyed Yukon, and it hadn't taken them long to work out what had happened. He had taken on both Macintosh and Yates, and when he had been left stranded, he had tabbed quick-time back to the prison. The timings would have dictated Adams to have put in a hell of a run.

"So, what's the plan, then?" King asked, breaking the silence.

"It seems daft, now," Rashid said. "What with losing Adams... but Dave and I secured some bikes for the guys to head back. Adams said it was his dream, and Big Dave was bike crazy back at the diner we stopped at."

"You soft bugger," Marnie said, reaching forward and rubbing his shoulder.

King chuckled. "I bet Ramsay loved that little lot on the expense account," he said, trying to break the tension. "So, the van is for Zukovsky and who else?"

"Marnie, Ramsay and myself. The idea is to regroup at the motel, take off in the morning. This bike festival has left the area rammed with people passing through. I thought we'd head back East on the I-90 and then head North into Canada. Simon Mereweather has arranged a freighter to take Zukovsky to Scotland, where he will be held at a safehouse. More of a castle, really. I'll chaperone him while Marnie and Ramsay fly out from Nova Scotia. With the guys heading East on bikes, I thought you and Caroline could head South for Colorado, maybe even head out to California and be a couple of tourists for a week or so. You can fly back non-stop from LAX."

Caroline reached forward and gingerly stretched to place a hand on King's shoulder. She squeezed affectionally, the emotion of finally being together, of what had happened back at the prison – of being injured, of Adams – finally caught up with her and she started to sob. She wiped her eyes and said, "That sounds wonderful, Alex. Let's just disappear for a bit. You've done enough, MI5 can just miss us for a while..."

Chapter Sixty-Three

Georgetown, Colorado

The motel was a log cabin style frontier lodge. The foyer was open-plan with a high ceiling with giant hand-carved crossbeams, the walls covered with mounted hunting trophies and a variety of horn and antler. Logs a whole foot in diameter were stacked alongside a fireplace large enough to roast an entire hog in. King guessed from the look of metal loops either side that somebody had at some time or other.

They were high in the Rockies, at an old mining town famed for its steam railway and unique loop bridge which allowed for the tremendous gradient down the mountainside. The motel was simple, run by two bearded men who seemed to watch *Bonanza* on a loop, and would have passed as extras on the show from their appearance and attire. King had gone out for tea, coffee and pastries and had ended up watching most of an episode before he passed through reception on his way to the car. He could have eaten from the breakfast the two men put out, but in truth, it hadn't been that good yesterday. And besides, he liked the excuse to drive the five-litre Mustang he had hired back in Denver. It was loud and fast and comfortable, and it made the idea of such a long drive seem like an adventure. It wasn't low-key, it was a dream car, and American icon, and it made him feel like a tourist. He nodded at one of the men at the desk as he returned, but the man was staring at the TV engrossed in a scene of Little Joe giving advice about woman to Hoss. King knew it wouldn't work out well for Hoss, or the woman for that matter. Those Cartwright boys didn't seem to have much luck between bandits, Indians and the highest accident rate in Nevada. King passed through the foyer with breakfast and headed up the steps to the lodges.

Overlooking a courtyard with an outdoor hot tub and a small indoor pool, King knocked on the lodge door and waited for Caroline to unlock. He always gave two sharp knocks, a long pause and then another knock. Caroline greeted him wearing just a silk negligee. King smiled. It may well have been packed as a tantalising treat, but it was light and soft and just the thing for wearing over ten puncture wounds and twenty stitches. He kissed her lightly on the lips and put the bag of pastries on the table and handed her the coffee. It was strong and black.

King's tea was white with one sugar. He drunk some from the sealed lid opening, cursed at the temperature.

"Utah today," Caroline said. "We can drive all through the high desert and pass through Monument Valley, find a place to stay before Nevada and see the Grand Canyon in a couple of days' time."

"Sounds like a plan."

"Vegas?"

"No," King sipped some more tea and picked up the tattered map. "Not my scene."

"You'd hate it," she agreed. She sipped some coffee and sat down on the bed. "There's nothing on the news, but there have been reports of prisoners being swept up by the military and the FBI on the internet. The sites are getting shut down, but they can't shut down *Facebook* and *Twitter* so easily. It's out there. Reports of a secret CIA prison subjected to a mass breakout."

King looked at his watch. It was his vintage Rolex, and Caroline had brought it with her from England. "Zukovsky should be at sea by now."

"With Rashid," she said. "I hope he has an uneventful journey. That Russian bastard can't be trusted for a moment."

King nodded. "He won't get the better of Rashid, and I imagine Mereweather put some security in place as part of the arrangement."

"Ramsay will be in Thames House by now. He'll need to be creative with his accounting for this trip," she smiled. "Not least for that bloody car you hired!"

"I think I deserve a break," King smiled, taking a Danish out of the bag and passing it to her. "We all do."

"I hope it was worth it," she said quietly. "There was a heavy price to pay." Adams had paid the ultimate price and it would sit heavily with everyone. Rashid had now doubted his idea of non-lethal ammunition. Had the man only had live-ammo, then the tables would have been turned. King felt guilt at having walked out into their trap, and Ramsay would shoulder the burden as the operation leader. As Caroline said; there was a heavy price to pay.

"There always is," King agreed. He bit into the Danish and chewed thoughtfully before washing it down with some more tea. He thought of the men he'd killed over the years, the women, too. The colleagues and friends he'd lost along the way. "And we never found Cole."

Caroline nodded. "That troubles you?"

"I don't think I've seen the last of him," he replied. He lifted his shirt tail and took the 9mm pistol out from his waistband and put it down on the table. He caught sight of them both in the full-length mirror. They looked a sorry pair with King's bruises over his face, slightly swollen ear and lip, and the way Caroline moved tentatively, nursing her coffee, the sheer silk of the negligee enough to disturb her stitches. "I don't like having to look over my shoulder," he added.

"Sometimes it's part of our job," she said.

King nodded. He knew the reality of his profession. It wasn't merely part of his job, but his entire way of life. He also knew that he preferred to be the hunter, not the hunted. And that he couldn't rest while both he and Caroline were under threat.

Author's Note

Hi, and thanks for reading this far - without you, I'd be out of a job, so it really is appreciated!

By now you will know there are other Alex King novels and you can find all the buying links here: **www.apbateman.com** You can also subscribe to my mailing list and newsletter, get in contact with me directly, read about the other books and reach Amazon to leave a much-appreciated review.

I hope to entertain you with another story soon…

A P Bateman

Made in United States
North Haven, CT
03 October 2022

24948851R00253